*For Maren,
the creator of the (for me) most beautiful
book cover in the world.*

Times like
Midnight Blue

Alina Bachmann

Bibliografische Information der Deutschen Nationalbibliothek:
Die Deutsche Nationalbibliothek verzeichnet diese Publikation in
der Deutschen Nationalbibliografie; detaillierte bibliografische
Daten sind im Internet über http://dnb.dnb.de abrufbar.

Verlag: BoD · Books on Demand GmbH, In de Tarpen 42,
22848 Norderstedt, bod@bod.de
Druck: Libri Plureos GmbH, Friedensallee 273,
22763 Hamburg

ISBN: 978-3-7693-8887-9

Cover: Alina Bachmann, Maren Nachtsheim
Translation: Alina Bachmann

Chapter 1

I t was already dawn when I woke up. Usually, I would still be sleeping deeply and soundly that early in the morning, but something – and I didn't mean the quietly snoring body that was lying next to me – prevented me from sleeping any further. I couldn't really explain what was going on, but some kind of unfamiliar unrest kept me awake. I wasn't nervous. Really.

Even though today was going to be the first day of school after the summer vacations and therefore the beginning of the new school year, it wasn't my first day of school in general. There was no reason to be nervous. And even less since I wasn't new to this school anymore. I had already made some friends, I was familiar with the teachers, and I knew what to expect from my school. Nothing was new to me. Nothing was unfamiliar. Still, I felt uncomfortable even long before school would actually start. What was going on with me?

I glanced next to me. Ramon was still deeply asleep. But there was no reason for him to already be awake; we still had plenty of time until my alarm clock would ring and notify us that it was time to start the day.

Maybe I wasn't used to sleeping next to another person. Being in so much physical contact with another person was a very new experience for me. Never before had I been in such an odd situation as I was now. Never before had I gotten that close to another human. Maybe my body simply needed more time to get used to the fact that I had less space in bed than before.

Restless, I turned around. I closed my eyes just to open them again.

I sighed.

I couldn't fall asleep; it was already too early in the morning, and the night was over. At least for me. I noticed that Ramon slowly woke up. His eyes were still closed, but a wide grin was forming on his face. Automatically, I had to smile, too. Was it weird to observe him like that? Maybe a little bit, but at the same time, it wasn't weird at all. I could see how he started moving his body until he finally opened his eyes, and his grin grew even wider.

"Hey, you're already awake?" he asked, still sounding asleep.

I nodded and stretched my joints.

"It's probably just my excitement for school," I answered ironically and looked out of the window.

The morning seemed dull and grey. This wasn't a great start for the new school year. Shouldn't it be summer at the moment? Since we moved houses, it felt to me as if the sun had vanished and been replaced by dark clouds that sometimes rained more or less onto our town. Everything was depressing and humid.

"I thought so," Ramon murmured, and I couldn't tell if he had understood my sarcasm or if he was still too asleep to figure it out.

In the meantime, it had gotten late enough for me to get up, so I made my way to the kitchen to lay the table. We could take the time we had gained from my early awakening to have breakfast together before we needed to go back to our regular lives. Ramon made his way out of bed as well and helped me.

"What are you doing on the weekend?" he asked casually while preparing his bread.

"My mom forces me to go on another happy family camping trip," I complained.

I wasn't keen on going on another camping trip with my mom, her new boyfriend, and even worse, his son. Although the last camping trip had been a few months ago – in fact, it even happened before our road trip to the mansion – I really wasn't looking forward to repeating this nightmare. There were a few things that I really didn't need in my life, and one of these things was camping.

However, I gave up on all of my hopes that my mom would finally realize how much I hated to camp. The only thing worse than all of these insects and spiders was that she wanted me to pretend as if we were one big and happy family. And I was tired of lying to her and even more tired of lying to myself. I wasn't as happy with our new family as she wanted me to be.

"Well, well," he laughed. "Where do you go?"

"As if I know… I think she wanted to go close to the mountains, but not some cool mountains like the Alpes – they would be too far away from home for my mom. I guess we'll stay close to here somewhere, but at least it's something different than the last time," I answered and noticed how his facial expression changed for a brief second. Everything happened so quickly, I couldn't even tell if he was confused, disappointed, or shocked. It was weird, but then again, everything that was somehow connected to Ramon was at least a little bit strange, and therefore I had gotten used to the fact that there were situations I simply couldn't comprehend at first.

"The mountains?" he repeated, as if he didn't understand me.

"Yes, mountains. Super high, pointy things that are standing around somewhere in the landscape, you know?" I tried to explain it for dummies.

"Ahh, that's what you're talking about," he said playfully surprised, and took a sip of his orange juice.

I could only laugh and shake my head while biting into my bread.

For a while, none of us said anything because we were too busy eating until Ramon finally broke the silence: "I think you shouldn't go."

Confused, I lifted my head and observed him carefully.

"Why shouldn't I? I don't think I have much of a choice."

"Well, you always have a choice. You could pretend you are ill or something like that," he lowered his voice at the end of his sentence as if he knew how dumb his idea sounded.

"Believe me, my mom wouldn't leave me home alone. Even if I was feverish, she would carry my ass up the mountain herself," I laughed.

I knew her too well, and when it came to family activities, she would never let me off the hook that easily.

"But you have complained about the other camping trip so many times already. Do you really want to get through this again?" he asked me.

I didn't know what he was trying to achieve, but it was somehow bothering me. I was annoyed by him judging me without knowing my life. He didn't know how stubborn my mom could be; she was even worse than me. Yes, he was right about the last camping trip. It was a horror trip for me, and I would give everything to not go camping ever again, but at the end of the day, it wasn't about the camping trip. It was about living in peace with my family.

"Yeah, I'm not super excited about it either, but there is nothing I can do about it," I answered annoyed.

It was so easy for him to talk like that. He already lived alone and was completely independent from his family. I, however, had to get along with mine on a daily basis. No matter if I rather wanted to stay home or not, I definitely wouldn't be allowed to.

"You could finally stand up for yourself. You are 17, and next year you will turn 18, and then your mother can't force you to do anything," he tried to convince me.

"But until then, I need to listen to her."
I couldn't prevent my voice from sounding sharper than I had originally intended.

"I only want what's best for you. And it would be for the best if you would stay," he admitted quietly.

"But why would it be for the best?" I asked dumbfounded.
Ramon's behavior was so odd and unusual; there had to be a reason for it, but I couldn't put my finger on what was wrong.

"You will only be annoyed and unhappy."

"Right now, I'm annoyed as well."
The words slipped out of my mouth without thinking.

"Sorry, I didn't mean it like that. But, Ramon, for real, I don't believe you. This can't be the only reason. What is really going on with you? Why are you so concerned about my camping trip out of a sudden?" I immediately apologized for my harsh words.
I didn't want to fight with him.

"There is no other reason," he said only slightly convincing.

It almost sounded as if he didn't believe himself either.

"I want you to be happy."

I rolled my eyes.

These were horrible arguments. They didn't count.

"Then you should accept that I will go camping with my family."

The more he tried to prevent me from going, the more I felt motivated to go on that trip. I couldn't even exactly tell why.

"Please," he almost begged me.

I shook my head and got up from my chair.

I had to start getting ready if I wanted to arrive at school on time. And thanks to this awkward discussion, I didn't want to be late.

"Do you trust me?" he asked after I had gotten ready for school.

"Yes, I do. But I still want to know the reason why you don't want me to go." I tried to be objective.

"I already told you I don't have any special reason. Just trust me. It would simply be better if you would stay here."

"Did you have another vision? Are you okay?" I asked out of a sudden because this was the only explanation for his strange behavior I could come up with. However, he hadn't had any uncontrolled visions since our second encounter. At least that was what he always told me. So, his strange behavior couldn't be caused by that. Unless...

Even though he tried to suppress it, he hasn't fully recovered from that night in the mansion yet. He was still exhausted and weak. He, himself, claimed it was due to the fact that he had used his powers more than ever, but I couldn't really believe him. It felt like there was more to it. And especially because I felt that way, it wasn't completely far off that his powers were out of control when he seemed to have zero control over his body as well.

"No, of course not. I didn't have any visions. Everything is under control," he answered quickly.

"Then what else is wrong?" I asked and put on my shoes.

I couldn't wait to go to school.

It seemed as if he was thinking about what to answer. He opened his mouth just to immediately shut it again.

"I knew it."

I sighed.

"But if you can't tell me what's going on, you have to deal with me going on that camping trip."

These were the last words I said to him before I made my way to school.

✳✳✳

It felt good to walk to school. I used to walk through these streets every morning. I knew them like the back of my hand, and everything felt so familiar.

So far, I haven't gotten used to living on the opposite side of town. Our new home was far away from my school and therefore far from Ramon's place as well, but at least now I lived closer to Jane and Finn. Everything had its advantages and disadvantages. Today, however, it felt nice to feel some sort of normality despite the odd morning.

More than just on time, I entered the entrance hall of our school, where I could immediately spot my friends. They were sitting at one of the tables in the back of the round hall. Just like they always did.

"Since when are you arriving on time?" Finn greeted me while laughing.

"Good morning to you too," I grinned and hugged him as a greeting.

"Qualification Phase 2, baby!" Julius shouted from the other end of the entrance hall.

"And hello, Julius. I almost didn't hear you," Finn said.

I quickly joined Jane and her friends for some short conversation before we had to go to the assembly hall to receive our timetables for the new school year.

"What class do you have now?" Jane asked us.

I glanced at my schedule to realize that I was about to have biology class. Although I liked this subject a lot, it would mean that I had to go there on my own since none of my friends were in that course.

Finn and Julius would have physics next. They were so lucky to be together in class. However, I wouldn't want to have physics as a subject in general, but I would have loved to start the new school year with some friends in my course.

"I have biology," I sighed.

Finn petted my back pitifully. He looked even more full of pity when Jane announced that she had PE next.

Having gym class on the first day of school was about the worst thing that could happen. Nobody, absolutely nobody, carried sportswear to school when they wouldn't know they belonged to the unfortunate people who had to do sports that day. The teachers, however, couldn't care less about that, which meant the students would be running around with sweaty clothes for the rest of the day.

Jane definitely was hit the hardest by her timetable, so I really shouldn't complain about my biology course. Despite my friends not being in that class, there were multiple other people I could talk to if I decided I wanted to.

Overly punctual, I made my way to the classroom. After all, I wanted to choose a good seat for the rest of the year. And if I was earlier than most of my classmates, I had a bigger selection to choose from.

Luckily, most of the other students took their time to walk from the assembly hall to our biology room which meant that I could choose my seat freely.

Most people probably wouldn't even care about their seat. Unfortunately, I was a little more complicated. I only felt comfortable sitting on the side of the room, preferably on the opposite of the windows – so no one could expect me to open them – with a good view on the blackboard while at the same time sitting far enough in the back, so the teachers couldn't tell if I was paying attention or drawing in my notebook instead. I simply wanted to avoid anyone noticing me.

Surprisingly, class started with the teacher announcing the attendance of a new student. How was that even possible? I've always thought if someone would change schools during the Abitur phase, they had to repeat 11th grade. After all, this was one of my reasons for staying at this school despite our move; I didn't want to repeat any grade if it wasn't particularly necessary. My other reasons for not switching schools were obviously my friends. I had to admit that school had become more fun now that I had made some friends, and I was also sick and tired of being the new girl again. I liked my life the way it was; there was no need for any changes.

Immediately, everyone looked around, searching for the new student, just to realize that there was no unfamiliar person in the room so far. A sighed of relief went through the room. I guess most people were happy about the delay caused by the new student, since this meant class wouldn't start immediately.

Suddenly, the door opened, and the new guy entered. I eyed him carefully. He was dressed fully in black, and when my glance arrived at his face, I realized that this person, who was still standing in the doorframe, wasn't a stranger to me.

I could feel my heart beat faster; it started racing. I tried to slow down my breathing. I wouldn't start having a panic attack. Not here. Not now. And definitely not because of him.

Everything inside of me felt the urge to storm out of the room and hide in the restroom until the day would be over, but rationality got the best of me. Or was I simply paralyzed by my fear?

"Great, you made it. Do you want to quickly introduce yourself to the other students."

Our biology teacher greeted the new guy friendly.

"I'm Matt, and I'm now in your biology class," Matt responded friendly.

What the hell was he doing here? I thought that he had run away after our last encounter in the mansion. Far away and preferably forever. I thought I had to never see him again.

So many thoughts were filling my head. Was this all just a coincidence? Was this planned? Was this another attempt by the magicians to pressure us somehow, or did he simply enjoy terrorizing people like me? Whatever occasion brought him here, I didn't want to find out. I didn't want to see him here.

Matt sat down on an empty seat, which luckily was far away from me, and unpacked his biology book as if it wasn't odd for him to be here. As if he belonged here.

In the meantime, he didn't pay any attention to me. Maybe he hadn't seen me. Maybe all of this was just one massive coincidence, and he didn't even know I was going to this school afterall. But why would a supernatural creature be interested in graduating school all of a sudden?

Our class felt like it lasted forever. And I couldn't really focus on much either. Matt's presence was distracting me too much. He made me feel restless, and my pulse still hasn't calmed down a single bit. Even though I could proudly claim I didn't have a panic attack, it felt like my body was prepared to run away any second. I was alert.

Fortunately, the first lessons at the start of the school year weren't too important, so at least I wouldn't need to feel guilty about missing out on important biology stuff due to being unfocused.

When class finally ended, I decided to follow my instincts. I was tired of feeling weak ever since that particular night in the villa. That was the reason why shortly after I had registered myself for boxing lessons. I wasn't very good at it, but more importantly, it gave me the feeling of being in control again. So, I decided to use my newfound confidence for something good.

I didn't stop observing Matt. Not when he packed his notebook into his backpack, and even less when he left the room. It wasn't until then that I noticed I had forgotten to pack my own things together. Quickly, I threw everything that lied on my desk into my bag and left the room to somehow be able to catch up with Matt.

A lot of thoughts were filling my head when I walked up the stairs, but I still couldn't answer the question of why I was following him. It probably was an incredible dumb idea to follow him all by myself without anyone knowing our shared history. I already knew he was strong. He was the reason why Ramon was still feeling weak. However, this was a school, and if he really wanted to kill me, he could've already done it in the mansion, couldn't he?

Completely out of breath, I reached the highest floor of the building. Matt casually leaned onto some lockers and looked at me expectingly. Now there were no doubts about his intentions anymore. It wasn't a coincidence that from all of the schools he could've ended up in, he had chosen mine. Of course, he knew exactly what he was doing, and he also knew I would follow him. He could read me like a book.

"You shouldn't be here," I pressed out from between my lips while I slowly walked towards him.

The corridor was completely empty. If he had the desire to hurt me, he could do it without anyone witnessing it.

"Neither should you." He shrugged.

He was right. I shouldn't be here either. I should be sitting in the entrance hall spending the break with my friends instead of following a stranger that could murder me any time if he desired to. So, everything was exactly the way it had been when I started to get to know Ramon.

"What do you want?" I asked demanding.

"I need Ramon's help," he answered with a normal voice.

I was surprised. Maybe I had expected everything from him but this. I didn't know him like that. His voice had always been scornful, degrading, sarcastic, everything but normal. I was so stunned that I didn't know immediately how to respond.

"Ehm," I stuttered.

"What about 'forget it'?" I added after a few seconds of awkward silence.

"I already expected you to say that, but why won't you let him decide for himself? You just need to bring me to him," he tried again.

"I will certainly not do anything for you. If I remember correctly, you attacked and hurt him during your last encounter. There is no guarantee this isn't one of your mean tricks."

"I already expected this as well. That you want to protect him," he said more to himself than to me.

"Well, then you have to get used to that. Save your energy! I won't let you get anywhere near Ramon."

And with these words I turned around to walk back to the entrance hall.

I was a little bit proud of me. I totally left him speechless.

What a grand exit!

The next two hours of art class went by much faster, and luckily, I could spend my time with Julius instead of Matt. The fear of seeing him in other courses than biology was haunting me for the rest of the day. Fortunately for me though, I didn't see him in any of the other subjects.

After school, Julius, Finn, and I were sitting at one of our favorite tables in the entrance hall waiting for Jane. We wanted to go out together and have dinner at a restaurant to properly celebrate the start of our last year of school.

"How long will she take?" Finn moaned in despair.

"Hungry?" I asked and laughed.

Finn was one of the most patient people I knew, but when it came to food, he could become incredibly fretful.

He only nodded saddened.

Luckily for him, it didn't take much longer for Jane to arrive. But she didn't arrive on her own.

"Can I introduce you to someone?" she asked excitedly.

I only looked at her in disbelief.

"This is Matt. He is new in our year. Isn't that incredible?" She continued talking.

Matt only waved at us casually.

How could he dare to get anywhere near my friends? They had nothing to do with Ramon. How could he dare to get near Finn after all he had done to him? Still, I couldn't let them know that something was bothering me about Matt's pure existence. They would start asking questions. And I couldn't give them any good explanations for that.

Even though I had promised Finn that I would explain everything to him one day, I simply wasn't ready to open up yet. Fortunately, he was very understanding. A lot of things had changed within me since we left the mansion, and if I was completely honest, I still hadn't figured out how to cope with everything.

There was more to the situation than just Ramon being weakened – and we still weren't sure whether it was the magician's work or not – there was also the fact that I wasn't quite sure who I was or what I wanted from life. I mean, I was so certain my life would end that night. A near-death experience like that would leave some scars on the soul, this I was sure of.

Now things would change even more with Matt in the picture. Maybe I needed to rethink my morals and tell my friends everything. What would happen if he would tell them our secret first? What if he would hurt them? I had to warn them. I had to get rid of him.

21

"Hey, nice to meet you." Finn greeted Matt friendly. If he would only know… There was nothing nice about it. And it wasn't as random as it seemed to be either.

"I thought he could come with us. He doesn't know anyone here and we could help him out," Jane stumbled.

Oh, I hoped he wouldn't do anything evil to her. I would pay him back double. Even though I had no clue how I could even hurt him, but I had to become creative if he would force me to.

Finn and Julius seemed to be excited about her idea, so I couldn't say anything against it. It would have been too suspicious.

"What a great idea," I answered, and I really needed to control myself to sound like I meant it.

We walked to the city center, and after discussing for a while, we decided to eat at a small Asian restaurant in the middle of the pedestrian zone. The others were eager to get to know Matt and to make him feel welcome. Why did my friend group have to be so open minded and friendly to everyone?

"How is it possible that you are new in our year?" I wondered out loud after we had ordered our food.

If nobody thought of it as weird, I could at least try to point it out for them. Maybe then they would realize that something was seriously wrong with Matt.

"I moved out of a sudden and your school has the best reputation in this city," he answered neutrally.

One could really think we had never met before.

"But why our year?" I pushed further. "I thought if one switches schools during the last year, they have to repeat 11th grade and cannot directly start in 12th grade."

His facial expression shifted from being totally relaxed to something darker for a second. I definitely made him feel uncomfortable, which felt like a small victory to me.

"There are exceptions where people don't have to repeat 11th grade, and luckily, I had the right connections and marks to go straight to 12th grade."

He looked comfortable again.

Damn. This time, he could save himself.

"Why did you need to move so suddenly?" I asked him. And I couldn't care less about Finn's confused glance.

"Luna, let him be!" Jane said strictly but friendly at the same time.

"Oh, it's fine. I have nothing to hide," Matt laughed and fixed me with his eyes. "If you really want to know the details, there were some complications within my family."

"A tragic backstory?" Jane slipped out.

Matt shook his head while smiling.

He could seem so likeable. If I didn't know him, I bet he could fool me too. But behind the friendly smile and the pretty eyes was an ice-cold murderer.

"It wasn't a big deal. Just a few differences in opinions that could be solved only through moving away." He reassured Jane, who already looked at him with pity in her eyes.

Differences in opinions? Was he hinting at the magicians or was he talking about Ramon? For now, it was better to lay low and not ask any further questions. Because everything I had done so far only allowed him to look even better in my friend's eyes.

In general, the afternoon went okay. I tried to get a grip on me and leave Matt be, and to my surprise, no one noticed my resentment towards him. It was a success for me.

But the afternoon was a success for Matt too, because at the end of the day he was added to our WhatsApp group chat. He had me exactly where he wanted me to be.

Chapter 2

I wasn't happy at all about my conversation with Luna this morning, but what else was I supposed to do? I couldn't bring myself to tell her about my vision. I couldn't tell her that her life was in danger all because of me, a person whom she trusted. How was I supposed to explain to her that I was feeling miserable ever since we left my Grandma's mansion? How should I explain this odd feeling that warned me that this was only the beginning?

I was positive she had already noticed I was going through something, but at the same time she couldn't estimate how extremely crappy I really felt.

I felt weak. I felt strange. I felt like I was about to lose control again, and I didn't even know why I felt that way. I had learned how to control my abilities before. There was no way I had to start learning this all over again. There was no way I was able to start over again. I was too exhausted. Too weak.

Overall, the situation I was in was hopeless, and I couldn't or didn't want to talk about it with anyone. Everything felt like a Deja-vu. A throwback to a time before I had started learning how to control my powers. But worse. More uncontrollable. And especially after all the progress I had made in the past, this setback felt like a disaster. And now I simply didn't have the strength to start again. I couldn't go on living like this for much longer.

But the closer the weekend came when Luna wanted to go on a camping trip with her family, the worse my nights were. I couldn't sleep at all because I knew I had to do something.

I couldn't let her drive away like that. And if I couldn't stop her from going on that trip, I had to at least do everything I could to prevent her death. As much as I loved looking for similarities between Luana and Luna, I knew that Luna's death would feel much worse to me than Luana's death could have ever been. So, I decided to let Tim know about my vision.

I wouldn't tell him everything, only the most important details. He didn't need to know how terrible I was actually doing. I could simply use somebody calm that would come up with a plan.

Determined, I was on my way to Tim's apartment. If I would come over to visit him, he wouldn't realize that I was scared as hell and exhausted. Because if I was really feeling like crap, I would never have the guts to visit him, wouldn't I?

"So, what do you want to talk about?" He greeted me friendly when he opened the door.

I sighed briefly.

He couldn't even imagine how serious this conversation would turn out to be.

Quickly, he realized that I didn't feel like laughing.

"I understand," he murmured while I walked past him and sat down.

"What happened?" he sounded worried.

This was exactly what I was trying to avoid.

I took a deep breath.

What I was about to say wouldn't be easy.

"I had a vision," I started and observed how Tim opened his eyes and mouth in shock.

"Shit," he whispered.

I nodded, then I cleared my throat before I could continue talking.

"I had a vision in which Luna died."

My eyes filled with tears and I couldn't stop it.

"Did you tell her already? Maybe we can prevent it. Maybe we can somehow change the future, or do you think you could have another vision, a more positive one where Luna survives?" He rambled without thinking too much.

It was obvious he was bothered by the situation as well. He was by my side when we lived through all of this for the first time, and if I was feeling too weak to start over, how should I know he wasn't feeling the same way? We had been at exactly this point before. This couldn't be an eternal circle. This shouldn't be an eternal circle.

"I didn't tell her anything so far," I started.

But before he could question me further, I responded: "I don't want her to think wrong of me. I'm scared she would think I want to see her dead, and

I also don't want her to notice how I'm losing control again. I don't want her to walk away from me, and I don't want her to be worried about me either."

"So, you say you'd rather watch her die instead of her choosing to leave you?" Tim tried to summarize the situation.

I never looked at it from this point of view, but something about the way he phrased it was correct. It sounded horrible, and the situation was way too complex to be summarized in only one sentence, but the words had come out of my mouth, so they must've been at least slightly true.

"Of course, I don't want to watch her die, but... I tried talking her out of going on the trip with her family without giving away too much," I explained my original plan.

"She is going to die while camping?" Tim asked.

I nodded.

"Did it work? Could you stop her?"

I shook my head.

I didn't know what else to say.

"Otherwise, I wouldn't be here," I sighed. "I hoped you could help me."

Tim thought about it for a second, then he nodded.

"Of course, I'm going to help you. But firstly, we should tell her about your vision. I don't think it will change anything if you explain the situation to her. I know you, and I know your powers as well. Whatever is going on right now, isn't normal. This isn't you.

Furthermore, she decided to help you despite your uncontrollable visions. You could've already killed her in the past. So why should she decide against helping you now, when she had already made her decision to stay at a time where you were doing much worse?" He was motivated and looked at me.

"What are we waiting for?"

Silence filled the room.

I didn't know exactly how I could respond.

"Yeah, about that. I was hoping you could try to figure out where she would go, so we can follow her and prevent my vision from happening," I tried to explain my new plan.

He just looked at me confused.

"Why don't you try to figure it out yourself?" he wondered.

I had no other choice but to explain again, and with further details, how I had already tried to prevent her from going and how she didn't like that. I had to admit that spending most of my life on my own had shaped me, and I sometimes had issues understanding how to react in certain social situations, but even I knew that it wasn't good for our relationship if I would keep pushing myself onto her with the same topic.

"Hm," Tim said. "Don't you think your idea is a little bit, how do I phrase it nicely, creepy?"

"It's not my best plan, that's for sure. But please, let's do it my way," I beseeched him.

Again, Tim had to think about it briefly, but eventually he agreed. His only demand was that I would tell her everything about the vision once we saved her.

Nervously, I was sitting next to Tim while he was trying to figure out her parent's camping destination during a casual conversation with Luna through WhatsApp. It was already Friday afternoon, and we were slowly running out of time. I didn't know when their journey would start. I didn't know their destination yet. And I didn't even know when exactly my vision would strike. It could've already been too late.

Luckily, Luna wasn't suspicious when Tim asked her about the camping trip, so she told him everything we needed to know for our plan to work.

I looked at Tim.

He looked at me.

"Let's go!" I said and got up.

"We have a mission!" Tim screamed and followed me as fast as possible.

We jumped into my car and started driving. On the way to the campsite, I explained everything I had seen in my vision to Tim, so he could be prepared as well. We both needed to be careful about potential issues that could endanger our mission. We had to find her before my vision would become reality.

I already was a mental wreck. How much more did I have to bear until I would finally break?

We didn't need to drive for long until we could already see the first mountains. Luna was right about everything. Her mother really didn't seem to want to travel too far. Now we only needed to find Luna or her family, which was probably the hardest part of our mission.

"Where do we want to hide on top of the mountain, and where will we sleep?" Tim blurted out.

Damn. I haven't thought about this at all.

In my head, everything seemed to be so much easier. But Tim was right, it was important to plan things like that in advance. We couldn't risk walking around the campsite like regular campers.

If Luna would see us, everything would be over. And with all the stress, I didn't even think about sleeping. I hadn't expected this mission to take longer than one afternoon, which was careless of me. Maybe this was the reason why Tim usually made the plans.

"We can sleep in my car," I suggested.

"Cool, I always wanted to sleep in a car," Tim answered happily like a small child.

I didn't expect such a genuinely positive response to my plan.

We started driving up the mountain, but we didn't make it all the way to the top on purpose. We stopped the car at one of the multiple parking spaces next to the road that would lead to the peak of the mountain.

Dusk had already begun, and the odds were too high that somebody would notice us or the lights of my car. Today, and I was sure about that, nothing bad would happen to Luna.

My vision should happen during day light, and Tim was texting with Luna the whole time; she was still alive. More or less relieved, I stretched my joints and pushed the driver's seat as far away from the steering wheel as possible so my legs had more space.

"We didn't even pack anything to eat," Tim complained eventually.

We probably couldn't have been less prepared, but it was a life-or-death situation, it only made sense that I wasn't thinking clearly. There was no time to think about something as ordinary as food, I had already lost too much time by hesitating to talk to Tim.

Eventually, we decided to search the mountain, firstly for some place where we could eat, and secondly for the hiking track I had seen in my vision. The first thing was surprisingly easy to find, and after we had dinner, Tim was keener on looking at all the hiking tracks that could possibly be the one.

It took us hours to find the right path, but eventually we found it. I could only guess that the adrenaline kept me going because my own weakness was, for once, not important to me. I couldn't believe how active I could be if it was for the sake of another person that meant as much to me as Luna did.

Even though we had found the correct hiking trail, we got lost in the woods a few times on our way back to the car (despite using Google Maps). Exhausted, we finally went to sleep.

"Ramon, it's 12 p.m." I heard Tim's voice.

He sounded dull and far away. I couldn't open my eyes to see where his voice was coming from. I wasn't feeling all too well, and if I was honest, I felt like I wouldn't be able to save her anyway.

How should I be able to change anything if I wasn't even able to open my eyes in the first place? My body was shaking. But I wasn't freezing. It wasn't cold outside.

Today was one of the few days this summer where the sun was supposed to shine. One of the few warm days in the past few weeks.

I fully woke up when Tim started shaking me. My mind was now completely awake, only my body was holding me back in my car seat like a magnet. I needed to get myself together. Just this one time. For Luna. After today, I could sleep for the rest of my life if I wanted to, but today, I needed to function. And while I was thinking about Luna, I finally managed to open my eyes.

"Damn, the night was a bit too long for me," I mumbled still half-asleep. I tried to play down the seriousness of the situation. It was impossible to tell if

Tim suspected anything, but even if he did, he stayed quiet.

We decided to drive a little closer to the hiking trail. On the one hand, because I was sure I couldn't walk that far, and on the other hand, we would be way faster by car than by foot. And we needed to be there rather sooner than later, in case anything was happening. At this time of day, our car wouldn't be as noticeable as it would've been yesterday night. At the weekend, a lot of cars drove up the mountain, it was a popular hiking and camping spot among tourists.

"Do you think today's the day?" Tim asked carefully.

I nodded.

I could feel that it was true.

"Okay, then let's not waste any more time," Tim said and jumped out of the car after we had reached our destination.

I took one more deep breath to gather all of my strength. I didn't know how exactly I should save her, but one thing was certain: I would save her. Even if that meant she would think of me as a stalker or a weirdo. She was worth it. Her life was worth it. I would do everything for her, even if I had to pay for it with my life. Finally, these thoughts helped me to leave my car as well.

Carefully, we moved in the direction of the hiking track. In my vision, her tents were close to the trail, so we had to be careful so she wouldn't see us here. Even though I wasn't fully sure if the tents from my vision belonged to her and her family, the odds were high that they did. And even if they had their tents somewhere else, we knew for sure that at some point, Luna would walk up this path, we had to be alerted all the time. We needed to be attentive while being invisible at the same time. Two things that neither Tim nor I weren't particularly great at.

It didn't take us long to find the tents from my vision, but Luna was nowhere to be found. Was it too late already? My heart started pounding, but my head was too rational to be panicky. As long as there was hope that it wasn't too late, I would stand here and wait. If I had to, forever. I had time. As long as I didn't know better, there was still a chance we could save her.

Luckily, Tim didn't say anything that could possibly trigger my insecurities. Actually, he was surprisingly quiet and calm. Although he always was a calm and relaxed person, he loved putting his foot in his mouth. His silence could only mean that even Tim had understood the seriousness of the situation, otherwise he would've tried to loosen up the mood with funny jokes.

We sat down in the shade of a large tree to hide from everyone. And we waited. So many thoughts filled my head. Was this really the right place? It had to be here. I was sure. Very sure even. I had seen this exact trail in my vision. The other hiking tracks looked way too different; this was the right spot without any doubt.

So, we continued waiting. Silence. The only noises around us were birds, which were happily chirping in the trees.

"And you are certain this is the spot?" Tim asked skeptically.

"Pssht," I said and put my finger on my lips to signal him to stay quiet.

We shouldn't risk being noticed by anyone in case my vision wouldn't happen. We needed to lay low, which meant staying quiet for most of the time. If Luna was really here, she could potentially recognize our voices.

"But yes, I'm sure that's it," I whispered.

Tim looked as tense as I felt. He had to be crazy to help me out this time. But on the other hand, he needed to be crazy to stand by my side for my whole life. And regarding that, it maybe wasn't that crazy anymore that we were lurking behind the tree waiting for something to happen. Maybe we should've tried this way earlier, when I had other visions, to see if they had to always have a deadly end.

Carefully, I stretched my neck to look past the tree trunk, which I had used as a backrest a few seconds ago.

"Do you see anything?" Tim asked quietly, but I couldn't answer. I was too focused on what was happening right in front of my eyes.

I saw Luna, and behind her a strange person appeared, who technically wasn't looking all too unfamiliar since I had seen him once before; in my vision.

I gulped.

It would happen now. I could feel it.

I had to do something. I had to jump up and pull her away from the slope, otherwise it would be too late to save her. Everything that was happening in front of me was what I had already seen in my vision. My vision was about to become reality and it would, as always, end deadly.

It seemed as if the world was moving in slow motion, but I was motionless. I was paralyzed. Was it because of my weakness or fear?

Luna hiked up the trail, a bit too close to the descent right next to it, in my opinion. The stranger from my vision was walking right behind her. He was too close to her. He stumbled over his own feet and held onto Luna to prevent a fall. She, however, started to tumble. She lost her balance and fell down the hillside.

I jumped out of my hiding place and buried my fingers in my hair. How could I be so incompetent? I couldn't let her die. I couldn't lose her. Not this way. Not through one of my visions. Not through something I could've prevented if I had told her the truth right from the start.

Just before I could storm to the hiking trail, I saw a dark creature leap itself down the descent. Everything happened so fast that I couldn't certainly say if it was real or just an illusion or even a dream.

The stranger that caused Luna's accident ran away, in the direction of the restaurant where Tim and I had dined the day before. If he was really going to the restaurant, it would mean that we had enough time to look after Luna ourselves without anybody noticing us. I immediately started to sprint away from our hideout. Tim followed me. My heart was racing even worse than before, and I couldn't deny the feeling of panic anymore. Still, I had to see her. Even if it was for the last time. I had to see how she was doing. Maybe there was something I could do for her. To save her. It wasn't possible that I was too incompetent. The only reason I was here this exact moment was to save her, and eventually I failed.

I looked down the steep slope and saw her. Her body was all curled up on the ground, the same way as in my prediction. It was too late. She was… She was…

Tears were running down my cheeks. I couldn't believe what had just happened. I couldn't stand looking at her anymore. I didn't want to look at anything anymore. Was there anything I could do in life, or was everything I started just doomed to fail?

I looked away and finally broke down.

Tim, who was still staring down the descent, carefully put a hand on my shoulder, but I just pushed him away.

I didn't want to be touched by anyone ever again. Because this was exactly what would happen if someone came too close to me; they would eventually die.

I didn't even bother trying to hide my tears. I couldn't care less what the other hikers or even Luna's family would think about me if they would see me here. I didn't care what my father would think of me, in case he would ever find out. It was okay to cry and it was okay to break down if one lived through so many tragedies like me. But the worst of all weren't the tears, it was the feeling of not feeling anything at all. Not even emptiness. Absolutely nothing.

How was it possible to show emotions and to be certain to have them, but you simply weren't feeling them? Not even a tiny bit. My head had emotionally shut down; my body couldn't bear the pain of another loss anymore.

"Ramon," Tim said, but I ignored him.

No matter what he was trying to say next, nothing, absolutely nothing, would fill the hole in me that her death had left behind.

"Ramon," Tim tried again to talk to me.

Why couldn't he simply let it go? Why did he not let me go when I tried to push him away from me years ago? Because then I would have been all alone from the beginning. I would have never dreamt about starting a new and normal life. I would have never waited for Luna in front of her school to talk to her. Without Tim and Luna, it wouldn't have been a wonderful life, but at least Luna would've been alive, and that would be worth all of that.

"Ramon, you should look at that."

"What?" I yelled at him. "What should I look at? Her dead body? Well, I've already seen it all in my vision."

"I don't think you've seen this in your vision." He stayed calm despite everything.

Still in tears, I let Tim turn my head to the side so I was facing the slope again. And when I looked down, I could see what he saw. Luna had moved. It was impossible. A death from this height must've been deadly. But she was alive.

Chapter 3

It was the first day of school in over a week. My mom made sure I was put on sick leave – even though the doctors reassured her that, against all odds, I was perfectly fine and didn't even suffer from a slight concussion or anything else – so I could recover from the accident. I was annoyed that I wasn't allowed to do anything, although I was feeling alright. Again, I felt weak, but not physically, and without any control over my life.

Every hour, my mom was entering my room to check whether I was still alive or had died from some unacknowledged internal bleeding. And even though I had told her multiple times that everything was fine, she didn't stop. She could be as stubborn as me, but I was used to it by now. That's why I was even more relieved when I finally was able to see my friends again after all this drama.

Obviously, they had already knew about the 'Miracle in the Mountains' – the media were talking about it every day, it was impossible for anyone to not have heard about it. But who could be mad about it? The most exciting things that were happening in this town were dogs running away or chess tournaments.; nothing exciting ever happened here.

But me surviving a fall from a height that was supposed to be deadly was some sort of sensation that wouldn't repeat itself any time soon. Nobody could explain why I was still alive, and I guess that made the accident seem even more exciting for the media. They finally had a story with a happy ending.

Personally, I didn't really know how to feel about everything. I probably read so much about the incident that it felt as if it happened to someone else. It didn't feel like it was me falling down that slope, and except for a few bruises and some ripped pants, nothing had happened to me. So, there was absolutely nothing that could remind me of the fact that it was actually me falling down the mountain. It really had to be a miracle.

My first day of school after the accident could be described as pure horror. Everyone treated me as if I was fragile and recently had a near-death experience, even though I had never been in any danger. All I wanted to do was to spend a normal day with my friends at school to be distracted from everything going on in my life, but my plan failed enormously. And even more, I hated all of the attention I was receiving.

The only good thing was that I didn't encounter Matt that day. He seemed to be ill, although I wasn't sure if he could even become sick. I had seen him that night in the mansion, and as quickly as his wounds healed back then, I'd always assumed he was invincible or something like that. But I was perfectly fine with not seeing him. And who knew, maybe there were special diseases that only supernatural creatures could have? If that was the case, I wouldn't feel sorry for him.

Even though my mom wasn't happy about it, I went to visit Ramon right after school. She would've preferred me coming straight home so she could take care of me again. Also, she still disliked him somehow. I, however, felt like I needed to see him. I had questions. Many questions. And he was the only one that could answer them.

Ramon hugged me tightly as a greeting and didn't say anything. I was quiet as well. But the fact that he embraced me as if I had almost died just confirmed to me that he probably knew more about my accident than he wanted to admit.

Everything suddenly fit together. His weird behavior when I had told him about the camping trip. His bad mood that he tried to hide from me. His tight hug, as if he didn't want to ever let me leave him again. Everything.

"You knew it, didn't you?" I asked after he eventually let go of me.

He nodded quietly.

"Why didn't you tell me?" I asked further after we sat down on his sofa.

"I didn't know how to tell you. I was scared you would lose your faith in me. Or even run away. I had everything under control, and I was so sure I could live a normal life, and then…" In the end, his voice got quieter.

He looked at the ground.

"But we already went through all of these uncertainties, and I decided to stay," I argued.

"I didn't think that far," he admitted.

"Are you mad?" he asked carefully.

"I had more than enough time to think about it, and since nothing happened, I have no reason to be angry, but in case you want to kill me again, please let me know beforehand so I can be prepared," I answered and smiled at him encouragingly.

He returned my smile.

"I wonder why I'm still alive. I mean, your visions are always deadly, aren't they?" Finally, I could ask the question that had been occupying my head for the past few days.

"That night…" I gulped.

It still was hard to talk about the night in the mansion.

"When Matt kidnapped me… He was certain your visions would always end deadly."

"As far as I know, they do. I have no explanation either."

And then he told me how he ran after me to save me from his vision. How Tim and he saw my fall down the slope and how some dark creature came after me.

All these things were new to me, since I didn't notice anything while falling; everything had happened so fast. It must've been this mysterious creature that had saved my life, or was it nothing more than an imagination made up by Ramon's mind to trick him?

I started to feel like I was trapped in an episode of *Beyond Belief: Fact or Fiction*. Unfortunately, I had always been pretty bad at distinguishing the true stories from the fake ones. In the end, it didn't matter who or what had saved me or if I even was saved at all, the only thing that mattered was that I had survived.

I observed how Ramon was trying to drink a glass of water with shaking hands and eyed him skeptically. It was pretty obvious he wasn't okay.

"I'm worried about you since that night in the mansion." Again, I tried to talk about the topic he always tried to avoid.

"You don't have to. I'm okay," he responded immediately.

"No, don't you dare say that everything is okay when I can clearly see how miserable you are. Your visions are back, and you look like you haven't slept in days. You always claim you are okay. Always. Everything is okay, but you are never truly fine. So, stop playing pretend," I finally exploded.

"Then you know as much as me. What else do you want to hear?" he shrugged.

I opened my mouth, ready to argue, but I didn't know what to respond, so I stayed quiet.

Eventually, it was Ramon who broke the silence: "I don't know what's going on with me. At the beginning, I thought it was the usual and familiar weakness I always have after trying out telepathic things, but it feels like it never ends."

"Do you have any theories why it hasn't stopped yet?" I wanted to know.

He shook his head.

Damn. Maybe we needed Tim's uncomplicated way of thinking to find a solution.

"Does Tim know?"

"I didn't tell him upfront."

"Maybe we should tell him, he could probably help us," I proposed.

"I don't want to worry another person. If he finds out about it himself or if I have another vision, I'll talk to him, but at the moment, I want to leave him out of this mess," he explained.

That was fine for me, for now, because I knew Ramon could be stubborn as well. But in the future, I wouldn't let the topic slide that easily.

"The two of us can find out what's going on by ourselves," he said after a while and took my hand.

I nodded and let him pull me closer to his body, so I could place my head on his shoulder. I was so damn worried about him. Since the night in the mansion. Since the encounter with the magicians. Since they threw this mysterious potion onto him.

I twitched. Maybe that was what had started all of this.

"That's it," I mumbled and looked into Ramon's confused face.

"It started with the potion of the magicians. Nothing else makes sense. It has to be the potion. I told you right from the start, but you didn't want to listen," I burst out.

"Damn, you could be right," he pressed out between his lips.

"But that would mean it won't get better by itself," I figured.

He just nodded with an empty glance.

I would love to know what he was thinking. I didn't even know how I should handle the situation how should he know what to do? It was obvious that there was no way to prevent another encounter with the magicians and then there was still the problem I had with Matt. Luckily, Ramon had no clue about his appearance in this town. Was Matt still connected to the magicians, or why else did he return to this city?

I was probably looking lost in thoughts because now it was Ramon who looked at me worried: "What do you think about?"

"We will have to meet the magicians again," I tried distracting him from my real thoughts.

I would continue keeping Matt a secret from Ramon. It would only enrage him, and he didn't need more stress than he already had.

Matt wasn't his problem, he was mine. And I had to deal with him. All by myself.

Chapter 4

Even I couldn't explain how Luna could have survived. Nobody could. It was the first time I had witnessed one of my visions being not deadly, however, this didn't calm me down much. Apparently, there were certain circumstances – and I didn't know whether they were supernatural or not – that could cause my visions to become invalid.

It was an interesting hypothesis that I needed to investigate. Unfortunately, all the methods to further explore this theory were ethically reprehensible. There was no chance I would trigger visions of my friends on purpose. It would be fatal, and my psyche had already signaled me that I couldn't take the loss of another person.

How much could humans bear until they would finally break? It probably depended on the person, but personally, I knew I had reached my limit. Additionally, there was no guarantee that exploring my visions would be helpful in any way. On first glance, it seemed like a miracle that Luna survived – even for her – so, maybe all of this was just one enormous coincidence or some kind of error. Again, there were so many unanswered questions, and again, I lacked answers.

Maybe everything would be easier if we would stop working against each other. If I had told Luna earlier how horribly I was actually feeling, maybe we would've realized sooner that the magicians were responsible for all of my issues. Then I would've told her about my vision, and she maybe would've not gone on that camping trip with her family. Maybe I had known it all the time in my subconscious that my behavior wasn't normal, I just didn't want to admit the undeniable connection to the wizards. Maybe I wanted to lie to myself to make things easier. So many maybes. But no answers.

I wanted to solve my problems alone and to leave her out of this mess. To protect her. But if I would try again to handle everything by myself, I would be exactly where I had started. Or had I reached my starting point already?

My visions were uncontrollable again and I noticed that I tried to avoid going outside more and more. Maybe Luna was right, and I should tell Tim about it. It would be way easier for me if I didn't have to pretend as if everything was alright even though it wasn't. It would be easier if we would stop keeping secrets from one another just to protect each other. We needed to work together to actually be able to protect each other, like we had done it that night.

It was early in the morning. The birds were already awake and chirping, and the sky changed its color from midnight blue to pink. The air was still fresh, so I did the most German thing ever and opened all of my windows to air the room. Although it was early in the morning, I wanted to start working already. I had planned for a while to wake up earlier to help improve my sleep schedule, but so far it has never really worked. Every time my alarm clock rang, I simply turned it off and continued sleeping. Every time, I didn't feel strong enough to get out of bed.

But today I did it, which filled me with pride. And especially because everything seemed to finally work out smoothly, there was no way I could've predicted what was about to happen.

He was just making his coffee to properly start the morning – usually, he didn't like coffee but he needed the caffeine to get through the day – when he sensed an all too familiar tingle twitching through his body. Immediately, he put his mug down on the kitchen counter. The tingle became stronger, and he noticed his view becoming blurrier and blurrier. He didn't want all of this to happen. He really didn't, but he couldn't stop it either, no matter how hard he tried. The vision overcame him.

His view was completely blurred for a second, and when he was finally able to see again, he saw a road. A road that wasn't used by a lot of cars at this time of the day since it was clearly night. And he saw Tim. Tim wanted to cross the empty street. Then he saw what Tim couldn't see anymore. A car that didn't bother about the speed limit raced at him. Squeaking breaks. Illegal street race. Despite breaking, the car was too fast. It couldn't stop in time. Tim was dead.

A clinking noise brought him back to reality. Even though he had put down the mug, he had managed to push it from the kitchen counter. He was mad, not because of the mug – he didn't care about that – he was mad about what he had become because of the magicians. They had managed to weaponize him against his own friends, and it was simply too much to handle.

Now he had no other choice; he needed to tell Tim everything. The magicians brought out the monster inside of him that he had tried to repress for most of his life. But now it was out of control and deadlier than ever.

"Is everything alright? You look pale," Tim wondered when I was standing in front of his door. Again.

I had immediately made my way over to his place to warn him. I needed every second I could have with him. This time we couldn't sit there and wait for another miracle to happen. Luna had gotten incredible lucky. How were the odds this would happen again? Probably zero.

If I were a mathematician, I would maybe claim the odds were never zero, they might have been leaning towards zero, but they were never actually zero.

However, I was no mathematician, I was a computer scientist.

Suddenly, so many thoughts were filling my head. What if today was his last day? What if we would never see each other again, starting tomorrow? Where would I be without him? Was he able to do all of the things he wanted to do in life? What would I do if I had only one day to live?

Usually, I tried to repress thoughts like this because the odds that I would die were kind of low. I was 20 years old; I was still pretty young. Well, maybe one could argue that the fact the magicians were after me would potentially raise the odds of me dying young, but nobody could tell if they would actually kill me. They probably needed me too much to murder me. And even if they were trying to do something to me, I could still… No. I would rather sacrifice myself than to murder another person. Not the magicians, and especially not Tim.

"Nothing is alright. We have a problem," I almost screamed at him in despair.

I sighed and sat down at Tim's table while he took a seat on the opposite side of the table and continued eating.

"Did you have another vision?" he asked seriously.

He probably had realized that the situation I was in was more difficult than it had appeared at first glance.

"Yes, and you won't like what I saw," I pressed out from between my lips.

My heart beat incredibly fast, and I hoped that Tim would find a solution. He always could find solutions to get rid of – for me – unsolvable problems within seconds. If someone could help me, it would be him. And this time he needed a good idea, because I had nothing.

If Luna hadn't been saved through a miracle, she would be dead by now. Despite us trying to protect her, we were too late to stop the vision. But this time, I wasn't allowed to be late again.

"Is it about me?" he asked hesitantly and chewed on his cereals.

"Yes," I whispered almost inaudible.

Tim coughed a little, maybe because of the surprise. Quickly, he chugged down his glass of water so the coughing could become better again.

"I need to admit, I was prepared for everything except that." His glance was empty, and all of the color in his face had vanished.

I didn't know him like this. After all the years I had known him, I had never seen him like this, and it tore me apart on the inside to watch him.

The one thing that could've happened all the previous years has happened, and he had known the risk had always been there. Still, it seemed surprising for the both of us. Especially after all the progress I had made with Tim's help. I was nothing without him. He was my Barbie, and I was his Ken; I was dependent on him.

All the years that I had spent alone, he had been the main character in my life, while I have felt more like a side character in his. And despite all of this, he had always come back to me. Even though he knew that every day could have been his last one. Live your life as if every day would be the last, my ass. How often would one think about making the most of every damn day, and at the end of it we were all stuck doing the same bullshit as always? It wasn't much different for Tim. If he had started living each day to the fullest a bit sooner, he might have left me alone with my misery, and maybe his life would've been longer than it was now.

At his request, I told him every detail about the vision, like the cause of death but also the time of day – at night.

He thought about it briefly, then he remembered: "Actually, I have a date at the cinema in the evening this week. I'm glad to hear it works out well if I'm walking through the streets late… Are you sure I'm alone? Have you seen someone else?"

"I'm not a love oracle," I tried to remind him, but, on the inside, I was glad he didn't look as serious as before. In the meantime, the color has returned to his face again.

"How could I forget about that."

Tim took another sip of his drink.

Then he continued: "But maybe you are right and I should rather cancel the date for now."

"That might be a good start," I felt relieved.

Now Tim knew everything, and he surely wouldn't walk through the streets at night. This was all we could do in the moment except for keeping our eyes open and hoping everything would turn out alright.

***

Although Tim had cancelled his date and didn't even think about leaving his house as soon as it started getting dark, I still felt desperate. His caution calmed me down, but at the same time I was incredibly afraid of the future. He was my best friend since I could remember, and he was the only one that was always by my side no matter what. I felt so damn guilty. How could I cause such a drama, he was my best friend? Within just a few weeks, I had managed to sentence two of the most important people in my life to death without even wanting this to happen.

It was the third evening in a row where I couldn't fall asleep without calling Tim first. Hearing his voice calmed me down; I then knew he was alive and well.

"All these precautions drive me crazy," Tim complained. Then he added while laughing: "Today, I almost got run over three times by bikes all while trying to keep myself as far away as possible from any car I could see."

In my opinion, it felt like he was trying to play things down. To make everything seem less bad. But it was pretty damn terrifying. He would not simply get hurt, he would die, and everything was my fault.

"Then you need to be more careful," I said without thinking about whether it was even possible or not.

"I'm trying my best, but it's hard," Tim justified himself.

"I know", I sighed. "But hopefully it is a once in a lifetime situation that we'll eventually get through."

"But how? Should I lock myself at home all day long or should I try to live my life as normally as possible?" he blurted out.

Usually, it was me who asked all of these questions that no one could really answer. It was odd to see Tim in my position.

"I don't know," I admitted. "Just be careful, okay?"

"Can't you somehow take your vision back?"

"I wish I would know how to do so. I'm really sorry." At the end of the sentence, I became quieter.

If I knew what I could do to make my prediction invalid, I would do it without hesitating. This situation sucked, and I was tired of living like that. How could everything escalate like that? These damn magicians. If I would find them again… Then… Well, what would I do to them? Killing them wasn't an option, and I was well aware of that. So, I probably wouldn't do anything to them except for discussing and hoping that Matt wasn't with them. At least I was physically stronger than the magicians, but I had zero chances against Matt.

The phone call with Tim didn't solve the problem. None of us had any idea of what to do next. Maybe my vision had an expiration date, and after that Tim could live his normal life again. Maybe he had to get into this life-threatening situation to be safe again. Maybe I could take a chance and this time save my friend.

That was the solution. He had to face my vision. Otherwise, we would never know when he would be safe again. But could we really risk it? Definitely not, but we had to. Otherwise, we would have to live forever with the knowledge that the vision could strike at any time. Otherwise, Tim would have to live the life I should've lived from the start for eternity. Isolated from everyone and everything.

Tim wasn't happy about my idea when I told him about it during our next phone call, but he knew that I was right. We had no other option. If someone could stop my vision from happening, it would be me.

This time, it was noticeable harder for him to trust me – I couldn't blame him since I was weak and my visions were going crazy, I barely trusted myself – but we had to try it. We had to leave all of this behind us so we could finally sleep again at night.

So many thoughts crossed my head while we walked to the street I had seen in my vision when it got dark. It was pretty easy for us to find the right street since it was one of the few bigger main streets in our city. Nobody would expect an illegal street race to take place here. Anywhere but here. Anywhere but this sleepy town.

Even though it was already dark, the air was still lukewarm. It could be a pretty nice evening if it wasn't for…

"Are you scared?" I asked Tim when we arrived at the spot I had seen in my vision.

"I know, I should be afraid, but somehow, I'm not. I trust you. You can't let me die this easily, you would be lost without me," he said jokingly.

As an answer, I carefully boxed against his arm. But he was right. Without him, I would be lost.

We continued starring at each other for a moment.

"In case this will be my last words, I want to thank you for the great time. If I die tonight, all of this was totally worth it."

I hugged him.

"We will make it!"

I tried to swallow the gigantic lump that was in my throat.

"And if we won't, you will follow me one day, and we'll see each other again on the other side. In case, you want to switch shores for me, or teams, or how exactly the kids would say it."

"Was that an outing?" I asked perplexed, and watched him shrug while already crossing the street.

So much about choosing your last words wisely. Still, I couldn't allow myself to think too much about the meaning of his words; I needed to stay focused.

Since we didn't know at what time my vision would strike, we had agreed that it was for the best if Tim would cross the street, carefully, of course, until something would happen. Even if it would take all night long.

More than an hour has passed, and we hadn't seen a single car drive by.

"Are you sure it's the right day for your vision?" Tim wanted to know after a while.

"I don't know, but I guess so. Can we even be wrong about the day if we never knew when it would happen in the first place?"

And because he didn't have a better answer to that, we simply continued what we had started.

Hours passed and we became more and more tired. I could notice that my focus wasn't as clear as it had been at the start, and my body started shaking again. I wasn't allowed to feel weak. It could happen any second. I needed to be ready. In case of an emergency, I needed to be able to stop the car telepathically.

Although it had been some time ago when I had moved something only with the power of my mind, to be more specific, the last time was during that night in the mansion. But nothing would stop me from being there for my best friend when he needed me the most.

Unfortunately, my body had other plans. The shaking got worse and took full control of my body. It didn't stop until I finally sank down to the ground because my legs couldn't carry the weight of my body anymore. Tim on the other side of the street noticed my fall.

"Ramon," he screamed scared, and ran across the street.

He wanted to come to me. Without checking for any traffic. Wanted to cross the street. And then it was time; the car came.

Out of reflex, I closed my eyes. I knew it would happen now. I could feel it in every cell of my body. I wanted to... I couldn't look at it. The last thing I could hear was the squeaking of wheels.

"Fuuuuuuuuuuckk," I swore loudly.

I dared to open my eyes again. I needed to know how Tim was doing. So far, I could still hope for a miracle. Maybe I could even save him if I called an ambulance in time. Maybe it wasn't over yet. Maybe there was still a tiny chance that my visions wouldn't always end up being deadly. Maybe...

Tim was curled up on the ground next to a puddle of blood that had formed around him. Although he didn't move, I was close enough to him to be able to see that he was still breathing. The car, however, was already gone. Hit and run. What an asshole. From the bottom of my heart, I wished the driver everything bad in this universe so that he would never have a decent day ever again.

I tried to get myself together and stand up. It didn't work particularly well, but it worked. As fast as possible, I stumbled in the direction of Tim and threw myself next to him. Slowly, he seemed to wake up again. He turned his head around, and his facial expression visibly changed from all the pain he was in.

"Tim? Are you alright? I'll call you an ambulance," I asked him immediately, even though I knew he wouldn't be able to respond.

The next day, I picked Luna up from school so we could visit Tim in the hospital. Of course, we had informed her about our plan before last night. And even though our begging attempts to not accompany us on our mission were unsuccessful, in the end, it was her mother who ruined her plan of joining us since she didn't allow her to spend another night at my place. She would never know, but she did Tim and me a huge favor by keeping Luna out of everything. She was already traumatized enough by the night in the mansion. And even though we all went through that particular night, I would always choose to protect her from any additional trauma. And after I had seen Tim being hurt like this, I could confirm that it was, in fact, a very traumatic event that I would have loved to miss out myself.

But now that he was in the hospital, no one, not even her mother, could prevent her from checking on Tim.

Tim was already awake when we entered the room.

"I'm still alive," he greeted us happily.

He looked so much better than last night.

"How are you?" I asked while taking place on the chair next to his bed.

"Everything is great. There were only a few wounds that bled a lot, but now everything is treated properly, and I'm doing fine again. Of course, I have this super ugly dressing around my head, but all that matters is that I survived. "

He scratched his head.

"But how?" Luna said astonished.

"I wish I'd know, but I don't. The only thing I remember is that something pushed me away just in time. The doctors could reassure me that the car never touched me. Otherwise, I would have probably died," he explained patiently.

"So, does this mean that my vision was again cancelled by something?" I concluded.

"Something or someone", Luna whispered.

Tim and I looked at her in confusion.

"Well, maybe it's somebody that saves us. Someone else with supernatural powers," she explained her train of thought.

Chapter 5

The past few days were very eventful, and it was difficult to have one clear thought in my brain. The incident with Tim only proved to me that it wasn't a coincidence I had survived. And if there was one thing, I had learned from my *Teen Wolf* addiction it was that if something happened twice, it could be a coincidence, but if it happened three times, it was a pattern.

So far, whatever happened had only happened twice, still I was certain there had to be more to it. The odds simply were way too low for a coincidence to break Ramon's vision twice. Someone had saved us on purpose, but who? Why did the person not show themselves?

At school, I was way too unfocused. During break time, Finn only looked at me worriedly. Luckily, he didn't question what was going on, because it would've been difficult for me to lie to him. Especially because I wanted nothing more but to tell him the full truth.

So far, it seemed as if he had accepted that I kept a few things a secret from him, which I found pretty mature. I had no clue if I could be so chill in his position or if I would already doubt the whole friendship, but that was just the way he was. He was simply Finn.

Unfortunately, Matt was still a part of our friend group and spent every school break with us. Every attempt to discreetly get rid of him failed, and I had to make peace with the thought of him being around us. How ironic.

A few days after Tim was released from the hospital, my mood lightened up again. There was one thing less to worry about, which was pretty refreshing. With Ramon's still declining health situation and my own problems at home but also at school, it was nice to have one person to not worry about.

Now that things have calmed down, I finally found the motivation to hang out with Jane again. We had planned to spend a relaxing girls-afternoon together after school. It had been forever since we did something only the two of us, so it was about time to start hanging out without the boys again. At least that was the original plan.

After school had ended, I sat down in the entrance hall and waited for Jane. It didn't take long for her to arrive. Together with Matt. These two were getting along a little bit too well, in my opinion, and I started to get worried about this unusual friendship. What if he would hurt her?

As far as I knew, they spent time together after school. She had even shared her love for different colored nail polish with him so that Matt started painting his own nails – or letting her paint his nails? – in black, of course. A different color would obviously destroy his mysterious bad boy aura. Oh, if Jane would know how bad he could be. She would suddenly dislike him.

"Do you mind if Matt joins us today?" She immediately asked after greeting me.

I gulped.

No, it wasn't okay. But she couldn't know that. She couldn't know that Matt was a supernatural lunatic that would kill us if he desired to do so and that he only sneaked into our group of friends to pressure me. She couldn't know that he would ditch all of us as soon as he got what he wanted. At least, that was my perception of the situation after he had dropped the magicians that easily.

I stared at Matt's triumphant face.

"It's fine with me. The more the merrier or something like this," I said only halfway believable, but Jane didn't seem to notice.

Accompanied by Matt, we made our way to the city center. All the time, I tried to keep the conversation as superficial as possible and avoided to talk about Ramon. Luckily, Jane didn't seem to notice this either. Usually, she always loved discussing my love life in every excruciating detail, but today she seemed to be focused on other things.

Matt was mostly keeping himself out of our conversation, as if he was just listening, and didn't even want to hang out with us in the first place. Sometimes, I still couldn't say what he was thinking or doing, and even more important, why he was doing it. What kind of help did he expect from Ramon? But as long as they wouldn't meet again, everything was fine. As long as they wouldn't meet, I shouldn't care about it. I should try to ignore his existance.

Since the weather was warm enough for ice cream, we decided to grab some and sit down on a bench. Still, I tried to only engage in a superficial conversation. What an odd thing to do. When we finished our ice cream, Jane had to go home. She didn't leave without telling us how much she enjoyed the afternoon and that we should totally repeat it in the future. It seemed as if she had a great time, and if she had a nice day, then all the torture I went through was somehow worth it.

As soon as Jane left, an awkward silence took over her place. I eagerly tried to figure out an excuse to leave the situation until I came to the realization that I didn't need a reason to leave. Matt didn't deserve any excuse; I could walk away any time. He still was the bad guy. He had kidnapped me in the mansion, not the other way around. He had hurt me. He had laughed at me. I didn't owe him anything, and I needed to stop being so damn friendly to everyone. I needed to stop being a pushover.

"I dare you to hurt her," I hissed at him, then I turned around and walked in the direction of my bus stop.

"Wait," he shouted and ran after me.

Even without using his supernatural speed, he could easily keep up with my pace.

"You don't actually think I would hurt anyone?" He asked me as if it was completely absurd to think something like that. As if he was harmless.

"The last time I thought like that, you hurt my boyfriend a lot," I pressed out between my lips.
I needed to get a grip on myself to not yell at him. How could he dare to pretend to be the good guy here?

"And if I think about it even more, what exactly happened to Ramon's Grandma?" I asked him.

"That was a rhetorical question. You don't need to answer it," I quoted him and added a fake smile.

Then I turned around again to continue my way to the bus stop. I didn't want to discuss with him.

"But I didn't harm you," he tried again to talk to me, and grabbed my arm. Surprisingly, his grip was loosened; I could easily free myself if I wanted to. So, I did before I turned back to him one last time.

"You almost broke my arm."

"Yeah, but I didn't actually harm you," he tried to justify himself.

"I don't know if you know, but humans are fragile creatures. Even a broken arm is incredibly painful," I said bitterly.

"You are so stubborn and unforgiving, do you know that?"

I walked faster. I didn't want to be here with him. Didn't want to talk to him. If I could, I would've loved to go to Ramon now, but the odds were too high that Matt would follow me, so I couldn't risk it.

"I don't want to hurt anyone, I promise. I only came back because I need Ramon's help," he stopped right in front of me to block my path.

"The only way I would bring you to Ramon is over my dead body. I don't trust you, don't you get it?" I tried to explain.

"And I never will. Not after everything you've done," I added.

"You never gave me a chance. It's no surprise you can't trust me." He raised his voice but it was obvious that he was desperate.

"I'm not the bad guy here."

"It doesn't matter. For me, you are. And that's enough of a reason to not trust you."

"What can I do to change this? We are running in circles." He correctly figured this out.

"And that's why we both should end the conversation and go home," I proposed and squeezed myself past him. This was a great exit. Again.

The bus stop was a bit further away from the city center, and most of the time I was the only person waiting there. Usually, it didn't bother me too much, but today I had an unwell feeling about it. A glance at the bus schedule told me that I had 15 exciting minutes of waiting time ahead of me. I sighed. Actually, I just wanted to be home and maybe cry a bit because my life was an absolute chaos, and I had no clue how to fix anything. But at the same time, I didn't want to go home either because then I would have to talk about my day with my mom and her new boyfriend – they both tried their best to pretend as if nothing had changed in my life – and I really didn't need that.

Suddenly, I felt two strong hands grab my shoulder and pull me away so quickly I could barely notice it. Everything happened so fast, I couldn't even scream. Out of reflex, I closed my eyes. I couldn't think clearly anymore, and the only thing I could feel was a tear leaving my eye and running down my cheek.

After I couldn't feel any more movement around me, I dared to open my eyes. The warm sunbeams were blinding me. I heard birds chirping, and a fresh smell of flowers was in the air. After looking around for a few more seconds, I figured out that I was standing on a meadow. Where the hell was I?

On my right side was a small creek floating down a mountain, a few meters behind me was a slope, and on my left side, there was no one other than Matt.

"Are you completely insane?" I yelled at him and started boxing against his chest.

Usually, I wasn't a huge fan of violence, but these circumstances were special, and, therefore, I could discard my morals at least for once. I have never been so happy that I joined a boxing club than in this moment, and I could only hope he would never try stunts like this in the future.

After a few punches, I stopped because I came to the conclusion that it hurt me way more than it hurt him.

"I needed to talk to you without anyone else around," he admitted and casually scratched the back of his head. Sun rays were shining on his dark hair.

"So, you thought you kidnap me again?" I hissed at him. "How can someone lack basic human empathy?"

"What does empathy mean?" He wanted to know.

At first, I thought he was simply being ironic, and would start laughing about me for some reason. So, I was even more confused when this didn't happen.

I snorted disparagingly.

Was he expecting me to laugh first? Matt still looked at me in confusion, and only then did I realize that he was dead serious about his question. So, I briefly explained the meaning of the word empathy to him so he could understand why I was mad. It also helped me calm down a little bit.

"I'm sorry I scared you. I was desperate."

"Socially incompetent," I corrected him coldly.

He laughed.

"Maybe that as well," he admitted.

I took a deep breath to be in control of my emotions again. It wasn't until then that I realized how fresh and clean the air up here felt. In general, this here was actually a nice place. If I would've been here by choice and not because Matt kidnapped me.

"Where are we?" I wondered with curiosity in my voice.

My rationality had taken over my body, and I had come to the realization that this was neither the place nor the time to start a fight with Matt. Up here was nobody except us, and I knew I had zero chances in a one-vs.-one against him, despite my boxing experiences.

"On the top of a mountain," he answered dryly.

"Yeah, but where exactly and why are we here?" I asked further.

"By car, it's 30 minutes away from the city center. By using supernatural speed only five to ten minutes, it depends if one travels alone or in company," he winked at me.

I could only roll my eyes at him.

"How often do you come here with someone else?" I wanted to know.

Now I was curious if he did this more often, kidnapping people against their wishes.

"Today," he turned around so that his back faced me and started walking a few steps. Away from the slope behind us. Only now could I see a small wooden cabin that was located at the beginning of the dense forest.

"Today," he repeated and turned back towards me, "is the first time that I brought someone else home."

"Does this mean you live here?" I asked dumbfounded.

I had never thought about where Matt was living. I might have expected him to live in some kind of apartment like every other human being. Or maybe at a dark and enchanted place like a graveyard or the sewers or something like that. Let's just say I had expected everything but this.

"Yes, this bachelor pad is all mine," he declared proudly.

What a bizarre guy. He knew what a bachelor pad was but not what empathy meant.

"Here I live and study everything about human behavior. You are really fascinating creatures, do you know that?" He continued talking while I followed him towards his cabin.

I must have been insane.

Before we entered, I said: "If there is a piano inside, you won't be able to ever convince me that you're not a vampire."

He looked at me and smirked.

"You watch too many movies, but I have to admit, I understand your reference," he shook his head in disbelief.

"You watched vampire movies?" I was flabbergasted.

"I wanted to understand why you asked me if I sparkle in the sunlight," he admitted almost a bit shy.

"But just so you know, I don't play the piano. I play the guitar," he enlightened me.

Then we entered.

I really must have been insane. Otherwise, I didn't have any explanation for why I followed him as if we were casually hanging out at his place. Trusting him would be the worst thing I could possibly do. I was probably better off if I had jumped off that slope earlier. But then again, falling from a descent would be the death of me. When I followed Matt, I had at least a tiny chance that he eventually would bring me back home safely.

The inside of the small cabin looked exactly how I would imagine a wooden house in the Alps to look like. The interior was very minimalistic and wooden. There was a bed, a couch, a commode, and a wardrobe. Only the chaos on the couch table felt a bit out of place. When I got closer, I realized that most of the chaos came from a number of teen magazines lying around. In front of the fireplace was the fur of a wild hog, including its head.

Disgusted, I starred at what used to be a graceful animal. Even if I was still eating meat, using animals as furniture or decoration simply felt wrong. Then again, did I expect anything else from Matt? He didn't even know the meaning of the word empathy; how could I expect him to have basic morals that even a lot of humans were lacking?

"Don't worry, it's not real," Matt said after he had seen my apparently obviously disgusted face.

"But where does it come from?" I asked skeptically.

"I bought it online. I just wanted this place to feel cozier, and I thought it suited the style of the house," he argued.

Somehow, he was right, it did suit the cabin, but on the other hand, it was still weird.

My glance wandered around, and I noticed that he didn't have a kitchen.

"You don't eat?" I blurted out.

"Correct," he confirmed my theory.

"Tell me again, how is your relationship to garlic?"

I looked him deep in the eyes.

He started to laugh.

"What do I need to do to prove that I'm not a vampire?"

"I don't know. But as long as you don't, I need to stick to my theory," I answered ironically.

Of course, I had realized that he wasn't a vampire, but it was fun to mock him. And if this was the only thing, I could do to feel superior – even powerful – to him, I would do it for as long as I could.

"But what are you?" I wondered after I had carefully sat down on the couch next to Matt.

"Definitely not a part of Team Edward. But to be honest, I don't really understand anyone in this triangle relationship," he answered sarcastic.

"That wasn't my question, and you know that."

"I don't know," he answered my question and shrugged.

I didn't expect this answer. He always seemed so confident and tough that I was sure he knew exactly who he was and where he belonged. But I was wrong.

"And why did you bring me here? In case you think I would trust you more if you kidnap me, you're wrong. Trust is something you earn over time and not through abduction," I stated my point and demonstratively crossed my arms in front of my chest.

"I took you with me because I think we met on the wrong foot, and up here, we can talk about everything without your friends around," he explained his train of thoughts.

"But you could've simply asked me and... – "

"And then you still wouldn't have come with me. You are way too stubborn for that," he interrupted me. He was right, and I knew it. Still kidnapping me wasn't a great decision either.

Not going to lie, I was pretty surprised by his knowledge of human nature despite not being one himself. Or maybe I was just an opened book; easy to read.

"Then what exactly do you want to talk about?" I pushed the conversation forward.

"I want to talk about what happened in the mansion. You need to understand that I don't work for the magicians anymore."

"How should I know you don't say this to spy on us?" I interrupted him quickly.

"Let me speak first," he said demanding, but chill at the same time.

He leaned back casually and sighed.

"I know the three magicians for a long time, to be more accurate, I know them for my whole life. They raised me when my biological parents had left me all by myself. Because of them, I even got the chance to develop my powers in the first place, and in exchange, I listened to their orders. Back then, it seemed fair to me. I never cared about power or hurting people. I simply followed their orders because I would be nothing without them, and they were the only people in this world I could trust. No matter how idiotic family behaves towards you, they somehow still are family, and the magicians were mine.

Of course, they used me, but they were the only people I had in my life. I could never hurt them. Still, I knew that I didn't want to live like this anymore. The only reason why I didn't leave them sooner is because they made a promise. I would help them find Ramon, and in return, they would give me the information I need to figure out what exactly I am. Only if I figure out who I am can I become fully independent from them and have access to my full potential because they enchanted me when I was younger and not as powerful.

Well, what should I say... They would've never let me go, and maybe deep down I knew it all along, so I ran away, and since them I'm trying to figure out my origin to break the bond between me and the magicians forever," he ended his very detailed explanation.

It sounded plausible, but I still couldn't trust him. All of this could also be another plan created by the magicians to fool us. I couldn't trust anyone anymore. How should I? After everything that had happened in the past months.

In case Matt was telling the truth, I felt sorry for him. But I couldn't help him. Under these circumstances, I simply couldn't and didn't want to trust him.

"I would love to help you, but it's too much to ask for. I'm sorry, but Ramon is my highest priority right now, and I will never lead you to him," I explained calmly.

I hated to admit that it was harder to let him down than it should have been. I was such a disgusting people pleaser.

He seemed disappointed. And it seemed so real.

I tried to smile encouragingly, but it didn't seem to work much.

"Thanks, anyway," he whispered and tried to smile as well, despite still looking pretty down.

"For what?" I asked confused.

"For listening and not completely freaking out that I brought you here."

I chuckled.

Maybe I could've helped him in some kind of way after all.

Shortly after our conversation had ended, Matt brought me back home safe and sound. The sun had already set, and the air was a bit chill. The last steps to the front door felt like forever because I had subconsciously started walking slower and slower.

If I was honest, I didn't want to be home already. Today was one of these days where I felt active and alive. I wanted to spend the whole night outside or at least stay up as late as possible. Unfortunately, I had school the next day, so I had to go home. I also would need my sleep, otherwise, I wouldn't be able to concentrate.

Before I unlocked the front door, I turned around to check on Matt one last time but he was already gone.

"Thank you for bringing me home safely," I whispered.

I didn't know if he could hear me, but it was important for me to say it out loud. He could've easily killed me, and nobody would have ever found out about it. But he had decided to let me go, even made sure I was safe, and I was actually grateful for that.

Chapter 6

Tim quickly recovered from the car accident, and despite the near-death experience that he experienced because of me, he didn't run away. Additionally, he was convinced that Luna was right, and it wasn't a something but a someone that had saved him.

Somebody saved my friends and always appeared after I had failed miserably. This could only mean that it must've been another supernatural being. Someone who was faster and stronger than the average human. Someone who was always at the right place at the right time. But no matter how many times I looked through my Grandma's book, I couldn't figure out what kind of creature would do something like that. There were too many possibilities. And in the end, we could only wait and hope this person would show themselves.

I was walking through a book store to buy some new travel guides. As long as my visions were shifting into being uncontrollable, traveling would be one of the things that were impossible again, but it wouldn't stop me from dreaming about it.

One day, we would figure out what was wrong with me, and then, I had sworn to myself, I would travel for months. I had saved the money for quite some time, now I only lacked the destination and the right timing.

So, I was not just buying another guide for dreaming, I was indirectly looking at inspirations for my future. Inspirations that would prevent me from looking for a new therapist. Because I didn't need another one, especially after my bad experiences with Mrs. Müller – who apparently dedicated herself to the community of flat earthers – I didn't want to give therapy another try. Still, I couldn't stop myself from thinking what if I really needed help. Fortunately, I was able to push this thought away every time it entered my head, but I didn't know if I could keep on doing this forever.

After some time, I had found some travel destinations somewhere far in the east. Happily, I paid my travel guide and decided to walk around further in the pedestrian zone. I had enough time to wander without any purpose, and if I had another vision, maybe I wouldn't feel as bad about it as I used to since I knew someone was ready to save the day. It was calming me down a lot.

Then I thought it would be a great idea to pick Luna up from school. It was already afternoon and her school day should be over soon. Additionally, today was a good day for me. My body wasn't shaking as much as it did the other days. Also, I didn't feel as weak as the last time we had met, so I needed to take advantage of this. I simply had to do everything to convince her I was doing alright, and if I picked her up from school, she might even believe me.

Like I did during one of our first encounters, I stood in front of her school while texting her that I would be waiting there, so I wouldn't miss her.

I observed the first kids leave the school almost running as if they were trying to escape from something. But they were just running to the bus stop as if their life depended on catching the first vehicle, like it was the only one stopping at this school. But after the first bus came another one. And another one

Luna took her sweet time, but I would be lying if I said I wasn't used to it by now. So, I sent Tim a text to ask how he was doing. Even though he was safe now, I was still worried about him.

Sometimes I couldn't read him, and especially now I was afraid he was just pretending everything was fine but suffering on the inside. Basically, everything I was doing to him. How paradox. Well, so much about working together and not against each other.

"Ramon?"

A voice interrupted my thoughts, and I looked up from my phone.

For a second, I couldn't breathe when I realized who casually headed into my direction.

"Matt?" I asked with obvious distaste in my voice.

"You are exactly as happy to see me as your little girlfriend."

"I dare you to do anything to her," suddenly I was panicky.

What if he was here because of the magicians? That night in the mansion they had threatened to harm Luna, and I couldn't think of another explanation why someone like Matt should be in a small town like this.

What if we should only believe that he had left the magicians that night, so we would feel safe, and he could strike all of a sudden and… No matter which explanation he had, it couldn't be a coincidence that I met him right here in front of Luna's school. After all, it was Matt. He must have had a plan.

"Don't worry about it. I'm not going to hurt anyone. I'm simply going to school here," he answered completely relaxed as if he could read my thoughts.

"Listen!" he lowered his voice. "I'm here because I need your help. But I can't explain the details now. Can we meet here at 7 p.m., so I can explain everything to you?" He almost begged.

I stared at him critically.

He seemed to be serious.

I nodded quietly.

"Don't tell Luna about it. She will only try to convince you not to come," he said before he vanished behind the next corner.

Maybe it was naïve to believe him after all he had done, but there had to be a reason he didn't murder Luna or Tim that night in the mansion, and maybe he could help me figure out the connection between Luna and Luana.

No matter how much I doubted his intentions, he was my only hope right now. And since he wasn't the only one desperately looking for help, it was possible for me to pretend that he wasn't the reason why my Grandma had died. At least for one evening.

It didn't take much longer for Luna to finally arrive. I greeted her with a brief kiss.

"I'm happy to see you, but why are you here?" She asked happily.

"I was nearby, and I thought we could hang out a bit." I shrugged.

"You definitely should be nearby more often, and you should also think more often."

I just shook my head smiling at her.

She had such a special kind of humor sometimes.

We spent the rest of the afternoon outside together. It was supposed to be one of the few warm days at the end of the summer. We had to stay outside and enjoy the last bits of sun, the last bits of the summer, before fall would come. The summer had been too rainy and too short this year anyway.

When it got later, I brought Luna back to her bus stop and excused myself with some lame explanation. Even if I knew it was for the best, it felt weird to lie to her. But Matt was right; she would never let me meet him. She was way too resentful, or I was too naïve.

Which of them was true? I would only find out after my meeting with Matt.

To play things safe, I told Tim about this meeting. I had promised Matt not to tell Luna about it. He didn't forbid me to talk to Tim.

I couldn't get rid of the feeling that I believed him, for some reason whatsoever, and he only came back because he needed my help. I really couldn't tell why I felt this way. Maybe because he had run away from the magicians. Maybe because he didn't harm neither Luna nor Tim, even though he had the power to do so. Or because I simply was too gullible.

Although Matt was a mystery to me, I couldn't believe that he was 100 percent evil. Was there even anyone who was 100 percent evil? Maybe I wasn't so sure myself where I would rank me on a scale from one to evil or I had some subconscious death wish, but I couldn't believe that Matt went through all of this because of another sick plan. And if it was like that, I was about to fall right into their trap.

7 p.m. I stood exactly where I had waited for Luna this afternoon. Matt wasn't there yet.

I sighed.

I wouldn't wait here forever. I would only wait that long for Luna. He would get 10 minutes of my time, maybe even 15 and at highest 20 but definitely not more than 30. But I didn't need to figure out how long

I would wait for him before I would go home because not even five minutes later Matt had arrived.

"You are late," I figured out.

"Sorry, I didn't think you would actually show up," he admitted, and for a second, he didn't seem as confident as he had been during our first encounter in the mansion. He almost seemed a bit intimidated.

"So, what's up?" I asked and tried to sound as casual as possible.

If I was honest with myself, I was frightened by this situation. Not knowing how things could possibly turn out scared me. And maybe Matt scared me too. I knew what he could possibly do, and I was in no condition to fight him.

"I have a problem, and you are the only person that can help me," he started.

There was no problem in this world that I could think of where I could be the solution for but it only made the situation more interesting for me. How the tables had turned. It was almost funny if the circumstances weren't that sad.

And then he started talking about his lonely childhood. About the magicians that took care of him while at the same time enchanted him with a spell that hadn't been broken yet. About his mission to spy on my Grandma and to get his hands on the spell book. About the setbacks when he found out that she hid it so well only I could find it (which I wasn't planning to do). And also, about the death of my Grandma – it wasn't easy to listen to that part – and his reasons behind it. Apparently, the magicians had promised him freedom if I would join them.

"How could they set you free, I thought you were under their spell?" I wanted to know.

Then I smirked about my poor choice of words.

"They would've told me what kind of creature I am. But they didn't tell me. Everything they said was a lie. After Tim knocked down the magicians with his baseball bat – by the way, super interesting choice of weapon – I realized this was my only chance to escape. It was pretty obvious you wouldn't join them, so I took what was mine: my freedom. After the death of your Grandma they had manipulated the storybook before you could get your hands on it. They claimed the pages would tell the truth about my heritage, but it was also just another lie," he answered my question very detailed.

"Then what is on the pages? Do you still have them? And what are the consequences now that you are still somehow bound to the magicians?"
I had questions. So many questions.

"I can't tell you everything that's on the pages by heart, but I offer you a deal: I give you the missing pages, and you help me figure out who I am," he only answered some of my uncountable questions.
I thought about it for a while. Would this be a good idea? After all, I had no clue what was written on the missing pages. What if they were completely useless

for me? I needed to expect them to be absolutely nonsense if Matt was willing to hand them over that easily.

But on the other hand, why should the magicians go through all of the trouble of hiding they ever touched the book if they wanted me to read these pages? Everything inside of me screamed to not accept Matt's deal. After everything we knew about him, this could be my personal demise, but what did I have to lose? I had already reached my Faust low; a deal with Mephisto wouldn't be able to break me anymore either.

"Deal," I said and shook his hand that was already held in my direction to seal our agreement.

"Thank you."

His thanking sounded honest which only reassured my belief; he was definitely serious about everything.

"You haven't answered all of my questions yet," I reminded him.

"Yeah, sorry. You had a lot of questions, and if I'm honest, I don't know the exact extent of the connection between me and the magicians. I guess they prevent me from using my full power, and maybe they can even track me because of that. Maybe they will find you too, just so you know what you got yourself into." He warned me.

"It's okay for me. But if they repress your full strength, I don't want to know what you are capable of," I said thinking about our fight in the mansion.

"You wouldn't even stand a chance against me," he bragged jokingly.

"Pfff, I held back my powers to spare you from losing."

We both started laughing because we knew I could've killed him easily if I had wanted to. But on the other hand, he could've killed me too if the magicians had ordered him to do so. Despite having different powers, we had surprisingly much in common. And it felt good to be able to talk to another supernatural creature. Except for Matt and the magicians, I didn't know any other magical creatures, and the magicians were the last people I wanted to talk to because I could trust them even less than I could trust Matt. Despite being the murderer of my Grandma, in the end, he was just another prawn in their game of chess. I would probably never be able to forget that, but wasn't it a sign of strength if I was able to start to forgive him?

"Luna won't be happy about this," I remembered.

"Maybe she will. I have a few good arguments that can convince even her."

I couldn't judge the huge smirk that had formed on his face.

Then we agreed to meet another day to tell Luna and Tim about our unusual alliance. Matt specifically asked for the help of all of us.

Before we said our goodbyes, he held me back for a second.

"Why did you decide to trust me? I didn't expect you could even forgive me," he admitted.

"I don't know." I shrugged.

This answer didn't seem to be good enough for him.

"I guess, because you didn't harm Tim. You hurt Luna, and you definitely hurt me because they had ordered you to do so, but they didn't know about Tim. They never told you to hurt him, and you didn't touch him. You let him do whatever he wanted to do. Since that night, I subconsciously sensed that you turned your back on the magicians. Nobody is fully evil or good. Humans can change, and I guess this also applies to people like us," I tried to explain myself.

Matt seemed to be content with this answer.

Chapter 7

E ven though I was happy about Ramon's spontaneous visit to my school, the thought of him accidentally running into Matt made me feel pretty uneasy. This unwell feeling only vanished after I saw Ramon waiting for me. Alone.

In the conversation after that – I tried to discreetly hint at Matt's presence in this town – he didn't show any signs of having met him. It seemed like everything worked out well. Or so I thought.

Until I received a message from Ramon the next day:

You probably won't be happy about it, but I met up with Matt yesterday, and we now work together. Can we talk about it in person? I would love to explain myself more. When are you free?

He couldn't be serious about it. How could he do something like that? After everything we went through because of Matt. The nightmares that were haunting me since that night in the mansion. The slight feeling of panic that rushed through my body every time I saw Matt in school. The feeling of being followed wherever I went. Every shadow, every silhouette, basically everything felt more threatening as soon as dusk was setting in. Since that night in the mansion, we all had our package to carry. We all had changed. We all had our scars, Ramon on his forehead and I on my soul. And all of that simply because of Matt.

On the other hand, Matt turned out to be more than okay. He hadn't killed me in the mansion, and even when he abducted me, he didn't harm me. And despite me not finding the strength to forgive him for everything he had done, he brought me back home. By now, I was convinced that he had only kidnapped me because he was desperate and really didn't know what else to do.

I didn't trust him. However, I trusted Ramon and his decisions. Even though I didn't find it particularly intelligent to help Matt, it wouldn't change a thing; I would help him, no matter how much I hated the idea of it. So, I had no other choice than to join this bizarre alliance.

Since Matt but also Ramon and Tim seemed to be astonishingly flexible, the day of the meeting depended on my schedule. Still, not 100 percent convinced about all of this, I agreed to meet up immediately after school. Then, at least, it would be over quicker.

"Who would've thought we'd walk somewhere together after school," Matt figured out while we walked to Ramon's place.

I just stayed silent.

There was nothing I wanted to say to him. I hated the idea of working together. It felt like we had just agreed to a deal with the devil. Sure, Matt wasn't the devil – as far as we knew –, but even the devil could probably be incredibly charismatic and manipulative, just like Matt.

"I didn't mean it in a bad way," he added to break the silence.

"Okay," I answered mechanically.

I was too occupied with my own thoughts. It was so incredibly naïve of Ramon to meet up at his place. Now Matt knew his address, which would be fatal if he was still working for the magicians. How could he trust him? He has probably never felt the pain of betrayal in his life. How could he possibly know this feeling? He was the one pushing all of his friends away, not the other way around. He had betrayed them somehow. And nobody was left that could have stabbed him in the back, and now he was blind.

I really hoped for him that Matt was sincere about everything.

"What do you feel right now?" Matt suddenly asked. This question came out of nowhere, and I couldn't repress a quick laugh about it.

"Where did you get this question from? Smalltalk for beginners?" I said while still laughing.

He just looked at me in confusion.

Again, he had probably asked a serious question, but still none of my friends would talk like this, especially not if the conversation was as dry and awkward as the mood between Matt and me. It was one of these moments where it was painfully obvious, he didn't have many experiences with social contacts or in general with humans. Then again, it surprised me how good he could play pretend in front of my friends. They would never expect him to be like he really was. He had convinced them he was human.

"I've heard humans have emotions and like to talk about how they feel," he explained himself.

Now I really couldn't hold myself back. I completely burst out laughing.

"If you have this information from TV-shows, then don't take it too seriously." I enlightened him and crossed the street at the – meanwhile green – traffic light.

"But…" he started but didn't finish the sentence.
He probably realized that the TV was an unreliable source for human behavior just like fantasy books were for supernatural abilities.

"And what do humans really talk about to break the silence?" His insecurity became visible.

"Great question."
I thought about it for a second, but there was nothing typical human that I could think of. Except for small talk. But nobody, absolutely no one, liked small talk. Also, wasn't it a bit late to ask such a question? He had already merged among humans. It would have been better for him to prepare before entering the

world of ordinary people. Then again, if he spent time with Jane, he wouldn't need to pretend to be something he wasn't. And now I could understand why the two of them were so close. She was a simple human. Not in a bad way, just in a way that made it easy to talk to her. She could ramble for hours about the smallest things, but she was also a good listener. I would claim she had the talent to figure out when to do either, so there never was an awkward silence while being with her if she liked someone. If Matt was with her, he didn't need to try to be human. She made him look human automatically.

"I have no clue," I admitted after some time.

"Well, I have enough time to learn."

I pressed the doorbell. It didn't take long for the door to open with a buzzing sound.

"Wait for me!" I heard Tim scream who had just arrived as well.

Quickly, he walked from his car to us.

He eyed Matt briefly.

Who would've thought we would ever meet each other in this constellation again? How bizarre.

Upstairs in Ramon's apartment, we sat down at the kitchen table because the sofa was too small for all of us.

"I understand that it's difficult for you to trust me, but I really need Ramon's and, if you like, your help as well. It's urgent, and if you can't help me, I will vanish as quickly as I have appeared. But please, listen to me first," Matt started the discussion.

"How can we know this is not a trap?" I blurted out. Even though I had tried my best to hold myself back and let the others do most of the talking, I couldn't stop the words from leaving my mouth.

"Because I didn't come here for no reason. There were certain *incidents,*" he emphasized the word incidents in a stretched way and with such a distaste in his voice that I haven't heard in a while.

"Incidents?" Tim wanted to know and looked at him attentively.

Of course, for him, everything was so new and so exciting. Tim only knew the summarized version of Matt's and Ramon's talk while he and I got to hear the detailed version from Matt personally.

"Ramon," Matt now explicitly looked at him, "I know you are doing worse, and I can help you get better again."

This would be enough to get Ramon's trust if he hasn't already gotten it. Why was I so skeptical again? I reminded myself that I wanted to be more open-minded, but at the same time I knew it would take some time until I would trust Matt blindly. He wasn't as bad as I had thought at the beginning. I realized that after my involuntarily visit to his place, but it was still hard to think of him as anything other than the bad guy. It was horrible.

"How do you know I'm doing worse?" Ramon asked confused.

"Your visions are uncontrollable," Matt answered and shrugged.

Now all eyes were on him.

How could he know this? It was impossible that he had heard this from somewhere. Did he know what was wrong with Ramon? Did the magicians share their plan with him, or why did he know so many things about him? There was no chance he had seen Ramon before they officially met again, so how could he know about his declining health?

"How do you know that?" Ramon looked tense.

Matt sighed.

"I'm tired of always saving your friends."

Still, we looked at him in disbelief.

Nobody dared to say something.

Everyone was thinking about what he meant by that. Did we just understand him correctly? Did this mean he was the one who had saved my life? Did this mean he was the one that had pushed Tim away from the car just in time? Did this mean the person I suspected of wanting to kill me was innocent, even my savior?

"But how?" Ramon stuttered.

It didn't make any sense that Matt was the Somebody who had protected us. Why should he? Why was he even nearby? How could he know where we had been at what time and when he needed to save us?

"And that's why I need your help." Again, he only talked directly to Ramon.

"I understand," he murmured.

Tim and I had mutated to speechless observers. He probably needed some time to cope with everything that we just heard, like me. If it wasn't for Matt, then I would be… I gulped. I didn't want to think about it.

"Thank you!" Tim was the first of us two who could say anything again.

I, however, still stared at Matt in disbelief.

"No big deal," he answered and gave him a very quick smile.

Silence.

Again, nobody dared to say a word.

Nobody knew what to say.

"You saved me?" I suddenly said as soon as I gained back my ability to speak. I couldn't hold these words in, even though I would've preferred to stay silent.

Matt nodded.

"For you, it wouldn't even be necessary."

"What's that supposed to mean?" I said offended and sat straight on my chair.

"You would've survived without my help, Tim, not so much," he explained calmly, and I realized how he repressed a smirk.

"What do you know that we don't?" Ramon wanted to know.

Matt and Ramon looked each other deeply in the eyes.

How could Ramon be so incredibly relaxed? I was way too emotional to somehow think rationally.

"I have read the missing pages from your book, and as promised, I will hand them over to you if you help me. On them are interesting information regarding your Grandma and her," he pointed his head towards me.

"What if I don't want to know what's wrong with me?"

I must've seemed pretty desperate because Ramon grabbed my hand below the table and held on to it tightly.

"Then you'll never see the pages, and we get rid of them immediately," he said while still holding my hand to calm me down.

I didn't know what else to say. Apparently, something was wrong with me, and apparently all of us – except for maybe Tim – had been well aware of that. But I didn't want to, no, I couldn't believe it.

Since the day I realized the old lady from the first floor was dead and I shouldn't be able to see her, I had this dull feeling something was wrong with me too. So far, I could successfully repress that feeling because other things were simply more important than exploring my emotions.

This subconscious realization of being different was the main reason why I had decided to help Ramon in the first place; but now I only wanted to run away and distance myself from everything that was supernatural. However, this wasn't possible anymore, I was already in too deep.

"Don't worry, it's nothing bad. You're not a vampire," Matt winked at me.

This only calmed me down a tiny bit.

"But if you really don't want to know, Ramon and I can get rid of the pages," he offered.

"Am I allowed to still read them?" Tim asked curiously.

How could he cope with this situation so well?

"Sure." I laughed about him being so chill about everything.

Tim was excited for a bit longer, then silence took over again.

Tense silence.

Now it was me who was observed by everyone.

"If it really isn't that bad, I think I'm ready to know what's wrong with me."

Was this my voice that was talking right now? It sounded so unfamiliar to me. Not like me at all. And I thought I was certain I didn't want to know what was going on. I sighed.

Apparently, my curiosity had won, and as long as it wasn't anything too crazy, I would be able to handle it. Or I would learn how to cope with it.

Of course, I was aware that it had to be a connection to Luana. A connection with the person that I knew way too much about without ever being able to properly meet her. And suddenly, I realized where my subconscious dislike against Luana and the constant denial of all our similarities came from. It came from a place that knew Ramon had been right all along. There had to be some kind of connection, otherwise, Ramon's Grandma wouldn't have kept her death notice. Otherwise, my mother wouldn't behave so awkwardly towards Ramon. Otherwise, Ramon's Grandma wouldn't own a picture of my mother. Everything pointed towards our connection, and it was about time that someone finally said it out loud.

"We won't overwhelm you, we will slowly explore everything together," Ramon promised and still didn't let go of my hand.

I could see the excitement in his eyes. A shining that I haven't seen in a while, to be more accurate, since we had left the mansion.

"Deal," I agreed to everything.

"I will give you my information about Luna and help Ramon to get better, and you guys help me to break the curse of the magicians for good, and if all of this is over, I will leave you guys allone immediately," Matt summarized our conversation.

Everyone nodded in agreement.

"Do we need to do some kind of ritual to fasten our pact? Like some blood brotherhood or something like that?" Tim asked motivated.

"No," Matt said and looked at him with small eyes.

"Okay, okay, then we won't," Tim pouted playfully. Because of all the awkward silences during our conversation, time flew by, and when we came to our conclusion, it was already dark. Quickly, I said my goodbye. It was time for me to go home. Ramon insisted on bringing me home, but I thankfully denied his offer. He only let go of his idea when Tim told me he could drive me home. This was okay for me since he needed to head in the same direction anyway. It wouldn't be a huge detour for him, in opposite to if Ramon would drive me home.

"Do you also need a ride?" Tim asked Matt when we left the building.

"No, thank you," Matt friendly declined his offer.

"I don't travel in cars," he quickly added, and before Tim could ask any further questions – and I could tell he had a lot of them and was just about to ask them – Matt had already vanished.

"Wow, that's so cool," I could hear Tim murmur amazed.

Why did everyone like Matt? Why was it so easy for him to wrap everyone around his finger, and why was I the only person that wasn't under his spell?

It wasn't until I was sitting in Tim's car that I looked at my phone. I realized I had completely forgotten that my mom, her boyfriend, and his son were at a concert tonight. So, I could've stayed a bit longer at Ramon's place. Still, maybe it was a good idea to end the conversation. Everything that needed to be said had been uttered, and I was sure I wouldn't be able to handle any more surprises today.

At home, I wanted to let in a warm bath to reflect on everything. There were a lot of things I needed to think about and maybe even learn how to cope with them, even though I had no idea how. It felt like some kind of Deja-vu. All of these feelings I had felt back then when Ramon had told me about his powers have returned. And exactly like back then, I needed a warm bath today. At least I would have all the time in the world, and nobody would knock on the bathroom door if I took too long. But when I started to let the water enter the bathtub, I could hear the doorbell ring.

Confused, I stood up and opened the door. I had no clue why I even did it. Usually, I would never open the door if I didn't expect anyone, and especially not at this time of day, but I probably was still too confused about everything to think clearly. And it could've potentially been my mom and her flock who forgot their keys or something like that.

But in front of me stood neither my mom nor my stepfather. In front of me was an old acquaintance. I almost didn't even recognize her because she had bleached her hair, and also, it had been some time since we met for the last time.

"Sina", I whispered in shock.

Chapter 8

Not even one day after our conversation with Matt, I could find the missing pages of the storybook in my mail box. They were a little bit wrinkly, but that was the smallest of my problems. They were readable, and that was everything that mattered to me. But before I would take my time and start reading them, I wanted to glue them back into the book where they belonged. It was more difficult than expected since my hands were still way too shaky. So, it took multiple attempts until I was fully satisfied with the result, but as soon as I was done, I couldn't suppress my curiosity any longer.

The first pages were about the magicians as supernatural creatures, and I only glanced over them quickly. I knew we would read the pages again during our next meeting with Matt, and I also felt like we already knew everything about them that we needed to know for now. The only thing that I was interested in was the connection between Luana and Luna.

Once upon a time, there had been an old woman, your Grandma. She, as well, had magical powers that were beyond your imagination.

Yeah, I had already figured that part out. It was nothing new for me, so I kept on reading.

*Her powers are hard to put into words, but she will try to do it anyway. She is known as **the Guardian of All Supernatural**. She offers shelter to magical creatures in her mansion so they can develop their powers and simply be themselves. A place where nobody needs to hide who they truly are.*

This, we had figured out already as well. But what exactly was the connection between my Grandma and Luna? There had to be a connection after everything we had seen. I took a sip of my sparkling water before I continued reading.

But this wasn't everything she did. She also heals magical beings and protects the supernatural world, so no ordinary human should ever know about it. Nobody knows as much about this world as her.

Was this the reason she knew about my powers? She probably knew everything about everyone with special powers simply by their existence. And since I was somehow supernatural as well, she knew about me too. Even if I had no proof for it, I was almost certain that my mom took my secret to her grave. My Grandma must've known about my powers because of some other supernatural reasons. And maybe my mom even didn't know what my Grandma was doing in her free time.

One of her abilities is being immortal.

What a great joke, I thought cynically.

She can only die if she decides to give away her powers to someone of her choice.

The rest of the page was a detailed description of the mansion and its function as shelter for supernatural creatures, something I had already figured out without Grandma's help.

Now, I needed to sort my thoughts. I had read all of the words, but I didn't understand their meaning. She could only die – I mean, be murdered – because she had given up on her powers prior to that. But who had she forfeited her powers to, and how did this even work?

Completely at loss, I scratched my head.

I decided to text Matt because he seemed like he knew more about this than he had admitted during our last conversation. In the end, he was the one that…

It was paradox that I believed and trusted him even though he was a murderer. But since I was a murderer myself and I even killed my own mother, I could only be a little bit mad at him. He had only done what he was ordered to do.

"I knew you would text me." Matt greeted me when I opened the door.

"Are you a clairvoyant now?" I asked ironically and let him enter my apartment.

"You are easy to read, Ramon."

Maybe he was right. One didn't need incredibly good knowledge of human nature to know I was still overwhelmed with everything related to supernatural things. And Matt was a little bit more experienced in that topic since it wasn't new to him like it was for me. He had spent his whole life among magical creatures.

While walking past me, he put a hand on my shoulder and said: "Don't worry, that's what I'm there for."

And again, he was right.

Confident, Matt sat down at the table where we all had sat together yesterday.

I eyed him skeptically.

I wished I would be only half as confident as he was.

"You know more than what is written on the pages, don't you?" I asked him after I had sat down as well.

"Of course."

"Then why did you throw the pages into my mail box instead of handing them over in person?"

"Because I wanted to wait until you'd realize that you need me."

He said it in such a neutral way that it was hard to understand what he was thinking. Suddenly, doubts overcame me. If I couldn't even properly judge his behavior, how could I even trust him? But it was as easy as that; he had saved my friends when I had failed. No matter how much I hated the thought of it, he wasn't the bad guy here.

"Okay," I just said.

I didn't know what else to say.

"I assume you have read the pages?" He figured.

I nodded.

"Then you should now know that we could only murder your Grandma because she had given up on her life to save someone else," he briefly summarized the content of the pages.

"Yes, but who?"

"You already know. I know. And she probably knows it by now too," he looked at me challenging.

"You can say it out loud, don't worry."

"Luna?"

My voice sounded more like a question than an answer.

"Bingo," he screamed unexpectedly loudly.

I cringed.

Maybe I had also become a little bit more sensitive to loud noises since that night in the mansion. But he was right. This information didn't shock me anymore. It was something that I had already expected. I just didn't want to admit it or even say it out loud because

I didn't want to annoy Luna with this topic. She shouldn't think that the connection with Luana was the only reason why I showed interest in her. Because it wasn't true.

"Well, yes, but somehow no," he started.

I just looked at him confused.

"Can I maybe get something to drink? My mouth is so dry," he asked politely and visibly enjoyed his moment of superiority.

"Sure," I murmured.

Still confused, I stood up and brought him a glass of water. Did he even need to drink?

"So," he continued. "Luna is already a pretty good assumption, but back then she didn't give her powers to Luna. She gave her powers to someone else. You know her as…"

"Luana," I interrupted him louder than I had expected it from myself.

He looked at me judging.

"Bravo, you're a quick learner," he admitted impressed.

I moved my hands to my forehead.

My head started to hurt. Today was not my day, but I needed to push through it. I wanted the information from Matt. And not doing anything wouldn't magically heal me either. I would be in pain whether or not I was talking to Matt right now.

"But what is the connection to Luna?" Matt asked rhetorically. "Exactly, there is a connection between the two of them – I mean even their names sound similar. How could you not realize there was a connection?"

He confirmed my theory.

"You knew Luana?"

"No, I wouldn't go that far. But I know people that kind of knew her."

He took a sip of his water.

I eyed him critically.

Was all of this a show, or was he really thirsty?

"Before you ask, even someone like me sometimes likes water. Do I need to drink to survive? Probably not. But it's simply a nice feeling when something cold is running down my throat," he explained after he had seen my questioning glance.

"Interesting," I murmured.

"Do you mean the magicians?" I wanted to know.

"With what?"

"With the people that knew Luna."

"Of course, I don't know that many people. They didn't know Luana personally, but they were very invested in her death. I don't know if you noticed it by now, but supernatural creatures can sense the presence of other supernatural beings. And the magicians were at the right place at the right time. They felt you. They felt your presence, Ramon."

This sounded creepy and a little bit disgusting as well. Did I even want the magicians to feel me?

"At that time, they were already following your Grandma around because they had heard about her owning a powerful weapon. At first, they only wanted to get their hands on the spell book, but later, they realized that it was you they really desired. If they had known it back then, they would've put their hands on you way earlier. However, they were nearby when things happened, and, well, they sensed you. You have always been easy to read. They quickly realized that something happened inside of you while you touched the girl."

Tears were filling my eyes and I noticed that my hand had turned into a fist. I was angry. But why exactly was I angry?

"When they saw her death announcement, their theory was only confirmed. They knew it was you who had killed her. Until not so long ago, they had simply assumed you'd pushed her in front of the car. They didn't have any other explanation for her death, and when I disproved their theory, at first, they couldn't believe me."

Matt briefly laughed about the dullness of the magicians.

"After the accident, they quickly stopped caring about you but not about your grandma. They started observing her, and when I was old enough, I did all the work for them. That's when they realized your grandma had a huge secret. One evening, she drove to a nearby graveyard in the middle of the night to dig out a coffin. You can probably imagine whose coffin it was. She revived Luana by transferring her power to her. And that's everything I know about it."

Even though everything made surprisingly much sense, I had a lot of arguments against it. To be precise, the arguments weren't even mine, they were the ones Luna had used when we had discussed a possible connection between her and Luana in the past.

"But what about the age difference? Luana was only one year younger than me. Luna is three years younger," I started arguing.

"Hm," he scratched the back of his head. "I can only guess what happened, only your Grandma knows the full truth."

"Then give me your best theories," I demanded almost begging.

"There are some spells that can only be done once in a century. Reviving is definitely nothing natural, so I don't need to explain to you that it most likely was a spell. She could have used one of these spells that need a special moon-planet constellation to work. It could also be that she wasn't sure if she should really revive her and eventually decided to do it after she had seen you suffer. Or she waited to be sure no one would remember Luana."

"How horrible. What if it's true and no one can remember Luana anymore?" The words slipped out of my mouth.

Memories were the only thing left after death. If nobody remembered you, have you even really lived?

"No matter which of these theories is correct, she probably made people forget about Luana. In the end, she brought Luna back to her mother. This was only possible if she had manipulated her memories prior to that."

This was too much for my head. Somehow, I had trouble imagining all of this. Somehow, I didn't even want to imagine it. And somehow, I could tell that Matt was right about everything he had just said. But if everyone had forgotten about Luana, why haven't I? Why could I still remember her?

At least now I knew why Luna's mother always looked at me as if she was scared. She probably disliked me because Grandma's spell didn't work that well anymore, or maybe it had never been strong enough in the first place. For some reason, Luna's mother seemed to remember me, and since this memory was from a time before Luna's existence, it scared her. She shouldn't have this memory.

"How should I tell Luna about all of this?" I talked more to myself than to Matt.

"You better do it as fast as possible," he answered and shrugged.

Chapter 9

Even though I was sure I had gotten over our friendship in the past year, I felt a stinging pain in my chest after seeing her now. Or was I feeling like this because I was over and done with her? Why did she need to come here and open old, already healed wounds again? At least I had thought I was over the past, but obviously all of this was just another lie I had told myself until I started to believe it.

So many emotions were filling my body. I would have loved to hug her, and cry, and immediately forgive her. But I couldn't. At the same time, I felt the urge to shut the door in front of her eyes. I already had enough problems, problems that were more important than our already broken friendship. But I also couldn't do that. So, I just stood there and stared at her in disbelief. None of us dared to say a word. She probably realized just now what a shitty situation the two of us were in.

It was her who had replaced me with someone better. It was her who didn't answer my texts anymore. It was her who let me down. After all the things we went through together. It was her that didn't want to be friends with me anymore. But it was also her who was standing in front of my door right now.

Anger and longing were rushing through my veins. No, I wouldn't start crying. I was too strong for that. I had changed too much. I had evolved. And she wasn't worth any of my tears.

She had been my only friend for most of my life, and I had loved her like the sister I never had. Maybe even more than just friendship, but before I could figure that out, she had let me down.

After I moved away, she had pretended as if we had never been friends. As if we had never met. As if nothing in her life had changed, meanwhile, I was missing her for months. She had ignored my messages and calls and all of this because of Derek. How should I possibly be able to forgive such disgusting behavior? I was worth more than that – I had learned this through my new friends. And still, I was standing here and debating whether I should start to cry or hug her.

She had treated me like crap, but as soon as she did the bare minimum to come back into my life, I would simply forgive her? What did she expect from me? What did I expect from myself?

This friendship was dead. Burnt and buried. And even if I would forgive her, things wouldn't be like they used to, and it was good that way. Subconsciously, I knew that. Still, there were hopes inside of me that they would be.

So many times, had I thought about contacting her again, telling her I missed her, but I had stayed strong for so long now. I didn't want to ridicule myself even further than I had already done. And if I thought about it a bit longer, I didn't even know why I missed her or what about her it was that I missed.

"You've dyed your hair?" I figured while still staring at her.

"Bleached," she corrected me.

Silence.

Again, no one dared to say a word.

"Listen, I'm sorry," Sina broke the silence.

Even though I had promised myself to be strong, I threw myself into her arms crying. This was the problem when it came to emotions, they were hitting strongly and uncontrollably. And this was my problem, I was too emotional.

Sina started to cry as well.

What an odd day. What a bizarre night.

We continued standing like this for some time. In silence.

At some point, we managed to free ourselves from the hug and sat down on the living room sofa.

"Why are you here?" I asked and grabbed myself a tissue.

My eyeliner, if there was any left, must've looked incredibly smudged.

"My life is hell," she sniffed and started to cry again.

If there were different kinds of supernatural creatures, I didn't want to doubt the existence of a hell, in which she obviously wasn't. But I held myself back. This wouldn't help the conversation, and in addition, would make things only more complicated. More complicated than they had already been.

"Derek and I broke up," she continued talking.

The way she said it would mean she assumed I knew they were together in the first place. Anger filled my body. Even though my mom, who was still in contact with her mother at some point hinted at this, I still found it outrageous of her to think I would know about it. As if her life and even more her relationship status were still important to me, even though she didn't think about me at all.

"Everything is shit. Derek and I broke up, his friends are suddenly against me. I don't know why they behave like that. I thought they were my friends as well. Suddenly, I'm alone, but not like we used to be back then. Because back then we were alone together, now you are gone too. I'm really alone. All alone, and it feels horrible," her crying got worse.

Carefully, I moved closer to her and offered her a tissue from the box that was standing on the living room table.

She thankfully denied my offer and rested her head on her hands.

I needed to get a grip on myself to not say anything I would later regret. Because of her I, had felt alone as well. But this wasn't a competition about who was feeling worse. Still, she had deserved everything that happened to her, and I didn't owe her anything. Why was she even so surprised that the tables could turn like this?

Oh, how much I would've loved to tell her all of this. To tell her that her life wasn't the most important thing on this earth and that the world didn't spin around her or that her problems were so incredibly irrelevant if compared to mine or even Ramon's. But right now, it didn't matter. All that mattered was that I was there for her now. Although she wasn't there for me.

Why was I so resentful?

It was about not making the same mistakes she did. Now, I had my chance to do things better. To be a better person than her.

So, I carefully laid my hand on her back.

"The good thing about this is that it eventually will be over. There is less than half a year of school left until we graduate. And if you want to study, you can go away wherever you want."

My words seemed to only calm her down a little bit, but her sobbing has stopped.

"Can't I move in here with you?" She asked.

"No, you need to do your own thing. This place here won't make you any happier."

I needed to speak slowly and controlled, so she couldn't hear the shock in my voice. As nice as it was to see her again, I definitely didn't want to live here with her. I had my own life, and as harsh as it sounded, she wasn't part of it anymore.

"You are right. But you seem to be so happy in this town."

Oh, little did she knew. Of course, I was doing better than in my hometown, but life had gotten so much more complicated than before.

"Everyone's different. Just because I'm doing just fine here doesn't automatically mean it would be the same for you. You need to find your own way, not follow my already walked path."

Did I eat a package of fortune cookies, or where did I take this pseudo deep philosophical quote from? As much as I internally needed to laugh about what I'd just said, it seemed to help Sina.

"But what if there is no path for me?" She asked scared, and I could hear she was about to start to cry again.

"Then you simply create it." I shrugged.

She lifted her head and looked me straight into my eyes.

"This city does you so well. I wish I would find a place where I belong too."

"You will, trust me. But now you have to explain one thing to me… Blond hair? Really?" I questioned her and started laughing.

"We all have our wild phases." She started to laugh as well.

"But before you think I did it only because of Derek, no. I bleached my hair after the breakup as a sign to myself. A sign that this was a new beginning and I was still in control over my life. It helped a little bit, so I can only recommend it," she explained and finally grabbed herself a tissue.

"I don't think blond would suit me."

And what should I say? At the end of the evening, we weren't two ex-besties that were totally awkward and feeling something between hate and love for the other one. At the end of the late evening, we were two people that found each other again. I had forgiven her because the past had become irrelevant; the present was what really mattered.

We had managed to talk about our problems from back then, and Sina even apologized multiple times. She had also shared her reasons behind her behavior towards me, and I learned to accept them. At the end of the evening, we were two people that were damn happy about having each other back again in their lives. And maybe this was my very first decision as an adult; I had decided to forgive.

My mom, on the other hand, wasn't very happy about Sina's visit. Especially because – as I later found out – her mother didn't know about her trip to our place and was incredibly worried. Before she agreed to take the next train back home, we needed to promise her she could visit me again in the fall vacations. The next day she would leave again because the last train for today had already left.

"Luna?" Sina asked while we were lying in my room in the dark. Me on my bed and Sina on our guest matrass that we haven't used since our last move into the still so oddly unfamiliar house.

"Yes?"

"I'm glad we talk again. I really missed you."

"I missed you too," I answered without hesitating.

My anger had vanished. Hate only made people weak. And I was so tired of being weak.

The next day was normal. Sina left, and I went to school feeling super tired. Finn noticed my lack of sleep, so I told him what had happened. We made a few jokes about bleached hair, not because it was looking ridiculous on Sina, but because it would definitely look hilarious on me.

In the evening, I received a text from Ramon. He told me that he had met up with Matt and read the missing pages from the storybook. Now he knew everything. He knew who or what I was and how everything was tied to Luana.

I suppressed my nervousness. Today, I wouldn't figure it out anyway. It was already too late for that, and I was still way too tired. But tomorrow, I would meet Ramon, and then he would explain everything to me. Did I even want to know?

To be honest, I hated everything about the conversation I had with Ramon the following day. It was obvious from the start that it would confuse or even deeply disturb me, but I didn't expect to be so internally stirred up. Up until this day, I was convinced nothing could shock me anymore; I was so wrong.

Ramon only said out loud what he and I – subconsciously – had already known: Luana and me were the same person. But how should I handle this information? Right now, I felt like my only option was to feel miserable for the rest of my life because I was the reason why Luana, me, wasn't buried in their grave anymore. I was allowed to live, but at what cost.

An empty grave.

An already forgotten child.

And although this child was somehow me, I still felt guilty.

Also, I had trouble processing the fact I had spent three years of my life dead and buried. How could my body survive? Was I some kind of zombie? Did insects chew on me, or what else happened six feet under?

And even if I had expected the worst, I hadn't expected all of this. Would I have an identical crisis? Maybe. Not just maybe. I probably already felt that way. Who was I? Luna? Luana? Neither? And why did it feel like fate to appear at the same places as Ramon? It suddenly didn't feel like a coincidence anymore that my mom and I had moved to this town. Exactly one apartment below Ramon. Some kind of higher power – and I refused to call it God since I wasn't religious and I would never be, but I could accept to call it destiny – was playing games with us. Maybe everything that had happened in my life so far was predestined.

At least now I knew why Matt had claimed it was unnecessary to save me when I had fallen into the abyss. I wouldn't have died anyway. All of this thanks to Ramon's Grandma; I was immortal.

I guess she didn't mean it in a bad way, but I felt like I would've preferred to rather be dead than alive. Now, my whole life felt like one gigantic lie.

Why did she pass her powers down to me? Why not to Ramon's mother instead, then these powers would've at least stayed in their family? All of these thoughts, I couldn't share with Ramon. He wouldn't understand them. Or would he even understand them best?

Although Ramon would've preferred if I had stayed at his place – it was the weekend and my mom was okay with me staying at his place during the weekend – I said goodbye to him. I needed to be alone to handle my life or my way too early death.

To be honest, I didn't know which of these things scared me the most.

Immortality. Something that so many humans were striving for. There were reasons for the success of vampires in modern-day literature. People were projecting their wishes on supernatural beings. They would have loved to be like them. But they would never be. Especially the idea of immortal love was romanticized through the modern picture of vampires. And even though I wasn't a vampire, I was immortal. But for me, there was nothing more repulsive than the idea of living together with the same partner for eternity. But it was less the relationship part that weirded me out, I guess I simply hated being immortal.

How cruel it must be to see everyone that one cares for die without being able to do anything about it? There was nothing I could do to avoid this burden, and maybe I could even understand why Ramon's Grandma gave up on her powers. I just couldn't understand why me?

I'd rather be one of these humans that were striving for immortality than actually living forever. I just wanted to be human, I guess.

I didn't feel worthy of the powers I had received. I didn't know Ramon's Grandma, and as far as I knew, she did so many great things for the world of supernatural beings. Great things that I could never do. At least not like her. I mean, I could do them, but I would never do them with the same passion as she did. There would always be some kind of pressure in doing what I would be doing. A pressure of becoming who she used to be.

It was pretty obvious this world needed people that were like her. A wise person who offered shelter and protection and, most importantly, understanding. But this was not me. And I was afraid I could never become this person either.

Meanwhile, I was still hopelessly overwhelmed by everything, and should I encounter any other magical creature than the ones I had already met before, I would probably run away, or fall into panic, or both at the same time. I wasn't ready to accept who or what I really was.

Luckily for me, it was the weekend, which made it easier for me to do what I had already decided to do. As soon as I had left Ramon's apartment, I grabbed my phone to call Finn. The old lady from the first floor only looked at me in pity. She didn't dare to say anything, knowing it would only make the situation worse for me. After all, I shouldn't be able to see her in the first place.

So, I called Finn and explained to him that we needed to meet in the city center, urgently. He would need to hurry up a bit because the stores were about to close. But fortunately, he didn't ask many questions and arrived as quickly as possible.

"You are really weird," he figured while we waited for the bus that would bring us back to my place.

"I know, but that's why we are friends," I reminded him in case he forgot.

It was so relieving to talk to a person who was human and didn't know shit about the world of supernatural creatures. Someone, who saw me as the person I yesterday thought I was. Someone who saw Luna and not Luana.

He only smirked at me.

"And you really want to do that?" He questioned my idea a second time.

I simply nodded.

"No matter how long it will take. Even if we'll need all night long," I confirmed while I mixed the blue powder with the white, creamy liquid.

A sharp smell filled the air. Immediately, Finn opened the window.

"And you don't care that I've never done this before and it could look like shit?"

"Yes. I need a change, and if it looks like shit, you need to convince me it doesn't."

That was what I liked the most about Finn. He didn't ask too many questions. He simply did things without second-guessing. And that was why he was here tonight. And that was why he held the dyeing brush in his hand and started massaging the bleach into my hair.

Despite the open window, the sharp smell didn't vanish immediately. It stayed in the bathroom for quite some time. How could hairdressers deal with that disgusting smell?

After some time, my scalp started to itch and burn a little bit. Was that normal? I had no clue. This was the first time I had done anything to my hair, but surprisingly, I wasn't worried about it. It was some kind of satisfying pain. The pain of a new beginning.

After 45 minutes, we washed the bleach out of my hair and, surprise, surprise, I was blonde.

"I had sworn to myself to never become a blonde," I laughed while looking at my reflection in the mirror.

Finn couldn't hold back his laugh either.

"Yesterday morning, we even joked about it, and now you are blonde," he summarized my life perfectly.

I glanced at the clock.

It was already late, but I had promised myself to keep on going until I was done. So, we continued. And I stuck to my word; I wouldn't stay blonde.

Finn cleaned the brush while I mixed the toner with some conditioner exactly like I had seen it in dozens of YouTube videos.

So, Finn and I stayed up even longer and dyed my hair *midnight blue*.

Chapter 10

All alone. I've never felt that alone in my life before, despite having so many people surrounding me. Again, I had started isolating myself completely for the last months. Except for the one day where I had picked up Luna from school, I hadn't left my apartment much. And if I continued to feel horrible, I would never do things like going outside ever again. It was so reckless and so many things could've gone wrong.

Just because Matt had the unexplained urge to save humans from my visions didn't mean I could justify having them in the first place. I knew I couldn't control these predictions anymore, and this was one of the things I simply had to accept.

The same way, I couldn't deny anymore that I was feeling worse with every passing day and I needed to change something urgently. I was simply too dangerous at the moment.

Now that we knew everything we needed to know about Luna and her connection to Luana, it was time to change my priorities. It was time to find out what was wrong with me and how I could change it. I deserved to give my life more quality. To make it more livable.

Every day felt like forever. Sometimes, I couldn't even leave my bed. Thank God, I was working from home, so I didn't even need to. I was a wreck.

The person in the mirror used to look better as well. Dark circles have formed below my eyes. At first, I tried to conceal them with make-up, but it turned out it wasn't worth the effort for me. The result was too underwhelming to keep on bothering about it. Maybe Luna could help me practice my make-up skills, but she seemed busy at the moment, so I didn't want to additionally stress her out.

And because I was feeling so unwell and weak, I didn't have many possibilities to avoid my visions except for isolating myself. So, I did it.

Tim went grocery shopping for me like he often did before the death of my Grandma. Fortunately, he understood my reasoning behind it and was always there to help me out, like always. I could feel how quarantining myself felt more difficult, and I started to become crazy.

Now that I knew what I was missing out on in the real world. Now that I knew that my life could be different than whatever misery I was living at the moment. Now that it felt like a major setback and I felt like a huge loser. Now, isolating myself hurt so much more than it used to. It was hard to stay strong.

But most of the days, I didn't even have a choice because I was feeling miserable. I had every possible symptom of a disease. It went from headache to shaking to nausea, basically everything that somehow kept me tied to my bed all day long. Eventually, I had gotten used to the symptoms. I had started to accept them. And as long as we didn't have any idea how to cure me, they would be a part of me.

I still had hopes Matt would find a solution that wouldn't involve the magicians, but so far, I didn't have the chance to talk about this topic with him. So far, I've always had other priorities than myself.

Matt and Tim were already sitting at my kitchen table when Luna rang the doorbell. The noise of the bell immediately caused a sharp pain in my head. Today was a bad day, like almost every day.

"Looks nice," I greeted Luna when she arrived upstairs and eyed her blue hair.

I would've never expected her to dye her hair but it suited her.

"I needed some change in my life," she murmured quietly and turned red. "I was afraid you wouldn't like it," she admitted.

I shook my head smiling at her.

I would always like her.

"Even bald you would still look beautiful. Just don't do face tattoos, please," I said jokingly.

"Thanks for the ideas."

When she noticed my shocked glance because I tried to imagine her with face tattoos, she quickly kissed my cheek and entered my apartment. Together, we sat down next to the others of our bizarre team. I laid the storybook demonstratively loud on the table in front of them.

Everyone automatically looked at me.

"Then let's diagnose our poor patient," I said, and tried to recreate Mrs. Müller's voice.

It was likely that none of the others would understand my joke since nobody else knew her. Also, nothing about this was really funny. It was only funny to me, almost as if I had an inside joke with myself.

Luna and Tim laughed about the change of my voice.

Matt only stared at me confused.

"You need to tell us what's wrong with you. Otherwise, we can't tell who you are," I explained and yawned.

I was tired and exhausted, but I didn't want to cancel our meeting today, I was way too curious.

"I save humans. Isn't that enough?" He asked untouched by everything he had just said.

I quickly flipped through the pages in the book and read through some passages.

"Guardian angel," I murmured.

"I'm definitely not a guardian angel," Matt argued visibly upset. "I'm way too cool for that."

He needed to smirk about his statement.

I ignored him and his protest and read a bit more of the text.

"Maybe you are right. It says they are almost exclusively female," I agreed with him.

"What else is special about you?" Tim tried to help me out.

"Supernatural hearing, strength, speed – no, Luna, I know exactly what you want to say."

I glanced at Luna, and she looked a tiny bit disappointed because she couldn't make another vampire joke. Still, we didn't want to give up that quickly, and since Matt didn't have any better ideas, I took a closer look at the page about vampires.

"Do you sometimes have the urge to drink blood?" I asked.

Matt looked at me annoyed.

"I feel like you don't take me seriously," he said and crossed his hands behind his head.

"We just have to talk about every idea so we don't overlook anything," I calmly explained.

"But no, I don't drink blood, and I don't have the urge to do it either," he finally answered my question.

So, it was official he wasn't a vampire.

"What about demons?" Luna asked carefully.

Quickly, I skipped to the right page and started reading.

"Yes, but also no," I answered. "It says that demons are created by a master. However, Matt claims he had parents," I explained.

"What if the magicians only told him he had a family? It wouldn't be the first time they lied to him," Luna threw in her thoughts.

She could be right, but she could also be wrong. And as vague as everything had been so far, it continued being this unprecise for the rest of the afternoon. Multiple pages of the storybook were almost fitting, but none was clearly about Matt.

In case we waited for some kind of metamorphosis on Matt's end, we were disappointed. Although Matt didn't say it, I was certain he would feel if we were on the right track. At least that was how it had been for me. When I had read the right page of the book, I knew who I was. Then again, it was pretty obvious the page was about me. My name was literally in the text. I never had to doubt it.

We tried until late in the night to help Matt, but nothing really made any sense. Either the creatures were more evil than good or the other way around. There was no being that behaved the way Matt did. And maybe we had sensed before that Matt was one of a kind, after today, however, we could be sure of that.

Maybe there was another page of the book left that was still with the magicians. Maybe even my Grandma didn't know what exactly Matt was. Then we would never know the answers as well.

Unfortunately, we were only as smart as my Grandma, since she was the one who wrote the book.

We were in a tricky situation, and I felt sorry for Matt. I felt sorry that we couldn't help him tonight. I trusted him. I had forgiven him. And now, I needed to admit that it was nice to know someone else who was born with supernatural abilities.

"This doesn't make sense," Matt yelled annoyed, and hit the table, which immediately broke.

Shocked, we stared at the broken table.

I could tell Tim was trying his best to repress a "cool".

"I'm sorry," Matt answered embarrassed. "My emotions got the best of me. I buy you a new table, I promise."

It was obvious how uncomfortable he felt it was almost funny.

"It's okay. I can understand your frustration." I nodded at him reassuringly.

"This here was my only hope," he said more to himself than to the others. "Damn. What am I supposed to do?"

Nobody said anything.

Nobody knew what to say to lighten up the mood. We had lost. We had no idea what else to do. I had never expected we wouldn't find anything at all, especially not after it was so easy to figure things out about Luna. But that was our problem. We needed my Grandma's book because we had zero experiences with magical creatures – except for Matt. He, however, had always been around them. We came from different worlds. Our knowledge was from different worlds. Maybe it had been obvious to everyone that we wouldn't be able to help Matt if he himself had no clue who he was.

We were only a bunch of amateurs, confronted with a world that we knew absolutely nothing about. Matt, on the other hand, was part of this world.

As much as I would like to stop hating on myself, I couldn't. The situation was already bad, but today made me feel even worse. My health was bad. Everything was pretty bad. And while the hours were passing by, nobody wanted to be that one person who would speak out the undeniable truth (that we won't find anything). So, we continued to stare at the same pages, looking for answers we would never find.

Meanwhile, I had given the book to Tim, who excitedly asked Matt everything he wanted to know. And while we sat around the table like this, I didn't realize how I slowly fell asleep on my chair.

Chapter 11

At latest when Ramon started to fall asleep, it became obvious that we couldn't hold onto the illusion of finding answers much longer. Everything was too complicated. I didn't know if it was just me, but I had expected this to be way easier.

Ramon had started to become quieter during the past hour, he probably knew as well that we wouldn't find anything. At least for today.

"I think it's time to give up."

I glanced at Ramon, who was deeply asleep.

Matt and Tim who, were trapped in their own world, just looked at me dumbfounded.

When they realized they were the only ones still trying to read the book, they understood that it didn't make any sense to further investigate Matt's heritage for today. In the meantime, we probably had read through the whole book thrice and nothing has changed.

"You are right. But we should definitely do this again soon. I'm certain we are about to solve the problem," Tim sounded wide awake.

How could he still be so motivated?

Matt didn't react to Tim instead, he just said: "Thank you. I really appreciate it."

The way he said these words sounded so honest. I couldn't believe I would think like this about Matt, but my opinion towards him has changed. On the inside, I chuckled a little bit. This was too absurd.

After Matt and Tim were gone and I had brushed my teeth, I decided to carefully wake Ramon up. Since that night in the mansion, where I had fallen asleep on a chair, I knew that this wasn't a comfortable sleeping position. And I wanted to spare Ramon the following neck pain as far as it would still be possible.

He grinned at me, still somehow half asleep.

"Do you stay here?" he murmured.

"Only if you get ready for bed immediately."

"I guess I don't have a choice then," he yawned and stretched his joints.

I kissed him.

"A foretaste," I said and winked at him.

Then I went to the bedroom and grabbed the first T-shirt of him that I could find.

Although I would've loved to stay longer at his place, I needed to get back home the next day. Fall vacation has started, and Sina would arrive at the train station tomorrow morning. Until then, I still needed to clean my room. It looked way too chaotic again. Tidying up has never been my strength.

And so, I spent the first day of my holidays cleaning up, which was exactly as exciting as it sounded; not at all. In the evening, my mom demanded we should have a gaming night as a family. After that, I went to bed.

It was an odd feeling to know Sina would stay at my place for almost two weeks, but it wasn't a bad feeling. It was simply different. After all, it was the first time we would spend that much time with each other after over a year.

Although a year wasn't much time, so many things in my life have changed. I have changed. My knowledge of what on earth was even possible has changed. My group of friends has changed, even my hair color has changed.

And with the knowledge that I had now, it was a mystery to me how I could still look into the mirror and recognize my own face. Because this person in the reflection wasn't me anymore. And actually, it had never been.

Was I more Luna or Luana? Would Luana have become the person I was today, or did Ramon's Grandma alter something about her, about me? No matter how much I thought about this, I would never find it out anyway. And in the end, Ramon was the only person that could even remember Luana, me.

All these thoughts and doubts needed to be repressed for the following two weeks because if I couldn't talk about my problems with Finn, then I would certainly not reveal them to Sina either.

Therefore nervous, I walked to the train station at 8 a.m. The train station in this town only had two gates, and most trains didn't even bother stopping here. If I was honest, this was probably the first time I spent a bit of time at the station. Usually, I always tried to avoid going here.

The closest bigger city was at least an hour away by train because the stupid machine stopped in every small town on the way there. If one was living in my town, there was no desire to go to the bigger city. Especially not if it would take that long to get there.

In case someone wanted to go shopping or to a restaurant, our pedestrian zone that was close to my school was more than enough. Since I didn't like going shopping too much, I only went to the city center for food, and there were enough restaurants for me. But I also knew that Jane, for example, was disappointed by the choice of clothing stores and often took the train to the city together with her other friends.

She had even invited me to come along before, but I had always declined that offer thankfully. Why I did this, I couldn't tell. I could've at least tagged along once to try it, but somehow I disliked the idea of long train rides since the few ones that stopped here were always crowded and didn't have AC. At least that was what Jane had told me. Since I was a bit claustrophobic, it didn't seem like a great idea to join her.

The train station was one of the ugliest I had ever seen. Although I haven't seen that many, it was so ugly it wouldn't surprise me if it even was one of the ugliest train stations in Germany.

To get to the trains, one needed to walk down the stairs that led to a sketchy-looking underpass. From there, more stairs would eventually lead to the gates. The walls of the underpass were dirty and painted in a monotone gray. The highlights were that some people had smeared their initials on the walls with edding to show that they had been here – what a weird flex. The train schedule hung behind an already shattered pane of glass. Next to it was the ticket machine. At least this one seemed to work, I figured after glancing at the display. It surprised me that it wasn't broken like everything else in this station.

The sharp sting of urine entered my nose. I knew exactly why I usually stayed far away from here. This wasn't a place one wanted to wait for a long time. It wasn't a pretty train station in a small town somewhere in the middle of nowhere with a beautiful entrance hall and fields surrounding it.

Here, there was no entrance hall, and benches or other seating possibilities weren't available either. The only thing coming close to that was an empty building right next to the train station. I didn't know what had been in there before it was emptied, but it definitely didn't make the place look prettier. All of this reminded me of German class in school where we once talked about aestheticization of ugliness. However, I was sure that even this station couldn't ever be seen as aesthetic, no matter from which time period one was looking at it.

I looked at the broken departures and arrivals board at the gate. Nobody cared about repairing or even replacing it. Nobody cared about the train station. The city always had other projects to care about; the train station was none of them.

Sina's train was late. What else should I expect? We lived in Germany after all.

It was 9.15 a.m. when she finally arrived. What an odd time. Still, it made sense that she would arrive that early. She didn't have much money and tickets for ICEs were expensive if they were driving during the day. The only chance at getting a slightly affordable ticket was to drive through the night.

"I told you changing the hair color can be great," she greeted me enthusiastically and eyed my, for her, new hair color. At first, I was a bit confused about it since I had gotten used to it by now.

"I hope you didn't need to wait too long," she added before I could think of an answer to her complimenting my hair color.

"It's okay. It's not your fault anyway," I yawned.

It was definitely too early for me to have an actual conversation.

"How was the train ride?" I tried small talk since my brain wasn't fully awake yet.

"Too long." Sina sighed.

And with these words, we left the ugly train station behind us.

It didn't surprise me that the train ride felt too long for her. The ICE was only stopping in the next big city, and from there she needed to change trains to come here.

Luckily, we didn't need to wait too long for the bus that should bring us home, it had started to rain by now. Stupid fall. I preferred summer.

"What's the plan for today?" Sina wanted to know after we had finished our breakfast.

"Great question," I murmured.

If I was honest, I hadn't made any plans for today. I had expected her to be exhausted after the long journey. And there weren't too many things to do in this small town anyway.

"We can relax today, and tomorrow I can show you the city center?" I offered.

"Great idea. I was afraid you would drag me through the city today. I'm way too tired," she admitted. And so was I.

"Don't worry. But tomorrow we need to buy a birthday present for a good friend of mine. I hope that's okay for you. It's his birthday soon, and I don't have a gift so far."

"Aha, a good friend of yours," she said very slowly and looked at me expectantly.

"One can be friends with guys without immediately falling in love with them," I explained to her.

There was a reason I hadn't told her about Ramon so far. She would want to meet him, and I didn't have any excuse for her to not meet him.

Even though we had our differences in the past, I didn't want to risk her life. Additionally, Ramon really didn't look too well; he probably didn't want to see anyone anyway.

"I know. But the Luna I know never talked to guys." She sounded almost a little bit sad when she uttered that sentence.

I imagined she was feeling especially sorry about how things went between us last year.

"Yes, but the Luna that talks to guys is pretty damn cool as well," I reassured her and smiled encouragingly.

"I hope so. I traveled for hours just to see her."

✳✳✳

Sina was impressed by the city center and its closeness to our school.

"If I would go to school in this town, I would be poor from eating out every day," she had said.

And she was right.

In general, I wouldn't spend that much money if I didn't have that many friends that wanted to do things with me. But it was worth it.

We walked through a small bookstore searching for the perfect gift for Finn. If I was honest, I was completely overwhelmed by buying birthday gifts, no matter how well I knew a person. Especially when I knew a person well. Because then I pressured myself extra hard to find the perfect gift. It was hard to describe this feeling, but obviously, I felt the same pressure now that I was looking for a present for Finn. After all, he was one of my closest friends, if not the closest friend I ever had.

Finally, I decided to buy him one of my favorite books. It was my way of gifting something personal to him. And I knew that Finn loved reading but never knew what to read, so I tried to help him out. Maybe it would motivate him to read a bit more in his free time. On my way home, we stopped at the closest grocery store to buy his favorite chocolate. Nothing was better than chocolate anyway.

The next day would be Finn's birthday. I had told Sina before she came to visit that there would be a party, but Finn had emphasized that he was fine with me cancelling in case Sina wouldn't feel comfortable going there.

Either way, I had promised him to celebrate with him, no matter if it was on his actual birthday or a few weeks later, after Sina would be gone again. Since I didn't feel like canceling, I let Sina decide if we should go or not. I could understand if she didn't want to go to a party where she didn't know anybody other than me, but luckily, she was excited to go.

"This is the first time we go out to party together. I wouldn't miss this for the world," she said and her face lit up.

And she was damn right about that. Back then, I would've preferred everything over partying. Maybe it was because I was older now, maybe it was the circumstances.

After all, if it wasn't for Finn, I didn't know if I would have ever thought about going to a party. He had this ability to make me step out of my comfort zone. And especially in the first months of our friendship, he did a great job at carefully pushing me onto new ground. He had made me a better person.

Was it really that simple to change someone positively? Because I was sure without Finn, I wouldn't be so openminded towards new situations.

"Then let's hope it won't be the last time," I responded.

"Never. This is only the beginning," she immediately said and hugged me out of nowhere.

The day of the party, we got ready together, which took way longer than I usually needed if I was alone. A glance in the mirror told me that we didn't look like sisters anymore. We didn't even look like we used to, which was the best metaphor for our internal changes as well.

Before we went to the party, my mom gave us a speech about responsible consumption of alcohol and that she wouldn't clean up after us in case one of us would throw up. She seemed to have a rather interesting idea of what we would do tonight. But then again, I didn't know how much alcohol Sina would drink and how she would handle it. Personally, I knew I could never drink as much alcohol as I would need to throw up from it. I never felt like drinking that much anyway.

"I'm a bit nervous to finally meet your friends," Sina uttered while we were on our way to Finn.

"You don't need to be nervous. My friends are so extroverted, it's hard to be disliked by them."
I tried to calm her down.

"Still. But…" she started.

"No buts. Everything is going to be chill. We will have a great evening, and everything is going to be okay," I interrupted her.

"But I'm not like you," she said in the second the traffic light in front of us showed a green light and we could continue walking.

"You don't need to be like me to be accepted by them."
Somehow, I couldn't imagine that suddenly I was the more confident person of the two of us. It always used to be the other way around. I always subconsciously looked up to her. Because back then, she was the self-

confident girl, and I secretly wanted to be a bit more like her and a bit less like me.

It was a weird swap of rolls, but I would lie if I said I didn't like it. Also, it was easier for her to think positively of me the further away I kept her from my real thoughts. Because if she or anyone else knew what kind of identical crisis I was going through at the moment, nobody would think of me as confident anymore. But maybe that was why it felt good to spend time with her. Right now, my inside didn't matter, and pretending to be whatever she saw in me was enough to make her like me.

"You're right, but I'm still nervous. What if they really won't like me?" she continued talking.

I just shook my head and laughed.

"This won't happen, and if it would, then so what? It won't change anything about our friendship."

I bit my tongue to not tell her about Ramon and his differences with Finn at the beginning. And even there, Finn had his reasons why he didn't like Ramon that much.

We had met under special circumstances, which had made our relationship unnecessarily complicated. Finn was the one I could vent to about Ramon's behavior, and if I hadn't been that involved in the situation, I could understand why he had problems liking Ramon at first. It was easy to dislike him. Finn, however, also behaved like an asshole towards him. Luckily, he had realized this by now, and in the end, they both somehow got along. They were far away from calling each other friends, but they were okay with each other's presence. And if we talked together, they didn't fully ignore each other, and for now, it felt like this was everything I could ask for.

I wanted to tell Sina all of that, but I held back. Otherwise, she would have questions about Ramon and why I haven't talked about him so far. It would lead to confusion, and I was too bad of a liar to handle a situation like that.

Finn opened the door when we arrived, but the party has already started. We had taken too long to get ready to arrive at a time when the host, in this case Finn, was less busy and the people were sober.

"I thought you wouldn't come anymore," he smiled and hugged me.

"Happy birthday!" I answered and handed him my present.

"Did you wrap it?" He wanted to know after skeptically eyeing the carefully wrapped gift.

"Nope, it was Sina," I admitted.

Finn knew from other parties that my qualities as a gift wrapper were very limited. I didn't have the talent for it. Sina, however, was way more creative than me. And she definitely was more patient when it came to wrapping things. However, she couldn't handle my poor attempts at wrapping Finn's present, so she offered her help. In the end, she did all the work, but the result was way better than I could've ever done.

"How nice of you," he turned to Sina.

Then he introduced himself.

The music was already turned to full volume, and the living room of Finn's parents was crowded; at least it sounded like it was. Which didn't surprise me, he was throwing a huge party. Parties were his thing and since his parents only allowed him to host one per year, he needed to take this chance and make it the biggest and best party of the year.

"Why didn't you bring Ramon? I haven't seen him in a while," Finn asked casually while accompanying us to the living room.

I could only hope Sina didn't hear his question, but a quick glance at her face showed me she wasn't paying attention; she was too distracted by all the people surrounding us.

"Do you already miss him?" I teased him.

"Well, you fought so hard for me to accept him. And now that I do, you stop bringing him. Are you guys okay?" He sounded worried.

"Yes, we are fine. He just doesn't feel well at the moment."

I was pleased with my answer. It wasn't even a lie.

"Oh, is he sick?" Finn didn't want to let go of the topic.

I knew he didn't mean to be rude or noisy, more of the opposite, he tried to be nice because it showed that he was worried about him because he did like him in a special way. Still, his questions made me feel uncomfortable.

"I don't know if he wants me to talk about it," I answered cautiously while I feverishly tried to think of a good excuse.

Right in this moment, I remembered Ramon complaining about therapy. He wouldn't be mad if I used one of his false diagnoses as a reason for him staying away from my friends. And until the day would come where Ramon would trust Finn enough to tell him the full truth, this would do it.

"It is more like a depressed phase, but don't tell anyone." It felt a bit wrong to lie about something like that.

In my head, it all sounded so much easier. But depression wasn't a topic that one should lie about. As far as I knew, and I had read a bit on the internet, after Ramon had told me about all of his 'diagnoses', it was a very complex topic that lost its meaning in today's world since there were enough people on the internet who romanticized the idea of having depression. Depression wasn't something one should want, still some people didn't get that memo.

When it came to Finn, I knew he wouldn't judge Ramon, no matter if he was depressed or not. He would believe my lie because it sounded plausible. And most importantly, he would keep this secret to himself. Another thing I liked about him. He kept my secrets as if they were his. And maybe that was the reason I felt so bad about lying to him.

On the other hand, I didn't lie to him because it was fun to me, I did it to preserve his view of the world. To protect him. Every time I thought about how I had felt after Ramon had told me about his powers... My whole world had crashed that day. No, I wanted to protect him from that for as long as possible. Because I cared about him.

Finn brought us something to drink, then he needed to go and greet some more of his guests that have arrived in the meantime. This was one of the disadvantages of a big party like that; he needed to be everywhere all at once.

Against my expectations, Sina didn't feel uncomfortable, more like the opposite.

"I didn't know people could party like this," she shouted excitedly, and only barely managed to be louder than the music.

This definitely wasn't the right place for a conversation. But this also wasn't the reason why we were here.

"This party is basically the exception. Other parties are smaller," I yelled back at her.

I didn't know if she understood me, but either way she stopped talking and took a sip from her drink.

"EVEN THE ALCOHOL HERE TASTES BETTER THAN AT HOME."

I was certain this had to be a placebo or she simply only drank the wrong brands of alcohol, but I didn't want to destroy the moment. If it made her happy to think of everything as better than home, then I wouldn't stop her from doing that.

After we had danced to a few songs, I decided to introduce Sina to my other friends. Despite the crowd, it wasn't hard to find Jane, Julius, and his boyfriend.

"Here you are," Julius enthusiastically hugged Sina and me at the same time.

Since I was already a bit tipsy from the alcohol, I almost lost my balance because of that.

"That's Julius." I introduced him to Sina.

She eyed him and introduced herself as well.

Jane put her smartphone away, which she was typing on when we arrived, and greeted us – a bit less enthusiastic than Julius did – but still cordial.

"Where is Matt?" I asked Jane.

If someone knew where he was, it would be her. I couldn't imagine he would let go of such a great opportunity to bother me.

"I don't know, he doesn't respond to my texts anymore. He didn't even say he wouldn't be here today." She looked hurt.

Whatever issues Matt and I had, they were in the past, and I was over them for good. He didn't seem to me like someone who would ignore people just like that. Something must have happened. I simply knew it. I already feared the magicians had returned until I remembered that he basically announced that he would vanish from our lives. However, I didn't expect he would mean to completely distance himself from all the people he had met along the way. The friendships he had made were not based on his supernatural roots. They were real. At least that was what I had thought.

When he said he would vanish, I thought he would simply leave Ramon alone if he couldn't help him. But now knowing that he was ignoring all these people without any good reason disappointed me. I somehow thought the relationships he had formed were more important to him. But looking at it from today's perspective, his last words towards Tim, Ramon, and me made a whole new sense. He didn't just want to thank us for our help; it was also a way for him to say 'farewell' or something like that. It was his way of saying goodbye. Forever.

I gulped and felt so incredibly guilty. I would have loved to help him, but I didn't know how. And if the storybook couldn't tell him what he was, what else could we possibly do to find it out for him? Damn. Now he disappointed Jane and Finn, whereas it was obvious Jane suffered more than him.

I was angry. How could he be so egoistical. In the end, we all had just been minions in his wicked game. What did he say during that night in the mansion? It was easy for him to play with humans, to manipulate, and to use them for his needs. What if we were nothing more than a way for him to pass some time? And I thought he had changed. Slowly, I became furious. I had told him from the beginning to not hurt my friends. Until now, I expected him to harm them physically, but whatever he was doing now was another way of hurting them. Maybe this was even worse.

"Maybe he needs some time to respond." I tried to cheer her up, knowing that the odds of him answering were low.

"I don't think so. Everything is so strange. I don't even know where he lives. What if something bad happened to him?" She blurted out.

It really seemed like she was worried about him.

"Something about him is wrong," she concluded while drinking from her beer.

Little did she know what was wrong with him. She would have a totally different image of him. But it wasn't my task to ruin the idea of him for her. At least not today.

Today it was most importantly, to cheer her up.

Sina looked at me insecurely and tried to whisper something into my ear, which I could only understand after she had repeated it for the third time.

"Julius looks like Derek," is what I thought I heard.

I chuckled.

It had taken me multiple months to notice this similarity. Maybe it was because it had been some time since I had seen Derek for the last time, or maybe it was because Julius had, by far, the better character, but now I could barely see any resemblance. Julius was unique, and this was what I tried to tell Sina as well. She seemed to understand what I meant by that because she let go of that topic. Maybe this party was good for her. As good as the party a year ago had been for me. These parties had proved that letting go could be so easy if one would simply try.

Time flew by. We danced a lot. We drank a bit. A bit much. We had fun. Despite the resemblance to her ex-boyfriend, Sina got along best with Julius and his boyfriend, who was a little bit shier. But this didn't surprise me. Julius almost was the definition of the word extroverted.

It wasn't until the living room slowly started to feel empty that I looked at my phone to check the time and realized that it was pretty late by now. Neither Sina nor me were particularly tired, so we decided to stay even though I would've already left if this was a regular evening. I always was the person that left when the party was at its best. But I could live with that. Today, however, was the first time none of my friends needed to try to persuade me into staying; I stayed because it felt like the right thing to do.

And in the end, all of the guests except for Jane, Julius, his boyfriend, Sina, and I had already left.

"I can finally breathe," Finn sighed after he said goodbye to the last group of people.

"Every year, YOU decide to throw these huge parties," Jane reminded him.

"And every year, I regret it, but so what," he laughed and sat down on the sticky ground where we were already sitting.

"How can people create so much chaos in such a short time?"

He was right. This was the main reason why I only celebrated my birthday in a small group. Too many people would create too much of a mess.

"But it was worth it. Your parties are always the best," Julius patted his shoulder.

"I hope so. I'm risking my graduation for these parties," Finn bragged.

"Just because you need to spend one day cleaning instead of learning for your Abitur?" I asked skeptically.

"Exactly," he admitted.

"We still have six months or so until the exams. You stress yourself too much," Jane tried to remind him.

"I work best if I'm under pressure," he answered just to realize he had contradicted himself somehow.

In the background, the music was still going, just way quieter.

"Isn't it weird that it's only six more months?" I blurted out.

All eyes turned to me as if they expected me to say something else. So, I didn't think about it and let the alcohol work its magic: "Well, it's only six months, which feels like nothing in comparison to all the years we have already spent in school. And everyone expects us to have a plan of who or what we want to be, but if I'm honest, I don't know anything. And all the time, I was counting the years until I would finally graduate, thinking I would have it all figured out by then, but now, where it is in reach, I'm panicky because it is the end of something familiar. Going to school is all I know. I can't imagine going to university because everything will change and new beginnings like this stress me out."

For a moment, everyone was quiet.
Even the background music seemed to stop for a second.

"I understand exactly how you feel. I always think I need to study law or medicine because my grades are good enough to get in. I work so damn hard for them to be good enough, but in the end, I don't think studying law or medicine would fulfill me. I'd rather study philosophy or music, but I don't know how I should explain this to my parents," Finn said.

I observed him.
I had never thought about what my friends would want to do after school. But Finn was right, I couldn't imagine him as a lawyer or a doctor. It simply didn't fit him.

"If you want to, we can switch reports, then I can study medicine." Julius offered and laughed.

"At least that used to be my plan until I realized my grades weren't good enough. So, I probably just study some arts and become a taxi driver. But in a pink cab to destroy patriarchy," he explained while looking at the ground.

It seemed to be the alcohol's work that he talked about something I was certain nobody else knew about.

"Damn, Julius. Why didn't you say this earlier? We could've studied together more often. I would've pushed you to your limits and beyond," Finn said sympathetically.

"You know I can be a diva. I hate asking for help, and now it's too late anyway." Julius shrugged.

Finn stood up and brought us new drinks.

"What about you, Jane?" Julius wanted to know.

"I guess I will travel before I study. Maybe I will go to Thailand or Vietnam. I want to explore other cultures and step out of my comfort zone," she explained and sounded so certain about her plans.

How could it be that she was the only one of us who had a real plan for the near future.

"I think I'll join Julius. Team Bachelor of Arts," I said and held my bottle up in his direction so we could drink to that.

"Team Bachelor of Arts," he yelled as well and drank from his bottle.

"To that we never lose touch no matter how far away from each other life will lead us," Finn shouted and we all agreed to that.

"Everything feels so surreal. Soon, we are supposed to be mature adults that make smart decisions in their lives, at least that is what people expect from us," Jane murmured nostalgically.

"I'm already an adult on paper, and I can reassure you, nobody expects anything reasonable from me." Finn laughed.

He was right. Sometimes it was easy to forget that he was the only one of us who had already passed the magical line of turning 18 a year ago. He once had to repeat a year of school because of his, as he called it 'rebellious phase', even though his grades had been perfectly fine before and after that one year.

"False friends change you," he sometimes said, but I accepted that he didn't really want to talk much about it. All I knew was that he had switched to our school after that phase. I concluded that he probably lost all contact with these "false friends".

Although he was already 19, he wasn't even the oldest person in our year. But there was always this one person in school that was way older than the rest.

And so, we continued to sit on the sticky ground and talked about philosophy and the world – I could now understand why Finn considered studying something like that – until all of a sudden it was dawn, and for the first time, I could feel how tired I really was. It was the first time, I stayed until the end of the night, and now I could understand why people in movies seemed to like it. There was nothing better than talking to your friends so intensely that you would forget the time. As if we were in our own world, a world to which the rules of time didn't apply.

It was almost completely bright outside when Sina and I were on the way back home. In the meantime, it had started to rain slightly, but we didn't care. It was a pleasantly cold rain that cooled down my tired eyelids a little bit. So, this was what it felt like to party through the night. Maybe I could get used to that. And for the first time since that night in the mansion, I felt a little bit more like myself. A little bit more alive.

It was late in the afternoon when I woke up again. I glanced at my phone and saw that I had one missed call from Ramon. I was confused, usually he only called if something important had happened. Immediately, I had a strange feeling in my guts. Was I worried, or was it just some leftover alcohol? I checked if he had sent me a text, but whatever had happened, it didn't seem important enough for him to write about it.

Sina was still asleep, so I carefully sneaked through my dark bedroom – thanks to the inventor of blinds – and locked myself into the bathroom. Then I called Ramon back.

I still had an unwell feeling in my gut. What if I had read the situation wrongly and Matt didn't leave us by choice? What if the magicians had returned for real? Under these circumstances, we would be absolutely doomed. So many thoughts were rushing through my head while my phone jumped to Ramon's mailbox. He didn't pick up my call.

Since I knew I would feel restless if I didn't get answers immediately, I called Tim instead, hoping he would know more than me. Luckily, he was one of these people that were always available. Therefore quickly, he picked up my call.

"What's going on?" he asked friendly.

"Ramon has called me, and now I can't reach him. Do you know what's going on with him?" I asked and couldn't prevent myself from sounding worried.

"Ramon has made an impulsive decision, he's on the way to the mansion." I heard him say through my phone.

I slowly ran my fingers through my hair. How could he be so stupid?

"Are you with him?" I wanted to know and hoped Ramon was intelligent enough to take Tim with him.

"No," Tim whispered almost inaudible.

He probably had just realized how big of a cluster fuck this situation was. Why was I sometimes the only person that thought about the possible consequences of certain actions?

Ramon on the way to the mansion all by himself was as bad as people in a horror movie that were convinced splitting up would be the right decision. It was incredibly careless and dangerous, and in the end we would all die because of this.

Chapter 12

The sun had already set when I – for the first time since the spontaneous start of my journey – reflected my behavior. Maybe it hadn't been my smartest decision to travel to the mansion, especially not alone. However, it had felt like the only escape from my current situation. My life didn't have any quality anymore since I had to isolate myself from everyone, and I couldn't continue living like this. I had to run away. From everything. From myself.

My loneliness laid over my chest like some sort of pressure. I had to do something against it; otherwise, I would have become insane. Now that I was gone, I could finally breathe again.

Traveling was the only way of realizing I still had some freedom left in my life. My apartment, these four walls, they trapped me like a cage. They didn't feel like a home anymore. Though, have I ever felt at home there? Maybe I needed to move, or maybe this short vacation in the mansion was all I needed to feel better.

My thoughts were still a little bit confusing, but at least I could now realize how reckless I had been. I shouldn't have started this journey alone. The magicians could show up any time, and as horrible as

I felt, there was no way I could fight them. I couldn't win against them.

If I had stayed in my apartment, maybe they would never find me, but now that I was in the mansion, it would be so much easier for them to locate me again. Unfortunately, I had realized all of this only now that it was too late to turn around anyway. It was the first time, in years of not being in control of my powers, that I let my impulsiveness control my life instead of rationality.

After all, I wasn't the same person I had been months ago; I was way weaker and more uncontrollable. Even the mansion wasn't the same. A few lost placers had heard about an empty villa and visited the building while I was gone. Some of them even left graffiti.

This was evidence for my theory that the magicians had left this place for good. It only made me calm down a little bit, but it did relieve me.

Did I feel lonely? Alone in a huge building like that? No, I didn't. I felt free, maybe a little bit overwhelmed by everything but definitely not lonely. If the magicians would come back, then so what? Let them come back, I couldn't change it anyway. Also, there was no reason for them to appear at the moment.

Back then, they didn't bother to spy on me themselves, they had let Matt do the dirty work for them. There was no way they would know that I had returned to the mansion now that he had left them. It was impossible. And if, for some reason, they did know, then I didn't care. Maybe I simply didn't want to drive back home again. Maybe I didn't care if I would return. Maybe I had subconsciously challenged my fate. Maybe. Maybe. Maybe. Slowly, I fell asleep.

The next morning, I woke up in my own sweat. I had trouble sleeping. Every time I fell asleep, I dreamt about the return of the magicians. Maybe the night in the basement had left more marks on me than I had thought at the beginning. Apparently, I repressed all these fears and trauma – I had enough problems already – but now that I've come back to the mansion, all the suppressed memories were coming back to the surface. And they hit me hard.

The mansion was one big trigger for me, but that was the best way to deal with trauma, wasn't it? You need to face your fears before they could get better. At least, Mrs. Müller had once talked about confrontational therapy. But if I were honest, I could barely remember her words.

Since everything about my journey was unplanned, I didn't pack much food into my bag. So, I decided to go grocery shopping and later clean the mansion a bit. It was not like I had anything better to do anyway. And additionally, it would distract me from my guilty conscience. I still haven't picked up any of Luna's or Tim's calls. I simply didn't know what to say to them. They would tell me I was an idiot, and I would agree. End of the story. There was nothing more to say, and in case they wanted me to come back, I wouldn't.

Right now, I wanted to be here. And I wanted to be alone. Otherwise, I would have asked one of them to come with me. At least that was, what I told myself. Because I had planned to take Luna with me, she just didn't pick up the phone.

I have always been great at lying to myself, but maybe I needed to be good at that to protect me from going insane through years of isolation. And if you told yourself often enough that you enjoyed being alone and didn't need other human beings in your life, then one day you would start to believe it.

If I hadn't learned in the meantime that things were different and I totally needed other humans to stay sane, I would probably still believe the lies I used to tell myself. Now I only had two options 1.) to drown in self-pity and isolate myself from everyone, keep my old habits, and hope the magicians would appear again to free me from my burden and tell myself I was happy or 2.) I would, if I was already in the mansion, not give up and fight through every day; maybe I would even find something helpful.

This villa was so incredibly huge, we haven't even explored all of it during our last visit. There could still be secrets hidden everywhere. Maybe I could even find my Grandma's spell book. The one the magicians were after. Then there would be a chance for me to find a cure so I could feel better again.

Nothing was lost, the future was still unwritten. I just needed to make my decision about which of the two options I would choose. But maybe I had already made that decision the moment I had started the engine of my car and drove over to the mansion. Because option 1.) I had chosen for way too long by now. It was time to get in control of my life. Just not today.

Today I was too exhausted. But tomorrow I would start to work on myself, and I would tell Tim and Luna that I was alive and well. In case one of them wanted to come and look after me, I would try to talk them out of it.

Even though it was naïve to believe the magicians weren't in the mansion and wouldn't return either, I could already tell how I felt better now that I was here. It was some phase where I needed to find myself, and if I could additionally find the spell book, my unplanned trip would've been totally worth it.

If there was one thing more powerful than the magicians, it was my Grandma's spell book. There needed to be a reason why they wanted to have it so badly. Too bad for them that they told me about it, because now that I knew I was the only one able to find it, I would do everything to keep it away from them. However, my memories were sealed, as if my Grandma knew what would happen, but it couldn't be that hard to unlock these memories. And if I could find them somewhere, it had to be here. I could feel it.

I started searching for the book in my Grandma's office. Although I was almost certain I wouldn't find anything in there since we knew the magicians had already looked through it, I hoped I would find anything that would point me in the right direction. So, I spent all week looking at old photographs and letters without really making any progress.

If Tim and Luna were here, everything would go faster, but doing all of this alone also had something oddly therapeutic. Even though I couldn't find anything helpful so far, it was interesting to see what my Grandma had done in the past, and maybe it also made me feel a bit happy knowing that most supernatural creatures were perfectly alright. So far, I had only met the odd ones out, and my expectations therefore were negative.

The letters that my Grandma has received, however, were positive and friendly, and somehow they made me feel proud to be part of this world. So, I spent too many days searching for the book by reading unimportant documents, but in the end, I learned a lot about myself and how curious I was to meet all of these other creatures once all of this would be over.

At some point, I could overcome myself and call Tim and Luna back. I had to reassure them that I was not just alive but also doing alright. Luckily, they could understand my reasoning behind this spontaneous trip and had new ideas where I should look for the book.

And it felt good to know that even though I was far away, they were still there for me, no matter how idiotic my decision had been. It was obvious Luna wasn't happy about the situation, she would've never let me drive to the mansion on my own. After all, she knew more details than Tim about how exhausted I really was. And even though it was a bit weird to read all of these letters written by strangers, they gave me strength and hope. Maybe one day this nightmare that was called my life would find an ending.

After I had searched through all of her office, I tried my luck in her personal bedroom. During our last stay in the mansion, we hadn't even entered it out of respect for my Grandma. Now, I needed to know if there was anything hidden for me in there. The odds were too high to not look through her room. And also, I highly doubted she would've cared about anyone in her room. She probably wouldn't even have minded if we three had stormed into her room during our last visit.

Maybe the reason for leaving her room untouched was not my fear of hurting my Grandma, it was deeper than that. Maybe I hadn't been ready to enter her room that shortly after her death because it simply was too painful for me. Now, it wasn't less painful, but since I was doing this also to become healthy again, the pain would at least be worth it. And that made it somehow bearable.

Her bedroom was tidied up and easy to look through. Still, I tried my best to not leave any mess behind. Therefore, looking through that room took me multiple days as well. The main reason, however, was that I couldn't stop myself from cleaning her room. She wouldn't like the dust on her bookshelf if she could see it from wherever she was now.

Looking through the other rooms was way quicker because they were less furnished, and I didn't bother cleaning them much. It was time to admit that I had come to my journey's end. Nothing made any sense. I had looked through every room in this goddamn mansion for the past few weeks, and I didn't find a single clue on where to find the spell book or how to unlock my memories. Frustration hit me. I was angry. Angry at me. Angry at the magicians. But also angry at my Grandma. If she was powerful enough to steal one of my memories, who could know what else she was able to do? Who knew which other memories she had taken from me?

Luckily, I calmed down quickly because being angry exhausted me only more than I already was, and I needed all of my energy because there was this one part of the mansion that I had not checked so far. For reasons.

Even though I didn't have high hopes of finding the book there, I decided to look through the basement. After all, this was the place I had heard about the book for the first time, and if my Grandma had a strange and well-hidden basement like that, who could know what kind of secrets I could find down there?

It made me uncomfortable going back to that place. And if I was honest, I was scared. In case something would happen, I was all alone and definitely not in the position where I could fight anyone. I could only hope the magicians didn't know where I was since Matt had left them, otherwise, I was in danger. They had already made it to the basement once without anyone noticing it… If I only thought about that night, my heart started to pound wildly.

He felt even more uncomfortable when he entered the basement room, where he had met the magicians and Matt for the first time. Everything looked exactly the way they had left it behind. But what did he expect? Somebody would magically clean up the mess for him? Obviously not. There was no one. Except for him and the others, nobody knew this basement existed in the first place, and after the magicians had disappeared, they had other priorities than cleaning up the mess that was made. They needed to treat his wounds as quickly as possible. Now that he saw all of the chaos, he felt a bit sad about it. For a brief second, he thought about picking up the jars and lifting up the shelf so the basement would look cleaner again. But it would only cost too much time and energy, and he didn't have much left. He needed to focus solely on finding the spell book. Cleaning the basement wouldn't help him find it.

Although it pained him to leave everything the way it was, he carefully groped his way through the small corridor that Matt had abducted Luna to back then. Maybe in the small room where she had been chained to the wall, he could find some traces of the spell book. Additionally to the poor lighting, he used the flashlight of his phone, which only made him realize how far away from everything he was down here. There was no reception. No one could hear him scream.

Of course, I didn't tell Tim and Luna that I wanted to investigate the basement. I had only given them the bare minimum of information, and they probably wouldn't expect me to go down there alone anyway. I, myself, didn't expect it either until I eventually did.

The basement was dark and I was alone in the mansion, but maybe that was the reason why I wasn't afraid; I simply didn't feel alone. I felt as if I could sense my Grandma here. And the closer I got to the small chamber, the more I was sure about it. Maybe she wasn't on this earth anymore, but she certainly was still in her home. Humans couldn't simply disappear like that, and just because someone had died didn't mean this person was nowhere to be found. I only needed to search for her in the right spots. And I did it. I was looking for her down here because it was the last place I had seen her. When I had broken down in front of Luna, I had some kind of dream – or was it another vision? – where she had spoken to me. So, it felt only right to find her in the basement. To look for her. Because without her, I wouldn't have been able to free Luna that night. Why did she appear exactly then when I needed her the most?

And suddenly I had a realization. There was no spell book. There never had been such thing as another book. It was dumb of me to expect a physical book just because the morphological composition of these words blinded me. Only because something was called a book didn't make it a real book. We lived in a world where even books could be bought and sold digitally as e-books. Only because it was called a spell book didn't mean it must be physically reachable.

All these weeks, I had looked for something I would never find. Everything was for nothing because I had looked for the wrong thing. The book wasn't a real book, it had to be a memory, and if I could feel something in this small chamber in the basement, it was only because my Grandma let me feel it, and since I could free Luna that night, it was only because my Grandma wanted me to free her. And why did she want Luna to be saved? Why did she want Luna to be safe if she was immortal anyway?

For now, I didn't have any explanation for that; my thoughts were still too messy. I didn't even know where all these ideas came from, but it felt like I was on the right track. I could feel that I was about to understand everything. There was only a tiny spark missing before everything would make sense.

I critically looked through the small room and carefully groped the wall with my hands as if I would feel anything else by doing that. As if the stones on the wall could answer all of my questions. As if they could tell me more about the spell book. But they didn't. Of course, it didn't help. Some things only worked out in movies or books and not in real life. And additionally, I must've looked absolutely ridiculous. I sighed and sat down on the ground. The walk down here had been exhausting, and I needed a break. I already felt a little bit dizzy. As soon as I would feel better, I would walk upstairs again. I should not stay down here for too long, the air was horrible and would only make me feel worse long-term.

Down here, I didn't find what I was looking for, however, I held on to the thought that I somehow had gotten closer to the book. Closer than I would've come in the overworld. It was definitely not hidden in any room of the mansion. If it was hidden somewhere, it was down here.

Where were my bizarre dreams when I needed them? Where was my Grandma when I needed her? But no matter how long I waited, she didn't come. So, I made myself stand up and went back upstairs. The further I walked away from the little room, the smaller my hopes to finally find the book became.

Before I started to walk up the endless, long spiral staircase to leave the basement behind me, I heard a noise. Scared, I looked around me. It was only a bottle that had fallen down from one of the shelves. It rolled in the direction of the small corridor that I had just left. Confused, I picked up the bottle. Inside a brown, not really pleasant looking liquid. I didn't want to know what it was, but it definitely wasn't what it once used to be. And if there was an expiration date on this liquid, it was definitely reached already.

Could it be a coincidence that this bottle had fallen out of the shelf now that I was about to leave? Down here, there was no wind, it simply couldn't be coincidental, could it?

Either way, it didn't answer my question if this was a trap or an attempt to communicate with me by my Grandma. Luckily, I didn't need to wait for long because one glance at the label could answer my question. On the label was only one word that was unmistakably written by my Grandma. *Luna.*

Chapter 13

I was absolutely unhappy about the fact that Ramon drove away, but I was even more livid he didn't know when he would come back. But I tried to hide it. I still had Sina over at my place, and I didn't want to explain myself to her. This situation was between Tim, Ramon, and me only. On the bright side, Sina's presence distracted me a lot, and I didn't need to think about Ramon too much. All the texts I received from him sounded surprisingly positive, and maybe he simply needed this vacation from his regular life. Thank God, he was self-employed and could easily work from everywhere or not at all.

But the vacations came to an end, and after Sina had left, I had more time to think about the Ramon situation, and my worries increased. He was already gone for longer than I had expected, and with every day my fears grew. The fear that he wouldn't come home again. The fear that something was holding him back. If I had no school and a driver's license, I would've already followed him. I hated being in that position of doing nothing, and even though he already sounded a tiny bit better than the last time we spoke; I, however, wasn't.

He barely texted or called me, and it got significantly less with each day. All of his texts were reduced to the bare minimum. This was not what a healthy and steady relationship should feel like. It didn't feel good.

The unknown was driving me crazy, and I felt panicky and sad at the same time. It wasn't until now that I realized how dependent on him I had become, and now that he was gone, it felt like I too had lost someone. But the worst thing for me was the fact that he didn't tell me when he wanted to return. I felt as if I had lost every single bit of control over my life I had left within the past few weeks.

I needed to urgently find out if the magicians were still looking for Ramon and how high the odds were that they would return to the mansion. So, therefore, I couldn't wait for school to start again. I would see Matt and I could ask him all of my questions.

The last few weeks, Matt has distanced himself from my friend group, he hadn't come to Finn's party, and he barely texted in our WhatsApp group. Although he had actually never written much, in the past few weeks it had completely stopped.

I needed to see him because now he was the only one that could help me. And things have changed. I now trusted him somehow. I was ready to talk to him about all of my problems. Especially about Ramon and his health. Maybe Matt could tell us what we could do to help Ramon feel better. Maybe he could help me convince Ramon to come back.

So, I was visibly nervous when school started again after fall vacations. I didn't think I had ever wanted to go to school that badly. But this mix between excitement and nervosity ended quickly when I realized Matt wasn't there.

His behavior was bizarre. I really hoped that nothing was wrong with him. What if the magicians had found him… I didn't want to know what they would do to him. I gulped. Maybe I shouldn't overthink it. I decided it was for the best to wait until the end of the week. Maybe he was ill – I didn't know if he could even be ill – or maybe he had other things to do. More important things. Maybe he needed to run away from the magicians and was doing perfectly fine wherever he was now. But I doubted this theory as well.

Still, I decided I would pay him a visit if he continued being absent until the end of the week and I could only hope he was still living in the small cabin where he had brought me to. Although it meant I would have to go on a hike.

The next day, Matt still wasn't at school, and since I was a very impatient person, I sent him a quick text asking him why he wasn't here. It surprised me that I hadn't thought about this sooner, it was the easiest and simplest way of communicating.

But he didn't respond; he left me on read.

Frustrated, the week passed without a sign whether he was still alive or not and, if I was honest, I had no clue if I would even find him if I looked for him. Because for now it seemed like he didn't want to be found. Why else should he ignore all of his friends? He was done with us. He didn't get what he wanted. We couldn't help him, and he kept his promise and vanished.

However, I didn't want him to. Nobody did. And I was sure that Tim and Ramon didn't expect him to cut all contact with us either when he said he would leave us alone. Yes, he had said he would vanish out of our lives, but we weren't done with him yet. We had only started to try and figure out who he was, and just because we couldn't find anything about him in the book wouldn't mean we had given up for good. And now that he was gone, I didn't want him to stay away from us, even though it was everything I thought I wanted a few weeks ago.

And because of all of these reasons, I started my mission to find Matt on a rainy Saturday morning. I had told my mom that I would meet Ramon because I didn't have a better excuse, and I knew she wouldn't ask any more questions once I mentioned his name. If she would know I was going for a hike, she would either be skeptical since I never go hiking alone or – even worse – she would join me.

I have only been to Matt's place once before, but I knew the general direction he had carried me. It couldn't be that hard to find him. There weren't too many mountains around us that were easily reachable in 30 minutes, I would somehow be able to find the way even if it would cost me all weekend.

Except for me, nobody has ever visited him, which sucked a little bit because it meant that no one could tell me where to find him. However, because nobody knew where he lived, I hoped he hadn't moved away and still hid somewhere around there. I hoped he didn't expect anyone to find him on top of the mountain. But then he totally misjudged me.

It took me forever until I made it up the mountain, and it took me even longer to find spots that somehow looked familiar to me. I cursed my bad memories and the fact that Matt had taken me up here with supernatural speed, which made it harder to remember anything. But I didn't want to give up just yet. Not even when the rain became stronger. As long as there wouldn't be a thunder storm, nothing could stop me from accomplishing my mission.

However, the strong rain made it hard to find my way around, but I kept on going. I couldn't stop, not yet. I had already come so far there was no going back, and if I was honest, I was a tiny bit lost as well. Why did he have to be so incredibly fast? Couldn't he be normal like Ramon? Then it would be so much easier to find the way to his place. Of course, I also cursed myself. While he had abducted me, I had my eyes shut for most of the time. I had been scared, and it was like a reflex, but it didn't make it easier to find the right way today.

After I was completely soaked and, in general, limited in my movement by the pouring rain, it became harder to watch my own steps. I slipped. The ground was muddy, and I couldn't hold my balance anymore. Now, I was not only soaked, I was also dirty. But I was not as unlucky as it seemed at first glance because when I stood up, I noticed I had already walked past a little creek. What did I expect? Did I really expect Matt's cabin to be at the end of a hiking trail? Of course, I had to leave the path at some point to walk through the dense forest, and now I have reached the point to do so.

On my right side was the creek, and I was certain it had to be the same one that was running by Matt's place. Now I only needed to follow it uphill, and it would lead me to Matt.

Filled with hopes, I ran through the forest until my lungs hurt. The way in front of me was still longer than previously expected, but I didn't stop, I continued walking. Until my body would give up, I would carry myself through the woods, at least that was what I tried to tell myself. I knew that I would have preferred to turn around and walk home. I needed to get out of these clothes and I only wanted to go to bed and watch a shitty TV show and sleep. But no matter how close I was to giving up, I didn't. I carried myself up the mountain.

I took some time to metaphorically pet me on the back. I was glad I had decided to wear my Dr. Martens this morning, so at least my feet were dry and it would be easy to clean my shoes after this adventure was over. But not even my favorite shoes could prevent my feet from hurting, and I was sure I already had at least one blister or two. But it would be worth it once I found Matt. If someone would have told me months ago what I would be doing for him, I would've simply laughed. This was insane.

Eventually, I found Matt's hut. I had definitely underestimated the way to get here. Now, I could only hope he would be home, otherwise, all of this would be for nothing. This was my last chance to find him. If he wasn't here, I didn't know where else to search for him. And if I was honest, I needed him now more than ever.

My heart pounded. I wasn't prepared for more disappointment in my life, he needed to be here otherwise it would drive me crazy. Additionally, I had no clue how I should find my way back home without him. I was exhausted, physically as well as mentally. And if I was doing only slightly better mentally, I wouldn't be looking for Matt right now.

I carefully walked closer to the house. I didn't know if he was alone or if he would have visitors.

I could see through the window pane that the light was turned on, which was a good sign. Someone had to be home. On tiptoes, I tried to look inside as quietly as possible. It wasn't until now that I realized how strongly my legs were shaking. I needed to stop peeking through the window before I would lose my balance and fall down. Now, I had the disadvantage of not knowing who was in there, but I had nothing to lose anyway. There was barely any reason for hikers to walk this way, it had to be Matt on the inside.

So, I knocked on the door.

No reaction.

"Matt? Are you in here? It's me, Luna, and I hiked all the way for you, it would only be fair if you wouldn't ignore me," I shouted and hoped he would hear me and open the door quickly.

I could hear steps coming closer.

I felt my heart pound.

Breath in. Breath out.

I tried to remind myself of breathing to avoid a panic attack. Seconds felt like forever.

Slowly, the door opened, and luckily, for me, the person on the other side of the door frame was Matt.

"You are here," I blurted out in excitement, and I could barely stop myself from throwing myself into his arms.

After all, we didn't know each other too well, and just the fact he didn't kill me didn't mean he would be my new best friend either. Sometimes, I needed to remind

181

myself of that because Matt felt familiar to me. Too familiar.

"Of course. Where else should I be?" he shrugged.

I raised my eyebrows and observed him critically.
He, however, looked as if he was trying to hold back a laugh.

"What?" I asked confused.
Now he couldn't hold back his laugh anymore.

"Wait, there is something in your face," he said still laughing, and tried to remove whatever it was by stroking my cheek with his finger.

"I can't get rid of it, but you should definitely check it out in a mirror. Maybe you can do something about it." He was still laughing and carefully led me towards a small mirror that was hanging on a wall.
To my horror, I realized that I looked horrible. My blue hair was bleeding out because of the rain and left blue stains on my cheeks. Also, my mascara was completely smudged, but this I had already expected.
I tried my best, but I could only get rid of the mascara below my eyes. The traces of blue color, however, didn't want to go away no matter how hard I tried to rub them away. Maybe I needed more showers until they would fade. Eventually. At least, I hoped so.

"You're doing weird things," Matt murmured and smiled while I sat down on the sofa next to him.

"For my friends? I do anything. But I guess you know this by now," I answered cheekily.

I didn't care if he saw me as a friend or something else. He intervened my friend group, and now he had to accept that I would call him a friend as well, even though everything inside of me was against it for a long time.

Also, this wasn't about him, more about the emptiness he had left behind when he had run away. And maybe I needed someone to talk to as well. Someone that could calm me down and tell me that Ramon would come back before the magicians would.

"Yeah, that's true." I could hear him say.

Then silence took over, which gave me enough time to notice how tired and exhausted I really was.

"I was worried about you." I broke the silence.

I wanted to be done with this conversation, so I could get back home. And to get over with it, I needed to start it first.

"But why? I'm perfectly fine," he asked astonished.

"You ignored all of us. You didn't come to school. Of course, I'm worried about you. We all are," I explained to him.

His facial expression changed, but I couldn't read him.

"I didn't want that. Sorry if I say it like this, but I don't understand human emotions, that's why I am a bit confused. I have told you I would leave you alone if we won't find something helpful in the book, so, for me, I simply kept my promise," he shrugged.

"Yes, but we weren't done yet. Maybe we'll find something if we continue searching. Also, what about the others? Do you really not feel friendship towards them? Towards no one?" I stuttered a little bit offended.

"Why should I? I'm a loner. I always have been. Friendships are overrated."

I sighed.

This would be a very exhausting conversation, I could tell.

"But you belong to our friend group like everyone else. Only because you claim to not feel anything towards us, which, by the way, I don't believe you, doesn't mean that no one feels the same about you. Jane is sad that you ignore her, and Finn missed you at his party. Those people enjoy spending time with you, and you have let us all down," I tried explaining myself.

"And what should I do, in your opinion?" He asked seriously.

"Come back. Please!" I said almost beseeching him.

Additionally, I tried my best puppy eyes.

I was probably looking disturbing because it always did, but it was worth the try. And I had already lost all of my dignity, the moment I had started my hike up here. I had nothing else to lose.

"I'll think about it."

"We need you," I started. "Not just Jane and Finn and Julius, but Tim and Ramon as well. We will help you because that's what friends are for. Nobody will be left behind, and promises will be kept. We are going to help you until we find out who you are. And you come back to school and help us find a cure for Ramon."

The words slipped out of my mouth before I could stop them.

"But if you keep your promise, why shouldn't I keep mine?" he wanted to know.

"Because running away is not a promise, it's cowardly."

He seemed to think about my words for a while, and I stared at him expectingly. Everything was depending on him. I needed him. He needed us. Why was he so hesitant?

"Okay, deal," he answered and nodded.

I couldn't even put in words how relieved I was.

"So, what's going on with Ramon? Anything new?" He asked helpfully.

I quickly explained the situation to him. I explained everything. How Ramon has driven back to the mansion alone, and that he was looking for the spell book, and how incredibly worried I was that he would meet the magicians again. I left out that I was still angry and disappointed and even unsure if our relationship could continue like that if he wouldn't come back soon. Matt wouldn't care about all of these emotions anyway, and I was sure he couldn't even understand why I felt this way.

"Hm," he murmured. "That really wasn't an intelligent decision, but I don't think the magicians are anywhere near the mansion at the moment. They are lost without me. They won't notice Ramon is somewhere else that quickly. If you ask me, they are on the way to this town, and in case my gut feeling is correct, Ramon is safer in the mansion than he is here," he shared his thoughts with me.

"Why do you think that?" I wanted to know and looked at him with my eyes wide open.

"It's simply a feeling. As I had mentioned before, there is some kind of connection between me and the magicians, and right now it feels like they are coming closer."

"That's not very calming," I figured and supported my head with my arms.

This was bad. Pretty bad. What if they were coming for my friends?

"At least Ramon is safe."

Matt tried to calm me down and added a smile.

It didn't help.

"If he finds the spell book, we have a decent chance to heal him without the help of the magicians."

"What do you mean?" I asked.

"Well, they threw a powerful potion at him, which weakens and prevents him from controlling his abilities. That's all we know so far. It's a fact that the magicians are going to come back. Not just because of Ramon but also because of me. That's, by the way, another reason why I left you guys alone. I could tell they were coming closer, but so can they. I basically accidentally lured them towards you, and I don't want them to find you," he said casually as if it didn't matter much. As if nothing was bad and he had everything under control.

I was surprised. I didn't expect him to be that selfless. Still, it didn't change the fact that I felt like crying finding out all of these things. I had already hit rock bottom. I wasn't ready to encounter the magicians again. Not now. Not that soon.

Of course, we all knew for some time that we would need to face them again eventually. At latest after Matt had stumbled into our lives. But it was easier to repress this thought than to actually prepare for another meeting.

"They will take advantage of the fact that Ramon is weak, and who knows what other things they have planned. Anyway, they will offer him a cure and hope that he is desperate enough to take it. So, they can force him to join them. But if we can cure him before they arrive, they will be blindsided by that. And we need every advantage we can get," he further explained.

"And that means?" I asked insecure.

"We already have one advantage. Since the magicians are tracking me, we can lure them wherever we want. And although we can't decide when they will arrive, we can choose the place where it is going to happen."

"Far away from the town and my friends," I immediately said.

That was the only way we could prevent innocent people from getting hurt.

"Exactly, but at the same time it should be a place that we know. In the best case, the magicians would think they have an advantage which, in reality, they don't," he thought out loud.

"Here. Your cabin. They would think they catch you by surprise when in reality we are prepared to meet them," I offered.

"Great idea," he answered impressed.

"If Ramon finds the book and we can heal him, we'll lure the magicians to your cabin." I summarized our conversation.

"But what if we can't heal him?" My fears came back.

After all, we didn't know when or if he would comeback. Neither did we know if his search would be successful. But he must come back. There was no way he wouldn't, would he?

"Then we still lure the magicians to my place. We only have a slight disadvantage. It's a fact that they are already on their way. We can't prevent that anymore."

"So, it all depends on whether or not Ramon will find the spell book." I sighed desperately.

The odds were so low that he would actually find it, and maybe it would be better for all of us if he wouldn't. Because not knowing where it was could protect him. But on the other hand, the book would be an enormous advantage, and we needed it desperately.

I hated everything about this situation, and even though I had little to no contact with Ramon at the moment, I was sure he wouldn't like the idea of meeting the magicians again that soon either. Thinking about facing them in the next few weeks, no matter what would happen in between, made me feel sick to my stomach. But even more important, Ramon needed to come back urgently because, without him, the fight was already lost. We needed every help that we could get.

"Maybe we should arrange another meeting with Tim and Ramon, so they can get familiar with this place. The advantage of meeting the magicians up here only matters if everyone knows their way around," he proposed.

I could only agree. The plan was good. And now everything we could do was to hope the other two would like the plan as well. So many things could go wrong, and just by thinking about them, I became panicky again. It was as if the same old nightmare would repeat itself.

And I didn't want to find out what else the magicians had to offer. If they were on their way, it meant they had found someone or something that could take

Matt... or... and I really didn't want to think about it because I didn't believe it, but I needed to be prepared for it... Or Matt would stab us in the back.

Of course, Matt brought me home at the end of the day. If I was on my own, it would have taken hours, and I wasn't ready for that. I just wanted to change from my wet clothes into something warm and cozy and maybe take a bath. Because I needed to sort my thoughts before I would call Ramon and beg him to come back as soon as possible. I needed to find some good arguments because, so far, he had dodged every single one of my attempts at making him come back.

"And don't you dare think about not coming to school. You know I'll find you," I said to Matt after we had arrived in front of my door.

"Don't worry. I won't fight you anymore." He laughed and disappeared in the darkness.

It was weird, and somehow, I believed him when he said he didn't feel a friendly connection to anyone. But he probably knew, as much as me, that there was something. Otherwise, it wouldn't be that obvious for him to fight on our side against the magicians.

Chapter 14

Although I wasn't 100 percent sure, everything made sense the more I thought about it. Even though her name on that bottle had almost immediately disappeared after I had blinked, I was certain it wasn't just a work of my fantasy. It felt as if someone had sent me a sign, and since my Grandma had helped me out in the basement once before, maybe she helped me out a second time. Maybe she knew I was lost without her and needed some help urgently.

If it was true and my Grandma had really given away all of her powers to Luna to save her – and we knew for sure it was true – then it was only logical that Luna would also have my Grandma's knowledge.

It was so dumb of me to think the spell book had to be a real copy of a book. It had limited myself to things I could touch and prevented me from finding the truth, even though I had been so close to her all the time. But I simply had been blinded by my own limitations. The only good thing was, if I was feeling that way, the magicians would have fewer chances at finding the book. I only needed to figure out what they knew and if I really had an advantage now that I knew where to find the spell book.

Additionally, I had to figure out if I wanted to tell Luna the truth or not because knowing she was the key to all of the spells would only put a target on her back. On the other hand, not knowing something big like this could make her vulnerable as well. Also, I was way too curious if my theory was even correct and if she could maybe cure me.

I should feel more euphoric now that I had an idea of where the spell book was, but somehow, I had the feeling that I would have a whole lot of other problems now that I had found it.

The following day, Luna called me in the night. I was already half asleep, but luckily for her, I had just looked at my phone screen while she called, otherwise, I would've missed it.

Although I had accomplished my mission in the mansion, it was a tough step to come back home and especially submit the news to them. I couldn't possibly imagine how Luna would react, and I definitely didn't want to pressure her even more, but we didn't have any other choice but to test her powers. I disliked seeing her overwhelmed or sad, so it was the easiest for me to postpone this conversation to the future. It was a problem for future Ramon, not present Ramon.

In general, I had spent so much time in the mansion that it had become even harder to leave and return back home. If I was honest, I hadn't thought about anything before I had started my journey. It was crazy, but if someone had told me about this trip six months ago, I would've assumed that starting would be the hardest part. Letting go of the familiar and heading towards the unknown. But now, where leaving had felt surprisingly easy, I realized that coming back home was so much harder. And sometimes you would only realize what had already been obvious before you just didn't want to admit; sometimes, home didn't feel like home.

No matter how much I liked the apartment I was currently living in, my real home was here. This place was where I belonged, and maybe it was somehow my destiny to step into my Grandma's footsteps, although our powers couldn't be any more different. She was the one that brought someone back from the dead; I only brought death.

Sleepy, I picked up the call.

"Ramon?" She sounded surprised.

She probably didn't expect me to actually pick up the phone.

"There is a tiny problem, and it would be great if you would come back home asap. Matt says the magicians are on their way to our town, and without you, we don't stand a chance against them," she blurted out.

My half-asleep brain needed a few moments until I could comprehend what that meant. We were all in huge danger.

In this moment, I didn't care why Matt knew the magicians were on their way, it was only important to know if we could have a chance against them. I, unfortunately, wasn't the most reliable person for that fight. How should I even fight if I couldn't control myself at all?

"Okay, tomorrow I will come back," I responded and suddenly I felt wide awake.

"And one more thing," Luna continued and sounded a bit skeptical.

"What else?" I asked tensely.

What else was about to come? Could things even get worse from here?

"Drive carefully!" she said after a short break.

I wasn't sure if that was everything she wanted to say, but I didn't want to question it any further either.

"I will." I grinned.

And maybe I was looking forward to driving back because it would mean I would see her again. If it wasn't for her and Tim, who would know if I would ever come back. But now I had two good reasons to drive back home, and suddenly, the thought of returning to my apartment in my hometown didn't feel that bad anymore.

And that was why I packed my bags immediately after waking up the next day and started my drive back home. It was about time, I had postponed it for too long already, but still, it was a nice feeling to break out of my usual life for some time.

I had texted Luna my estimated time of arrival, and she insisted on coming over the same day. My heart beat faster than ever when I saw her in front of my apartment. It felt so good holding her in my arms again, and we probably had a lot of things to say, but they had to wait until tomorrow. Tonight was one of the few evenings where we could be Luna and Ramon that have a normal relationship. Tonight, we could be like the other couples. And saving the world could wait until tomorrow.

So, we spent a wonderful evening together. We ordered in and watched bad Netflix movies, and maybe I was a bit angry at myself that I had been gone for so long and therefore wasted so much time that I could have spent with her instead. I wasn't good at talking about emotions and even worse in having a relationship, but I didn't want to lose her, even though it might have looked like that to her in the past few weeks. And even less did I want to damage our relationship by driving away. I would have loved to simply stop the time during this evening to live in that moment forever. Around us, the world was about to crash – again – but here, when we were together, everything was alright. At least for this one evening.

The next morning, however, reality caught up to us. And no matter how beautiful the past evening was, today we had more important things to do than to sort out our relationship. Today was the day Luna and

Matt wanted to explain why they were so certain about the return of the magicians and how we could stop them. Additionally, it was my turn to tell Luna about my search for the spell book.

The mood at my kitchen table – the headquarters of our unsimilar alliance – was tense even though the morning had started so peacefully. Luna had made pancakes, and we enjoyed breakfast together, and every time I glanced over at her to see how she was doing, my world was okay again. Even if it was just the simplest of things, it made me happy to watch her.

At some point, Matt and Tim arrived and sat down at the still laid table while I offered them the leftover pancakes. Despite having done everything to try to lighten up the mood as much as possible, it was super tense.

"Great to see you're back," Tim said and took a bite from his pancake. "Very good," he added, eating noisily and nodding towards Luna.

"Yes, it was about time," I said vaguely.

I didn't want to overwhelm all of them right from the start and brag about my findings. Especially not now when I was neither certain if I had found the book nor if it would be of any use for us.

"I assume Luna has already told you the magicians are nearby." Matt led the conversation in the right direction.

I only nodded in silence.

I had a lump in my throat, and I felt as if my mouth had become terribly dry out of a sudden. It felt like I couldn't talk anymore. So, I quickly stood up and grabbed a glass of water, took a huge sip, and looked at Matt expectingly.

"We." He looked at Luna. "Came to the conclusion that we need to lure the magicians to a special place to gain an advantage. It should be a place that we all know, and it should be far away from this town so nobody will be suspicious," Matt explained to us.

Tim observed him skeptically and asked exactly the same question, which had formed in my head as well: "Why are you so sure the magicians are on their way? Did something happen?"

As a response, Matt explained his connection with the magicians in further detail. Now we were able to fully understand which effect the bond had, and we could understand even better why Matt wanted to break free from the magicians. As long as their bond was intact, he would never actually be free.

Since the magicians were basically attracted by Matt like moths by the light, we only had one option; to trust him. His feeling needed to tell us when the magicians would arrive in this town, and even more important, how we should stop them for good.

"And where should we lure them?" I wanted to know and took another sip from my glass.

"We thought Matt's cabin would be a good place. You two haven't seen it yet, but we can change that.

It's perfect. He lives far away from this town, and none of our friends know that he lives there either. Also, we can catch them by surprise if they think they could surprise Matt because he is at home, but in reality, we are prepared for their attack," Luna blurted out.

I didn't know what exactly she meant when she talked about being prepared, but I didn't want to question it because it was possible she had no idea what she meant herself, and I didn't want to ruin her excitement about the plan by pointing out its flaws.

Of course, I wasn't happy about the return of the magicians, but as far as I understood, there was no other option than to face them. There was no way they would simply turn around, now that they had come so far already. Not when they had almost reached their destination.

"So, the idea is neat. I mean, we have an immortal omniscient, a supernatural lunatic, the deadliest weapon on earth that is not able to control his powers, and me. I don't want to rain on your parade, but it sounds to me as if we have a tiny disadvantage no matter what we do." Tim figured, and I couldn't stop a small grin forming on my face. After all, he was right. We had a huge disadvantage.

"Actually, we hoped Ramon would find the spell book somewhere in the mansion. That could've been helpful," Matt admitted and seemed a bit abashed.

"About that," I started, looking down.

It was time to tell them the truth.

I gulped.

"I think I found it," I said and immediately felt all eyes on me.

"But that's great. Maybe we can even heal you before we beat the hell out of the magicians." Tim was excited.

"It's not that simple. The book is no book," I tried to explain.

"And the spoon is no spoon. We all have watched *the Matrix* before," Tim commented on my poor attempts at explaining the situation.

"What's that supposed to mean?" Luna looked skeptical.

"Well, I'm not sure if it's even true, but when I was in the basement of the mansion, I had a crazy idea. What if we have focused too much on our idea of the word book while searching for it, so we actually overlooked it all the time? What if the spell book only exists in theory because writing down the spells would bring too much power and therefore too much responsibility with it?"

"So, you want to tell us you remember the spells from the book?" Luna wanted to know.

"Not exactly. But I think I know who can remember them," I said and looked around me.

Still, the others were staring at me in disbelief. My glance shifted towards Luna. I couldn't read her facial expression, but it seemed as if she understood what I meant before I needed to say it out loud.

"I think Luna is the key to the spell book," I eventually said.

Immediately, the others glanced at Luna, who now rested her head on her hands and sighed.

"You think it's because of your Grandma? When she gave me her powers, she also gave me her knowledge?" She pressed out between her lips.

"Exactly, that's what I think," I agreed with her.

"Hm," she just said.

Everyone still stared at her, but she couldn't see it, her glance was still too focused on the ground below her.

Nobody dared to say anything, everyone waited for her to say something to break the silence.

"I don't know what to say. It makes sense, but shouldn't I have any idea what I could do to save you by now?"

She carefully looked at me.

"We could have a séance to help you out," Tim said thrilled. "Last week, I bought an old Ouija board at a garage sale, we could use it," he added quickly.

I didn't even question why Tim would've bought something like that in the first place. I had accepted that some things I really didn't need to know. And in the end, he must've had a hang for the supernatural, otherwise our ways would've parted years ago.

"Why the hell did you buy it?" Matt looked at him judgmental. "Everyone knows ghosts don't exist."

"You, a supernatural being, want to explain to me what exists and what doesn't?" Tim argued and looked at him playfully skeptical.

"Matti Boy, there are things on this earth that go beyond your imagination and who knows, maybe you will eventually realize that there are beings that even you don't know about."

"Don't ever call me Matti Boy again or else..." Matt responded coldly.

"What else? I'm not afraid of you." Tim provoked.

What a great team we were.

Within a second, Matt had packed Tim and gently pressed him against the wall.

"You don't want to find out," he whispered and let go of him again.

"Maybe I am a little bit afraid of him," Tim admitted and sat down again.

"Good, that we have figured this out. Do we have any other ideas?" Luna looked around.

"I already expected that. Tim, when can we use your Ouija board?" she decided after no one answered.

"Really?" Tim asked surprised. "I will prepare everything. This is going to be great. When should we start?"

Everyone should have a Tim in their life. No matter how hopeless the situation was, he stayed positive, and I really appreciated that.

After everyone else was gone, Luna stayed. I knew exactly what was about to happen, and somehow I had hoped we wouldn't need to have the following conversation or at least could postpone it as far into the future as necessary so it would become irrelevant again.

"I think we need to talk," Luna said and insecurely looked at the floor.

Immediately, I could feel some kind of panic. Did these words ever mean something positive?

It wasn't even like I was surprised that she wanted to talk all of a sudden. It was shit of me to completely shut her out of my life for the past few weeks. I had barely responded to her messages or calls; she didn't even know how things were going for most of the time. But this didn't mean my feelings for her were gone. It only meant that I was too busy with myself to take care of others.

"I don't think I need to explain why I was unhappy with how the past weeks went?" She started and nervously fumbled her wristband.

"No, I know exactly what you mean," I said and gulped.

"You left me behind. Although you knew exactly, I was worried about you. You mostly ignored me and barely shared any information with us. How should I know how your search for the book was going if you never talk to me? And maybe you wouldn't have texted me at all if I hadn't always texted you first. Just the fact that you drove to the mansion by yourself was horrible for me. You can't believe how worried I was. In your condition, you actually shouldn't be anywhere by yourself." She summed up the situation.

And I couldn't do anything but to let her talk and to reflect my own behavior. She was right about everything, still I couldn't take it back. Mistakes have been made, and no matter how much I wanted to change them, I couldn't.

"But the worst of all, was the uncertainty when you would return. If you had told me from the beginning when you were planning on coming back, everything would only be half as bad. But the fact we couldn't properly communicate…" She added under tears.

"I know. Believe me! If I could change it, I would," I threw in.

"But that's not the point. And relationships don't work like that," she almost yelled to release her anger.

"Maybe I don't work in relationships. Maybe I'm better at friendships," I answered also more emotional than before.

I had no clue if I meant what I had just said. I didn't want to lose her, but she was right, things couldn't go on like this.

"But that's not how friendships work either." She sounded desperate when she said it out loud.

Silence.

I didn't know what to say. And I was scared of asking the question, whose answer I didn't want to hear.

"What do you want to do now?" I eventually asked after the silence had become unbearable.

"I don't know."

She sighed and looked at me.

"Of course, I still have feelings for you, but I think we have reached this point where it simply isn't enough to keep the relationship going. Now, we need to focus on the magicians and on your wellbeing and less on…" She gulped.

It was obvious the following words weren't easy for her.

"And less on us," she finished her sentence.

Although I had already expected this answer, it still hit me harder than expected.

She threw herself in my arms crying, and I started to cry as well. She was right about everything. Even though we both had feelings for each other, it was too hard to act according to them at the moment. First, we needed to focus on ourselves, and maybe then we would find a way to focus on us again. Right now, simply wasn't the right time for it.

"It's okay," I tried to cheer her up while being super overwhelmed with the situation.

"I will still help you with everything. I don't want this to stand between us. I just want each of us to focus on ourselves and when everything is over and things are less complicated, maybe we can work things out again." She spoke my thoughts out loud.

"So, we stay friends?" I asked the most cliché question one could ask after a breakup.

She nodded and seemed relieved that I wasn't mad at her.

But how could I?

I knew she was right all along.

Chapter 15

My serious conversation with Ramon went surprisingly well, and it seemed as if he could reflect his behavior, which was relieving. He would always be important to me, but the past few weeks were shit and things couldn't go on like this. And with the magicians around, it didn't make any sense to focus on having a relationship. When things were over, we would have all the time in the world to try again. But right now, things were too difficult. The only thing that made me feel more uneasy than the breakup was Tim's idea.

If I was being honest, I didn't really like the idea of having a séance that much. It wasn't the idea itself that threw me off, it was my own fear of ghosts.

When I was younger, I had always disliked horror stories about ghosts, and especially a certain ghost lady that appeared in mirrors and shared a name with a cocktail – seriously, one with tomato juice, who drinks something like that? – scared the hell out of me. Things escalated, and there were times I couldn't walk past our hallway mirror as soon as it started to get dark. Even brushing my teeth was too creepy for me, I could only do it when it was still bright outside.

The older I got, the less afraid I became. And I can proudly say that I, by now, didn't care about mirrors or ghosts anymore. Still, I felt a sick feeling in my guts every time someone told me something slightly creepy. A séance was probably the worst case for me, and everything inside of me screamed as soon as Tim mentioned it, but I didn't have much of a choice, so I agreed. If Ramon was right and I had, in fact, inherited his Grandma's knowledge, we needed to try out everything that could possibly help us to access it.

We didn't have much time left before the magicians would arrive, we desperately needed every advantage we could get because there had to be a reason they had waited multiple months to try to find us. They were well prepared, and we weren't.

We needed Ramon's full strength. We needed my full consciousness, and if there was hidden knowledge trapped in my head somewhere, we needed to find it. If we wanted to stay alive, we had to try out Tim's idea because no one else had any better idea. And that was why I had agreed, despite only the thought of it making me shiver.

It wasn't helpful that Matt, the person who knew most supernatural things, was convinced ghosts weren't real. But if his knowledge was the benchmark, he shouldn't exist either.

We decided to meet again at Matt's place the next day. The séance needed to be held at a quiet place without much disturbing noise and a lonely cabin on top of a mountain seemed to be the best place we could possibly find. The only other fitting alternative would be the mansion, which could be neat because if the ghost of Ramon's Grandma was still somewhere, it probably would be there. Unfortunately, we didn't have enough time for another trip to the mansion; the magicians could arrive any moment, and I had school tomorrow.

I had told my mom that I would drive to Ramon's place after school and even sleep over. I left out the tiny detail that we had broken up, though. She would only ask questions. Questions I couldn't answer. There was no good excuse for why I would sleep over at Ramon's place despite our breakup. Because it technically wasn't even a lie. I would actually sleep over at his place. But it was also the only way to justify being away from home for a whole night. And I couldn't tell her that we would have a little chitchat with some ghosts. She would think I completely lost my mind. Especially since she knew my relationship to ghosts has always been complicated.

Also, she didn't need to know everything in my life. I was already 17 years old, and next year I would turn 18, and maybe I would move out, maybe I wouldn't. After all, I didn't have any exact plan of what to do in the future. Maybe I should start finding myself first. For now, I have spent all my life living as someone else because the real me shouldn't be alive at all. But on the other hand, this was my real body. The body that was driven over by a car back then. The body that had been buried. So, technically, I was myself in some abstract way. But somehow, I was not. And somehow, it made me feel sad that somewhere in the east was an empty coffin buried in the ground because the body that belonged to it was walking around here.

I wondered whether it was possible to contact my previous self through a séance or if everything that had once belonged to me was still inside of me.

Maybe I would have to have another séance in the future to answer these questions. Now we had different priorities. But – and I promised it to myself – if we would get out of this alive, I would get my driver's license, and I would buy a car, or rent one, or convince my mom to use hers, and then I would drive to my grave and look at it. Maybe it was still there for some reason whatsoever.

I couldn't think of a good excuse why it should still be there, because all the people that could have possibly paid for it – so, only Ramon's Grandma – were dead. No one else knew about Luana except for Ramon and his family. And even though everyone else had forgotten about her, I wanted to make sure I would always remember her. Despite not being able to remember ever being her.

I hated the idea of nobody remembering her/me. It made me sad. After all, there was only this one life, this one chance, to make yourself immortal in some kind of way. Death was not what I feared the most. Being forgotten was what truly scared me.

Tim had promised us to prepare everything for the séance; he was our guy with the plan. Although he had never lost his inner child, he always was in control of everything. He was the only one that always knew what to do. And I was the one that shivered simply by thinking about preparing anything for the séance. I just wanted to get done with it as fast as possible.

When I was a child, I was afraid of ghosts, but now I knew Matt and Ramon, and they were real, and they made me believe in things that I wouldn't have believed in when I was younger. Why shouldn't ghosts be real either?

It was starting to get dark when Matt transported all of us to his place. I was glad I didn't have to walk up to him myself. I wasn't really keen on trying to find the way in the dark. I was an easy-to-scare person, and walking through the forest in the dark simply wasn't on my bucket list.

Additionally, I highly doubted I would be able to find the way again. The last time I had visited Matt, I could only find him because of a lucky accident, and it wasn't even dark back then. And even though it wasn't that late today, we could tell that winter was slowly coming, and I hated it. Less sun, and, since we lived in the flat part of Germany, I couldn't even remember the last time I had seen real snow. Winter without snow simply wasn't the same.

Especially in the past years, the seasons have changed, one could already feel the slight effects of climate change. The summers started to become shorter and the winters longer. Still. Neither the summers felt like real summers because they were too dark and too rainy, nor did the winters feel like winter because there was no snow. If things would go on like this, maybe one day all of the seasons would vanish completely and merge into one big blob.

When we arrived at Matt's hut, I was astonished he had even prepared some things for the séance. The windows were darkened and he had lightened candles, which personally I found risky with all the wood around us, but Tim said it was just fine, and that candles belonged to a séance, and since he was the only one with a plan, I tried to not worry too much about the possible fire hazard. We simply needed to be careful, and everything was going to be alright. But no risk, no fun, was I right?

I, however, could do perfectly fine without the tingle that only the bare idea of a séance gave me.

Together, we sat down at the folding table – which Matt had provided only for this event – and Tim put his Ouija board down. Matt turned the light off and sat down on the last empty chair. Nobody had any idea what to do next. My heart was almost in my mouth.

Things were about to get serious. I was so tense, I felt sick.

I disliked the thought of summoning ghosts. What if we talked to an evil ghost that would murder all of us one by one? Maybe I had watched too many horror movies, Finn loved that genre, so we had watched some of these films together even though I was never really excited to see them. It simply wasn't my favorite genre.

And, rationally, I wasn't able to die. I was immortal. So, I literally had nothing to fear.

"On the internet, I mean, my sources have told me we need some kind of leader that guides us through the questions," Tim started.

In the candlelight, I could still tell that everyone was now staring at him.

"Although I am the person that knows the most, I won't be able to do it. Since it's about your Grandma, you will be our leader," he said towards Ramon.

"But how should I do this?" Ramon asked astonished and insecure.

I knew he didn't like the idea of leading anything at the moment, he must feel overwhelmed. But Tim was right. Ramon had a connection to his Grandma, they were related after all. If she didn't want to encounter him, then she would certainly not appear for any of us.

"It's easy, I'll share my wisdom with you," Tim said enthusiastically.

I couldn't tell if he knew how serious all of this was or if he just found it super exciting. It probably was a mix of both.

"Then let's go!" Ramon tried to hide his insecurities behind a laugh.

"So, we need paper. Here we go." Tim searched in his bag until he eventually found the paper and laid it on the table.

"Each of us gets one piece of paper and writes down exactly one question. I will explain the next step once we are done with this. I don't want to intellectually overwhelm you guys."

I grabbed a note and looked at it sternly. There were so many questions I could ask. So many questions whose answers I wanted to know. I could ask for the spell that would cure Ramon. I could ask for a spell that would help us prepare for the magicians.

"Can we ask questions that are a bit selfish?" I asked the others.

Ramon looked at me in pity, almost as if he knew what I wanted to ask. And maybe he really did know, I was too easy to read.

"It's okay," he nodded. "We all have a question to ask." He tried to give me a cheerful smile, but because of the candlelight it looked a bit creepy.

I sighed.

I knew it was wrong, but I needed an answer to one of the questions that had lived rent-free in my head for months by now. To be exact, since the day Ramon had shown me the missing pages from the storybook. And I would hate myself if I would never find out the answer to it, even though it was selfish. But I couldn't know if we would ever be able to contact Ramon's Grandma again, I didn't even know if it would work out today.

What if she was only trapped in some kind of in-between world until she would find her peace and this séance was the one thing that would liberate her? Then I would never know the answers to my question.

"Are you sure it's okay?" I asked again.

I was still uncertain of what to do. Usually, I wasn't selfish, but maybe tonight I needed to be. But it was so damn hard.

"Of course, isn't it selfish as well if I ask how to become healthy again?" Ramon asked rhetorically.

He was right. Still, it wasn't easy for me. After all, he meant everything to me, and it should be my task to ask these questions for him. But since he seemed okay with it and I was sure he would be angrier if I wouldn't ask my question, I wrote down something else:

Why me?

"Are we all done?" Tim asked us.

Everyone nodded.

"Perfect. Then we can all hand our papers to Ramon. Ramon, you will read all of the questions and then sort them based on which questions are important and which aren't. The séance could be over at any time, so we should start by asking the most important questions first," he explained.

We listened to him and handed our notes to Ramon, who quickly glanced at each question. It was absolutely silent. My heart beat so quickly, and I felt the urge to run away or at least leave the room. This situation was unbearably scary.

"Should I tell you the order of questions?" Ramon wanted to know.

"No, that's irrelevant. It's important that we know the question we currently ask. The rest doesn't matter. Also, nobody but Ramon can ask further questions. Only the leader can talk to the ghost, otherwise, it will be too chaotic, and we won't learn anything from it." Tim continued his explanation.

I didn't know what the others had written down on their notes, but I could only hope Ramon had set his priorities straight. I was afraid he would choose a different order of questions than I would've done if I was in his position. My bad gut feeling grew stronger.

"Okay, the first question is: 'Why Luna'?", Ramon started the séance.

I gulped.

I knew he would make the wrong decision. If the séance ended after one question, which was possible, I would hate him forever. My question was irrelevant, it was way more important to find out how to help him.

In case the séance would end soon, I could never forgive myself for being that egoistic. I would hate myself forever.

Tense, we stared at the planchette that was below our fingers. Tim has told us we should write down every letter or number the planchette stays on for longer than one or two seconds. My nervousness reached its peak, but I only became really afraid when the planchette slowly started to move.

I quickly glanced at Ramon, who also looked tense. I guess he hadn't expected this to work either. I wondered what Matt was thinking right now. He seemed so sure when he told us ghosts weren't real. But I could ask him about that after the séance was over. Now, I needed to focus.

The planchette stopped. I. The planchette moved further down. T. That must be the first word. But the planchette didn't fully stop. Multiple letters followed our first word until nothing moved anymore.

"It was time to go." Ramon read out loud what he had written down.

Everyone compared it to their sheets and we nodded. But we didn't feel much smarter after all.

"But why did you give your powers to her?" Ramon asked further.

I became restless. He shouldn't waste that much time with this question. We didn't know how long we would be able to hold the contact. We needed time for more important questions about the spell book and his cure. My question was so irrelevant in comparison to the ones that really mattered. It made me feel so uneasy that he didn't drop it.

Suddenly, I didn't care why exactly I had been chosen. Maybe there simply wasn't any deeper reason for it and everything was just a huge coincidence. There were more important questions to ask, but I couldn't complain to Ramon because he was the only one allowed to talk, and I didn't want to risk ending the séance.

The planchette started to move again.

S-H-E-W-A-S-T-H-E-R-I-G-H-T-O-N-E.

I guess this answered the question of whether it was a coincidence or not that I was chosen, but it still didn't explain what I had that other people didn't.

Ramon didn't need to further ask, the planchette started to continue moving over the letters.

S-H-E-W-A-S-P-U-R-E-A-N-D-Y-O-U-N-G-A-N-D-D-E-A-D.

If these were the only requirements, it did explain why I was chosen. The number of young and dead children around Ramon's Grandma probably wasn't that high.

I-D-I-D-I-T-F-O-R-Y-O-U.

Although no one dared to say it, we all knew this message was directed at Ramon.

Ramon's Grandma didn't know me, she couldn't have done it for me. In general, immortality was a gift I had never asked for. Why should I want to live in a world where all my loved ones grow old and die while I was doomed to stay?

This wasn't a world I wanted to be part of. Ramon, however, had an advantage due to my surviving; he didn't need to feel guilty about murdering me anymore.

"Thank you for your answer," Ramon said a bit confused if he was behaving correctly.

"My next question is: 'How can we heal Ramon'?" He read out loud.

Finally, he was asking the right questions.

Again, the planchette moved wildly across the board, and again we started writing down letters.

T-E-M-P-U-S.

I had no idea what that was supposed to mean, and it seemed like the others didn't know either. I glanced around and everyone seemed to be confused by that answer.

"Maybe I forgot to mention that the answers can be given in a different language as well," Tim said embarrassed.

One could tell he was feeling uncomfortable, none of us could've prepared for that.

"But we don't speak Latin." Ramon figured out.

It was beyond my knowledge how he could figure out which language it was that quickly.

"Well, isn't this just the name for the tenses of words?" Matt asked casually.

Of course. He was right. Now I could remember the word. We had talked about it during German class in combination with the words casus and genus. But what did all of this have to do with our problems?

"Does she want to tell us to just wait and the time will give us answers?" Tim tried to interpret the answer.

"But why does she need to change the language? We could understand her perfectly fine before, why did she speak Latin all of a sudden?" I wondered.

"Maybe we aren't talking to Ramon's Grandma. Maybe it's just some ghost that is playing with us?" Matt said annoyed.

He hadn't been fully in on the idea of the séance, and our first setback here only proved to him that it was a waste of time. The situation became even more tense.

"What exactly is this supposed to mean?" Ramon interrupted.

M-E-M-E-N-T-O.

"That's bullshit," Matt said angry.

"Stop being so pessimistic!" I hissed at him.

His negative view annoyed me. It wasted our time. And we didn't know how much time we had left to ask more questions. And before Ramon could ask any other question, the planchette wrote the word E-N-D. The fire of the candles flickered for a second, and the light in the cabin was turned on by itself. A shiver ran down my spine.

The séance was over.

Our last chance to gain valuable information was lost.

First, none of us said anything.

We were all too astonished by what had just happened.

"Insane." Tim quietly murmured.

It took a few more seconds for me to find my words again.

"We could've used the time that you took for complaining to ask more questions. And now we aren't smarter than before," I yelled at Matt.

Then I started to cry. I was desperate and I felt guilty because Ramon prioritized my unnecessary and selfish question over the others. And now we still didn't know how to help him.

"We can try tarot cards next." Tim had already thought of another plan, but nobody really responded. The others probably have given up, like me.

"All of this was for nothing. We probably have been pranked by someone," Matt answered furious.

"First you tell us ghosts don't exist, and now they have pranked us? Why don't you believe in restless souls that are trying to find some peace?" Tim asked him curiously.

How could he sound so calm? I was in a rage.

"Because I haven't been completely honest with you," Matt admitted and looked down.

He seemed insecure for a second, which was pretty rare. Quickly, he caught himself again and put on his mask of self-confidence and no emotions.

"Of course, ghosts are real, and maybe I haven't had the best experiences with them in the past. There are multiple reasons why some of them surprisingly aren't the biggest fans of me. So, technically, it would be possible if one or two of them wanted to get revenge," he admitted.

"So, you think they fed us wrong information on purpose?" Ramon wanted to know.

"Yes, maybe. I have no other explanation for the shift in language otherwise. Tempus? It seems weird to me to use a Latin word that has something to do with verbs. That doesn't seem like much of a help," he justified himself.

"Then we aren't any smarter than before."

Ramon sighed and rested his head on his hands.

I needed to restrict myself from making a Faust joke; this situation wasn't the right time to quote Goethe. But then again, when was the right time for that?

"We don't know if the messages are real or fake, and we can all be mad at Matt, but it won't help us either." Tim tried to calm us down.

He was right, but still, I was incredibly angry. But not at Matt; at myself. I should've asked another question. As Ramon had correctly figured, we weren't smarter than before. It was just easier to project my anger on Matt than to admit that my question had been the problem. As long as I existed, Ramon would prioritize me, and maybe I knew that. It didn't make sense that I had asked this question. I should've chosen a different one.

"It's a fact that we are going to treat the messages like they were real as long as we don't have evidence pointing against it. So, how could we interpret the words?" Tim took over the leading role again.

"It could mean that she wants us to wait and time will tell us what to do," Ramon repeated the most obvious assumption.

Tim wrote this theory down and looked at me.

"Maybe we should change our point of view like tenses that also change," I answered insecurely.

I had always been good at overanalyzing things. 11 years of school, and all of the analyses I had done in German and English class had taught me how to interpret every sentence of a poem or a novel in the most obscure way. Unfortunately, I wasn't really good at finding the most obvious explanation.

"Matt?"

"Maybe we should learn the different tenses," he answered ironically.

Tim wrote his idea down without commenting on it.

"What if we really need to take a closer look at the tenses?" Tim was thinking out loud and nobody dared to interrupt him.

"Present, past, future," he murmured.

"I think I like Ramon's idea the most," Tim figured after some time.

"But how should we interpret the change in language? In case the message is real, there must be a reason why she changed to Latin," Ramon argued.

It was obvious he wouldn't be happy as long as the theory wasn't fully debated. He wanted to know the truth, and he wouldn't give up before he would find it.

"A change in tempus." Tim was thinking again.

"A change in tense. A change in time!" He exclaimed.

We only glanced at him in silence. But he didn't expect us to react. That was one of the great things about Tim, he was doing Tim things, and he didn't expect us to understand them, and, in the end, something incredibly genius would come out of it. We didn't need to do anything; he functioned great by himself.

"She wants us to change the times. It totally makes sense. If we could travel back in time, we could prevent the magicians from throwing their potion at Ramon. And then he will be healthy and powerful. That's the solution." He was ecstatic.

"And how do you want to go back in time?" Matt asked skeptically and eyed him.

"It's easy. All I need is a DeLorean and… –"

"Tim, we're not in *Back to the Future,*" Ramon interrupted him gently.

"I know," Tim pouted, "I admit, I don't know how we should travel back in time, but I'm sure it's the answer. Ramon, please tell me you feel it too."

"Yeah, I totally feel a tingle in my big toe on the right foot," he answered sarcastically.

Tim rolled his eyes.

"Okay, okay. Your theory does sound like it could work," Ramon admitted.

"Perfect, now we only need to figure out how to time travel," Tim said as if it was something ordinary, something one was doing every day, like going to the supermarket for groceries or brushing the teeth.

"And what about the second message?" I wanted to know.

"Maybe that is the magic spell for finding a time machine," Matt said mockingly.
It was obvious he didn't take the discussion seriously. I had no clue what had happened between him and the ghost world that he was so certain someone was playing with us, and I really didn't want to find out either. It must have been something truly horrible, and I was getting along with him so well at the moment, I didn't want to ruin it.

"We will find this out as well. Can someone google it?" Tim asked us and completely ignored Matt.

"I don't have reception up here." I figured after checking my phone.

"I could get us a dictionary," Matt offered unconcerned, as if he didn't care whether we would find something or not.

"That would be great." Tim couldn't even finish his sentence; Matt had already vanished. Sometimes I wished I was superfast as well. It was pretty damn impressive.

It didn't take Matt long to return together with a heavy red dictionary, which he audibly put down on the table next to the Ouija board. I shivered on the inside. Unfortunately, this book looked way too familiar and only reminded me of school.

I was so glad I didn't have Latin classes in school anymore. As soon as I could, I had gotten rid of it. And although I had sworn to myself to never touch a Latin dictionary again because my relationship with that language had always been complicated, things have changed and my Latin phobia wasn't important right now. Exactly as unimportant as the place where Matt could've possibly gotten the dictionary from.

"Wow, where could you find it that quickly?" Tim asked impressed.

"Let's say I borrowed it," Matt answered dryly with strong emphasis on the word borrowed.

Tim didn't seem to question it, but I did.

There was no way he could've borrowed it from anyone. It was too late to buy it in a store either. None of the shops here were open after 6 p.m. Maybe in the bigger cities, but not here.

Again, it reminded me that Matt wasn't fully good. Matt was still Matt. I gulped. No, I trusted him. If it would come to the ultimate showdown with the magicians, he would fight on our side. There was no reason to not trust him. At least, I tried to convince myself of that. He was one of us, and after all, we weren't 100 percent good either. A serial killer, a corpse, another murderer, and Tim. What a bizarre quartet.

Tim looked through the pages of the dictionary and started to read: "remember."
This wasn't much of a help.

"Maybe we need to sleep and think about it tomorrow," I offered.
It wouldn't help us if we continued discussing for hours. I was tired, and so far, the debate was leading nowhere. Maybe tomorrow we could change our point of view and find a solution. But for today, I needed a break. A break from everything supernatural.

"No, we are about to figure it out, we can't stop now." Tim just shook his head and continued to flip through the pages of the dictionary as if he would find an answer somewhere.

"Maybe she wants to tell you that you should remember something," Ramon said.

"But I don't remember anything. It's not like I'm not trying." I sighed in despair.

"That's fine, but maybe it will come if you keep on trying."
Ramon hesitated a bit but then still hugged me as if he could sense I was about to cry again. I was completely done with life at the moment. Our friendship worked so well too.

But before I could give in and actually start crying, Matt's glance suddenly jumped towards the door.

"It's time," he whispered, and we all knew what he meant by that without him actually saying it out loud. My heart was in my mouth. This was going to be our demise.

Chapter 16

How long until they arrive?" I wanted to know and reflexively grabbed Luna's and Tim's hands. I don't know if I expected them to catch me in that moment, in case I would break down, or if I wanted to show them, I was there to protect them. Because I would. There was no way I would let any of them die. Maybe it simply was a mix of both.

We weren't prepared for what was about to happen at all, even though we knew sooner or later we had to face the magicians again, but to be honest, until now I had hoped for a miracle to happen. A miracle that would save us. Or at least heal me before they would arrive.

"Not long. I can already hear them," Matt answered seriously.

"We should get outside so they won't surprise us," Tim said and stood up to grab his baseball bat, which he had carried around with him for the past few days. He wanted to feel armed as well.

It still looked ridiculous, but he and his bat had saved us once, so who was I to judge? Also, he had officially forbidden me to make fun of his bat. Unofficially, however, we all looked pathetic.

Quickly, we grabbed our winter jackets and made our way outside to the pitiful enlightened clearing in front of Matt's home. Now everything looked more threatening than it had hours before when we arrived. When it wasn't all too dark.

The cold wind made our breath visible. But the freezing temperatures weren't the worst thing we needed to handle tonight. We all knew that.

On the horizon, we could see a few lights that slowly but regularly moved towards us. I needed to gulp.

"Are these the magicians?" I heard Luna ask quietly.

"Yes, and it seems like they have somebody or something on their side. Something that fills my place."

It was admirable how calm Matt sounded, even though we could hear the worry in his voice. He was as unprepared for what was about to come as we were. How could we be prepared? We didn't even know what would expect us. There was no way we could have prepared ourselves. A creature still bound to the magicians, an immortal person that didn't have any special powers, a human with a baseball bat, and me, who couldn't even control his own powers and was about to break down any second; we were doomed.

"So, we basically are some kind of Suicide Squad." I heard Luna murmur as if she had read my thoughts.

"Oh, then I want to be Harley Quinn," Tim yelled excitedly and swung his baseball bat through the air.

We laughed for a brief moment, relieved that we could forget the tension for a second. Unfortunately, we couldn't relax for all too long, we needed to focus on what was happening in front of us. The lights were still in sight, and they were not turning around.

The closer the magicians came, the worse I felt. I could feel my breath going faster, and I needed to concentrate on slowing it down again.

The lights turned out to be torches, we could figure it out when the magicians stepped out of the forest and onto the clearing. There was still enough of a distance between them and us, and somehow, they didn't seem to be interested in coming much closer, but this didn't change the fact that I didn't feel safe anymore. If they had only come here to talk, they would've come alone. But they weren't.

Next to them was a dog-like creature walking on all fours on an incredibly pathetic-looking leash. Despite the distance, I could clearly see the sharp and long fangs. Its size was larger than every dog I had ever seen. Although I had never seen a bear in real life, it wouldn't have surprised me if their creature was as big as one.

The magicians pushed their big torches into the soft soil next to them so we could see their faces in the light. My breath stopped for a second. Their clothes looked the same as they did six months ago, and even their body shapes were the same, but their faces had changed; they had become younger.

It wasn't super obvious but still noticeable. How could this even be possible?

"Nice pet!" I shouted in their direction.

"Brutus, indeed, is a nice creature if you are going to cooperate with us," Titus responded with a fake friendly voice.

They should know by now there was no way we would ever cooperate with them.

"What if we won't?" I asked.

"Then, this won't have a good ending for you." Lucius grinned, which looked even more threatening in the shadow of the flames.

"Well, too bad we won't cooperate with you," Tim bravely uttered.

A slight smile hushed over my face.

I was proud of him even though this wasn't the right place to be brave. In contrast to Luna and Matt, he could be harmed quite easily.

Titus raised his eyebrows in confusion, he probably wasn't expecting Tim's answer. But who could blame him? Nobody would have.

"And what are you saying, Matt? Or are you afraid of saying anything?" He now spoke to Matt after he had found his words again.

"What am I supposed to say? You are not welcome here. Nobody has invited you," Matt hissed at him.

"Is this how you treat your old friends after everything we have done for you?" Lucius pretended as if Matt's behavior hurt him.

"You're not the heroes you think you are. Neither for me nor for the world," he answered dryly.

"Neither are you," Lucius answered with the same tone of voice.

And unfortunately, he was right about that. We weren't the good guys either. No, I wasn't allowed to let them inside my head. They were just trying to manipulate me; again. But this time I shouldn't listen to them.

Of course, they knew my weak spot, but it wouldn't work this time. This time, I wouldn't even let it come that far. I would stay strong. And it would be much easier this time because all the people I needed in my life were around me. They couldn't surprise me anymore.

"So, do you prefer the diplomatic way or the violent one?" Titus casually asked as if he wanted to know what we would like to eat for dinner.

"What about not at all?" I proposed.

"Don't you want to be cured? You look pretty weak to me, and you have probably figured by now that we are the only ones that can help you." Carefully Titus came one step closer.

"Leave Ramon alone, damn!"

Matt also stepped in the front.

"And why exactly should we do that?" Antonius grumbled. "Why should we do anything for you after you left us?"

"Ramon is my…" Matt glanced quickly in my direction, as if he was waiting for my confirmation.

I only nodded cheerfully.

"Friend," he ended his sentence and sounded a bit weirded out by that.

It must've taken him a lot of strength to call me a friend of his, so I almost felt flattered by that.

Antonius laughed loudly as if he just heard the best joke in the world. It was an uncomfortable laugh that was echoing through the fresh night air.

"We don't have friends," he suddenly sounded serious again.

"And that's the reason why you will never get Ramon." Matt grinned confidently.

I couldn't repress my smile as well. He had chosen exactly the right words. Everything would be fine, wouldn't it?

"That's enough!" Lucius said and looked at Antonius as if this was some kind of sign.

Then suddenly, everything happened so fast. Antonius let go of the monstrosity of a creature, named Brutus, which immediately wanted to jump at us. Just in time, Matt threw himself against it with a loud bang, then they both rolled to the side. In this moment, I could only hope Matt had everything under control. My brain couldn't process the whole situation that quickly, my mind was still too dazed. What had just happened?

"Leave Matt alone! Leave all of us alone!" I screamed at the magicians.

I hoped they couldn't hear the desperation in my voice, but I was almost certain it was impossible to

233

not notice. From the corner of my eyes, I could see Matt and the creature that was almost as tall as him fight against each other. The air was filled with growling and the clenching of teeth. Whatever this monster was, it was strong.

In fact, it wasn't even surprising they didn't come alone. And it wasn't surprising their new companion would be incredibly strong, since they needed to assume Matt would be fighting against them. And Matt already was tough to fight. He was our only hope to beat the magicians forever.

As soon as my brain was able to process what was going on, I ran towards the beast. However, I didn't know what I was about to do. Physically, I had absolutely no chance, but I couldn't have cared less. The magicians wouldn't let me die anyway, would they?

"You can't help him," Antonius shouted.

In the meantime, he had come closer and wanted to hold me back. I grew angrier and angrier. So did my desperation. And somehow, I made the fatal mistake of looking into his eyes for a brief moment.

My view turned into a blurry mess, and an all too familiar feeling filled my body. Damn. I couldn't control it. I couldn't do anything about it. I could only watch how Antonius broke down before he could even come one step closer to me. Cause of death? A broken neck. Without me even touching him.

All of this had only been a product of my panic. The magicians had changed me. They had turned me into a timebomb. And they were the ones that now had faced the consequences of their actions.

I would be lying if I said my powers weren't impressive, still, this demonstration of my abilities was not planned and incredibly disadvantageous for us. But it was their fault.

They wanted to make me lose control over my powers. And it was just a matter of time until something would go wrong. Until someone wouldn't be mysteriously saved. Unfortunately for the magicians, Matt was too busy fighting Brutus, so he couldn't even think about if he could save the magician in time.

Have you ever looked into someone's eyes the moment they were dying? Up to this moment I hadn't. The empty glance of Antonius, the snapping of his neck while invisible powers twisted it. All of these things would be burned into my mind forever, and I wasn't able to do anything against it.

Shocked, I stared at the dead body that used to be a living human being just a few seconds ago.

"You went too far with this," Lucius yelled angry, and shot a questioning glance at Titus.

"This is all your fault. You made me what I am now," I shouted at them full of hate.

But the two magicians completely ignored me. Instead, they murmured something inaudible to me. In case they were using another spell, I wasn't prepared for that. I had never seen them use magic, the last time, they completely depended on Matt and his powers and let me believe they were old and confused. What if I had made the mistake of underestimating them?

I became panicky while still observing them. Whatever they were doing over there, I couldn't stop them. Of course, I could've tried to simply murder them as well, but firstly, there was no guarantee it would actually work, and secondly, the easiest way wasn't always the correct one to choose. I wasn't a monster. I still somehow was human, and the way I felt about Antonius's unwanted death, I didn't want to feel like this again. Especially not on purpose.

'Do you know the difference between you and a murderer?' Luna had asked me once when I had a miserable day and felt responsible for all of the deaths I had caused through my visions. 'A murderer doesn't regret what he is doing. He simply continues and maybe even enjoys it. You are not a murderer. And there are reasons that in court, there is murder and there is involuntarily manslaughter.'

Even though her words made kind of sense, they had never really changed the way I felt about myself. It was a fact that I had killed all these people. But now I understood what these words really meant. It was the first time I realized that although I was doing evil things, I wasn't an evil person. I had never murdered anyone so it would give me any kind of advantage in life. I had never murdered out of fun either. My visions simply happened.

The only thing good without limitation was the good will. And maybe I could still make the right decisions despite all of the horrible things that I had caused. In this case, the best decision was to let them live and to find another solution. Violence was never the answer.

The magicians were done with murmuring and looked at me.

What had they done? I felt exactly the same as before. What a genius plan of them. Did they really try to confuse me without doing anything? Were they even able to use spells, or was everything just a big bluff?

"Nothing happened," I figured confused.

"Not everything is about you." Lucius grinned evil.

Hectically, I glanced at Luna and Tim, who only shook their heads. In the same moment, I heard a loud scream from the left side. Now, I looked at Matt, who was lying on the ground. Right below the beast, which was about to hit him with his claws. Despite his supernatural speed, Matt didn't dodge the attack. Again, he screamed in pain.

Until now, I didn't even know that he could feel pain, but I guess there were better ways to find that out.

"Help me! I can't move anymore," he yelled in panic – and it was the first time I saw him like this – before the beast could hit him again, which was followed by another cry of pain.

Chapter 17

Matt's screaming made me snap out of the trance, which I had fallen into since the magicians had arrived in front of us. Everything felt so surreal. So distant as if this was just one horrible nightmare. I didn't even feel afraid anymore; I didn't feel anything.

It was like the same traumatizing events from last summer were repeating themselves, and I wasn't ready for this yet. All the things I had tried to forget about and repress were now catching up with me. Everything I wanted to prevent, especially the feeling of losing control, hadn't worked out. Never again did I want to feel as weak as I did that night back then, and still, I was standing here, paralyzed by my own fear.

Although I knew my life had never been in any danger and wouldn't be today either, I was worried about my friends, and now that I could hear Matt cry, my feelings for my friends made me snap back into reality. Suddenly, everything didn't feel like a dream anymore. I could sense the danger. I noticed that I was freezing and that I would've preferred to be anywhere but here. Then again, who would've wanted to be here right now?

Now I realized what happened. One of the magicians had already died. This wasn't like last summer; it was worse.

Who could tell what they would do to Matt, damn? Was Matt even mortal? The only ones that could answer this question were probably the magicians. I needed to do something urgently, but what? And before I could've done anything that might have changed the situation we were in, Lucius pushed another person in front of him. A person that I hadn't noticed before because he was hiding behind the magicians and now looked at me with his eyes wide open in shock. Finn.

"This isn't fair," I murmured.

And it wasn't. I had promised to tell him what was going on, and until today I hadn't fulfilled my part of the deal. But this didn't mean that I never wanted to tell him. It only meant that I needed more time.

After all, it wasn't only my secret. I would've revealed Ramon's but also Matt's true identity with it as well. It wasn't fair that everything was revealed to him like this. He deserved to learn the truth from me. He deserved to learn the truth because I wanted to tell him and not because the magicians wanted to use him for their plan. He deserved a better friend than whatever I was. I was nothing but a huge disappointment.

I felt like I was trapped between a rock and a hard place. Should I try to help Matt or firstly get to Finn to bring him somewhere else where he was safe?

"We can do this, okay?" Tim nodded at me cheerfully. After all, he was the only one still standing next to me.

"Are you sure?" I asked on the verge of tears.

"Sure, so far, we have always managed everything. And now, you drag Finn into the woods behind Matt's hut, he should be safe there," he whispered.

I nodded in silence and observed how Tim raised his baseball bat and ran towards the beast. Immediately, I tried to look away and clear my thoughts.

They didn't hold Finn back so he could run to me any time, in theory. But what if they did something to him? Was he under the effect of a spell? Could I even trust him?

I couldn't answer any of these questions, I had to simply have faith that this wasn't a trap, no matter how hard it was to believe in anything good. And even though everything inside of me was hesitant.

"Finn, I'm so sorry," I said, and carefully made a few steps towards him.

"Luna, what's going on?" he asked in confusion.

"Didn't Luna tell you?" Lucius acted surprised.

He knew exactly what he was doing. What a son of a witch.

"What should she tell me?" Finn looked panicky in my direction.

"Don't listen to them. Just follow me, and I'll tell you everything," I promised.

"Like she told you everything in the past months?" Lucius argued.

"No, this time I really tell him everything. He deserves to know the truth from me and not from you. Come with me," I begged.

Hesitant, Finn came closer.

Also hesitant, I tried to walk towards him.

I still didn't know what they had planned. Why did they bring Finn here? To pressure me? But was that it, or have they done something else to him? Things couldn't be that easy, could they?

The closer Finn came, the more confident I felt that it was the real Finn, and even his facial expression became more and more relaxed. He almost looked relieved when he reached me.

"Is it really you?" I said under my breath.

Yes, it wasn't the most intelligent question to ask, but, in that moment, I didn't care. I needed his confirmation no matter if it was the truth or maybe even a lie.

He nodded.

Before the magicians could say anything else, I took his hand and dragged him into the forest behind Matt's cabin; far away from the wizards. Exactly what Tim had ordered me to do.

We only stopped running after I was totally out of breath.

"Why are you here?" I panted and tried to breathe.

"Those three talked to me on the street, and the next thing I remember is being here," he explained not struggling for air at all.

He was way sportier than me.

"Did they do anything to you?"

"I don't think so, but I can't guarantee anything."

I leaned onto a cold tree trunk and tried to hold my balance. All of this was too much for me. Here in the forest, it was almost pitch-black, only the flashlight of Finn's phone was giving us a little bit of light. Of course, I had forgotten my phone in Matt's cabin because of all the stress.

"What is going on, Luna?" He asked again and looked at me seriously (at least I thought I could feel his glance on me, but I didn't really know if it was true because of the darkness).

"I don't know exactly how to start." I started and thought about it for a while.

Then I began to talk. About Ramon and his powers, the road trip to the mansion, and about Matt, who we had met there for the first time. I also told him about my near-death experience during the camping trip and the magical powers of Ramon's Grandma.

"So, Ramon can kill people, Matt is completely insane, you are immortal – what exactly is Tim?" Finn summarized everything I had told him.

"Tim is Tim; a normal human being with a baseball bat." I smirked.

He chuckled, and for a moment, I was glad he was here with me in the dark, cold, and somehow not that scary forest. I wasn't afraid anymore because I knew the real monsters weren't hiding in the bushes or between the trees; the real monsters were on the clearing, far away from us. We were safe.

And then, suddenly, the scales fell from my eyes, and I knew what the magicians were planning. Finn wasn't here to pressure me into anything, he was here to distract me. The real puppet in their plan was Tim. He was the most fragile of all of us, and additionally, he was the closest to Ramon. Whatever was going on in front of Matt's place, I had to go back. I needed to protect Tim. They couldn't harm me in any way, and knowing that should be enough to make me feel braver than I would usually do. Nobody could harm me.

"Finn, we need to go back." I figured anxiously.

"But you haven't finished your story yet," he said while pouting.

I took a deep breath.

He was right. I could only hope Matt and Ramon were in control of the situation for a little bit longer while I would tell Finn the rest of the story. If not now, then when? Also, maybe he could even help us, and we were not in a position where we could do anything without additional help.

So, I tried to sum up everything as shortly as possible. I explained to him why Matt had vanished and

243

basically ghosted all of us and how frustrating the séance was. After all, we still didn't know how to cure Ramon. All of these things, I told him while we slowly made our way back to the clearing.

"So, you basically have two options," Finn said and looked at me.

"What?" I asked confused.

"Well, either you cure Ramon or you prevent him from being ill in the first place."

I looked at him in disbelief.

How could he process everything that easily? Why was he being so helpful? And why had I reacted that poorly back then? Why could I still not have any clear thoughts?

"But to prevent them from throwing the potion, I would need a time machine," I stuttered.

Time machine.

Time.

Tempus.

The séance was a success, we just didn't see it. But now everything was making sense, and it was almost as if I knew exactly what to do next. Tim had been right all along. We were just too blinded by Matt's pessimism to notice it.

"Finn, you are a genius," I said and threw my arms around him.

"I don't know what I did, but I accept your compliment."

Euphoria was running through my veins. It felt like a door in my head has opened, a door that was damn well locked before. A door that had separated me from all of the answers. Was this the key to unlock the memories of Ramon's Grandma?

I couldn't really tell what opened the door, nor could I say where it would lead to, but that wasn't important right now. We were one step further than before, and that was everything that mattered.

I had no clue how we should be able to time travel, but after everything that we have been through, it didn't feel impossible anymore. More like the opposite. It felt like the only logical conclusion. I just needed to tell the others, and then we... No, I didn't need to tell them. I needed to make it on my own.

This time, nobody could help me, it was all on me to figure out how to proceed. Nobody except for me had these memories. I only needed to find them. Then I could travel back in time and prevent that Ramon would be hit by the potion. It wouldn't change the fact that we would have to meet the magicians another time, but at least we would be prepared. We would have one enormous advantage; we would have Ramon with his full powers.

Chapter 18

How could the magicians even find Finn in the first place, and where was Luna going? So many thoughts were filling my head but, I tried to push them away. This wasn't the right time nor place to be distracted. As difficult as it was but I needed to concentrate and trust Luna to keep Finn and herself safe.

My glance hushed from one magician to the other one. I was relieved that they were still standing at the same place. Nobody would try to hurt Luna. And in case one of them would only look in the direction she had vanished in, I wouldn't hesitate to do something, I thought stubbornly, even though I knew there was no way I would kill any of them. I couldn't, and I didn't want to murder anyone consciously. I wasn't a killer. I was a regular human. And who was even more human than me was Tim, who was putting himself in danger just to save his friends.

"What do I need to do so you call back your furry friend?" I shouted in despair.

I couldn't do anything. Even if tried to do something supernatural, there was no guarantee it would actually work. Maybe I would make things even worse. Additionally, I had absolutely no clue what I could possibly do. Tim was already occupied hitting the beast with his bat. As surreal as it might have sounded, but he was better armored than me.

Matt was still lying on the ground; he was still paralyzed.

"Join us! You know there is no other way for you anymore. We have the fate of your friends in our hands. Your own health is standing in your way, Ramon. Without our help, you will never be able to live a normal life," Lucius explained neutrally.

Damn. They were right. In theory. They were the only ones that had a solution, but I was sure this couldn't be the only way. There had to be another way. The magicians had already tried to get into my head in the mansion back then. I knew exactly how manipulative they could be. What if everything they were saying right now was just another attempt at manipulating me? I needed to be careful, but I always was when it came to them.

"Never," I answered bravely.

It was risky to contradict them, but this was a risk I had to take. I needed to keep them distracted until Matt would be himself again. Until he could move. He would find a plan. He knew the magicians better than any other; he would know what to do.

"Matt will be paralyzed forever."

Lucius shrugged as if he had read my thoughts.

"Why?" I asked dumbfounded.

"Do we have to explain everything to you twice?" Titus shouted slightly annoyed.

After I didn't answer his question, he continued talking: "We are the most powerful magicians when it comes to dark magic. The only one more powerful than us could be you if you would play by our rules, of course. You would only need to do us one little favor, and then we will leave you alone forever."

"Like you wanted to free Matt after he did everything you ordered him to do?" I interrupted him angrily. I didn't believe a single word coming out of his mouth.

"We have let him go, but what do you even know about Matt? You don't even know who or what exactly Matt is. He doesn't know himself what he is capable of. Why should we keep someone as useless as Matt if we now have Brutus." His glance wandered to the beast that had managed to walk past Tim and straight towards Matt. Tim was now lying in the grass, holding his leg in pain.

Damn.

"Do you really believe your little friend can stop our beast? All of its power comes from the three of us, and now that you have murdered Antonius, all of his power has been transferred to Brutus. It's even stronger now. And as soon as we give our sign, it's ready to kill. Everyone."

I starred at them astonished.

They were right. Could I really believe Tim had a chance against this beast when all he had as a weapon was a dumb baseball bat? I knew that he had spent more time at the gym after that night in the mansion, but there was no way he had enough muscles to harm the beast. Was there even a way for any human to have enough strength to be able to harm a supernatural creature? Probably not. After all, I could speak out of experience how limited my powers had been in comparison to Matt.

"Because we are not evil, we'll give you a choice. Who of them do you want to save?" Titus gave me an ultimatum.

"What do you mean?" The words slipped out of my mouth even though I could already imagine what he was talking about.

Damn. And again, I needed to accept that the magicians had power over me with whatever they were about to say next. Exactly like they did in the mansion.

"Your morals are making you weak," Titus said, and made a dramatically long pause while observing me.

I shivered.

"Ramon, Ramon, Ramon," he smirked. "Are you still convinced you can save them all?"

I didn't know what to answer, and before I could find the right words to say, he continued talking: "By now, you should have realized that you can't save everyone."

He glanced at Matt, who was still lying on the ground paralyzed, and then at Tim, who again tried to fight the beast. He looked exhausted and he wasn't really fighting it much either. He was more trying to dodge its paws. At least he managed to distract it from Matt. At least for the moment. However, it was obvious he wouldn't be able to fight much longer.

"Matt is controlled by us, he had always been, even during the time when he thought he was free. And right now, we still control him. Don't you see how strong we are? Come with us, and we let your mundane friend live." Lucius looked disgusted while uttering the word mundane, as if being a human was a bad thing for him.

I tried to concentrate. I wasn't allowed to listen to them. It was a fact that I needed Matt. I had no clue about spells or even magic, but something must have caused Matt's paralysis, and if everything the magicians had said was true, I somehow must be powerful enough to help him.

What if I could concentrate enough to move Matt. I could open and close doors simply with the power of my mind, how difficult could it be to throw a 1,90-meter-tall teenager into the forest and out of the danger zone?

If I had worked on my powers in the past few months, this certainly wouldn't be a problem for me. But under the circumstances that I was in, there was no way I could successfully do that. It was impossible. Too high was the risk of me accidentally hurting him. What if I would even kill him by trying to save him? Could I even kill him? So many questions, so few answers, and actually, I just wanted to scream to clear my head and to sort my thoughts. Instead, I sank to the ground shaking, because my knees couldn't hold the weight of my body anymore. Everything around me became a big blur.

Maybe I was just exhausted from life. From living like this. Maybe I wasn't even as powerful as the magicians thought. Maybe they mistook me for someone else. There was no way I was good for anything. I just wanted all of this to be over. And with these thoughts, my view became black.

I hadn't fainted for too long, but I was pretty confused when I started to become conscious again. Nothing around me has changed. The magicians still looked at me expectantly.

"Do you like the taste of our powers?" Lucius asked factual.

"Grrrr," I growled under pain.

It was the only sound I was able to make. It was only now that I realized how badly I was actually doing. No matter what the magicians had done to me in the past, this here was way worse. And they got me exactly where they wanted me to be.

"We will give you one more minute to make your decision. You either join us or your little friend won't survive until tomorrow," Titus reminded me of his ultimatum.

"Ramon, it's fine," Tim shouted before I could even process what the magicians wanted from me.

"No, it's not. I don't want anyone to sacrifice themselves for me anymore," I yelled back.

I could feel how my eyes were filling with tears. As fast as possible for me, I used the last bits of strength left in me to run towards Tim. Even though he wasn't that far away, it felt like eternity until I reached him. It seemed as if time stood still, even Brutus stopped fighting. He was sitting on the ground like a well-behaved dog, waiting for his signal to attack again, right next to Matt, who was still paralyzed.

"We knew from the start it would be dangerous. And still, I never hesitated to help you. I'm not dumb, Ramon. I know what I have gotten myself into." He stayed calm, still I noticed how tense he was.

"What if I don't want to let you go? You are the only one that stayed, even though there was a time I would've given everything for you to leave me. Tim, everything I've always wanted is for you to be safe." Now the tears were rolling down my cheeks, but I didn't care.

He was my best friend. The person who had always believed in me, even at times where I couldn't do it myself. Everyone should have their own Tim. Everyone needed their own Tim. Why did I have to let go of mine now? I wasn't ready for that. Not after I had lost everyone else already. Why me? Why did everyone have to leave before me?

"If you help them, nobody will ever be safe anymore." His glance wandered towards the magicians.

"But," I wanted to argue.

"No, let me finish. It's okay for me. Really. I'm just grateful for everything. For all the experiences and for the time we spent together and I hope you feel the same. I'm glad that I didn't let you push me away. My life would be so boring without the constant adrenaline rush only you could give me. Friends like you are hard to find."

How ironic that he said all these positive things about me when he was the better person. People like him were rare, maybe even unique.

"Are you really sure?" I asked him again and sniffed.

He only nodded.

For one moment, we just starred at each other, and none of us said a word. In my memories, we are still standing there, crying in silence.

I had never thought about how Tim would die, the only thing I had expected was me being the cause of death. But somehow, I had expected things to be different. I had expected I would have more time to say goodbye to my best friend. But that was the tricky thing about death. Sometimes it came all of a sudden and not even I could be prepared for it, and other times it was dying in installments.

What exactly was true for Tim, I couldn't say. On the one hand, everything came way too sudden for me to process, but on the other hand, his life was hanging on by a thread since the day he had decided to stay in my life. Every day he survived was a success, and people who would argue against it were lying. We both knew he would never live the life he deserved if he was hanging out with me.

"Ramon," Tim interrupted my thoughts, "I don't want anyone to buy flowers for my funeral. Because who wants flowers when they're dead? I want people to plant trees instead. Why should another being die just because I am dead – damn, it's so weird to talk about yourself like that – and I want to spread life and to be remembered like that."

"Noted," I said, and a slight smile formed on my face.

"And something else. I want you to play the songs *pray for plagues* and *my life would suck without you* during the funeral," he added.

"You are an idiot." I grinned.

"And something else."

"What else?" I asked.

"Don't forget me!"

After he had said this, he turned around and walked back to the beast.

"How could I ever forget someone like you?" I said, but I doubted it was loud enough so he could hear me.

My tears continued to roll down my cheeks, and it felt as if I was alone in this world.

I didn't want to see how the beast was attacking Tim, but at the same time I couldn't look away. I was still so occupied watching everything that I didn't immediately notice someone pulling on the bottom of my pants. Confused, I looked down and saw Matt. I didn't even realize that he had gotten closer to me. Everything happened so quickly, and if I was honest, I still was under the assumption that Matt couldn't move at all.

"I can slowly move again. Just distract the magicians, I have a plan," he whispered.

It was impossible the magicians could've noticed this – they were still too preoccupied looking at Brutus admiringly. And although my world was as dark as it hadn't been in a while, there was still a little beam of hope inside of me.

Maybe everything would be fine in the end, and maybe Tim hadn't died for nothing.

"Are you happy now?" I screamed at the magicians. If I should distract them, I could at least release all of my frustration and anger.

I walked away from Matt to give him an opportunity to vanish without immediately being noticed by the magicians. Angrily I stomped towards them.

"You will never get me, never, do you understand?"

Unfortunately, I was walking a bit too quickly towards them and forgot to keep a tiny bit of safety space between us.

"What if we simply take you with us? What do you want to do against it?" Lucius said while glancing over to Titus.

They packed me.

Scared, I screamed.

And in this moment, I knew there was nothing I could do. The magicians held me tightly and dragged me towards the forest they had come from. There was no escape anymore. I could only hope Matt had a good plan.

At least this was the best distraction he could have wished for. While the magicians dragged me behind them, I could watch a dark shadow stand up from the ground and vanish in the darkness of the forest. His plan needed to work, please.

Chapter 19

Finn and I were desperately thinking about where we could possibly find a time machine when I could hear a loud scream. It was impossible to say what had happened, but something told me that this wasn't a good sign.

Reflexively, I started running even faster towards the clearing. I didn't care that soon I wouldn't be in the safety of the woods anymore. If it was necessary, I would throw myself in front of Ramon to protect him at any moment. I knew he would do the same thing for me as well. But not knowing what was going on with my friends was the worst part of everything.

All of a sudden, I bumped into something hard that I couldn't see because of the darkness. Immediately, I was thrown aback a few meters and fell to the ground, hurting the palms of my hands while landing.

"Luna?" I heard a familiar voice.

I blinked multiple times and held my head with my hand. Then, I grabbed the hand in front of me that Matt had pointed in my direction to help me up.

"I'm sorry. I was just looking for you. You need to listen to me now. I have a plan, but we don't have much time," he apologized in a haste.

As soon as I was standing on my legs again, I only hugged him. Who would've ever thought I would be so relieved to see Matt? I certainly wouldn't.

"I'm so glad you are okay," I said euphoric although it was kind of ironic.

Matt was probably the person I needed to worry about the least since he was supernaturally strong and maybe even immortal. In general, he was Matt, and somehow you just knew he couldn't be in too much danger. But in this moment, I simply forgot about everything. My fears. My worries. Everything.

I knew he had a plan. And I had a plan myself, more or less. Everything would turn out alright. Carefully, Matt peeled out of my embrace, and it wasn't until then that I realized that not everything was fine. And things wouldn't turn out alright just now. And then I realized that my plan wasn't a real plan, and everything wasn't actually as simple as I had thought a few seconds ago.

"What happened?" I asked immediately.

"The magicians have Ramon," he said quietly.

I didn't know how to react. How could we let this happen? I thought we had one mission, which was to prevent exactly that.

"But, but, but," I stuttered.

"He wanted to distract the magicians so I could run away unnoticed. I have a new plan, and if everything works out, we can free Ramon. But not just that, we can even cure him."

"That's a huge promise. I have a plan as well – how familiar are you with the topic of time travel?" I wanted to know.

"Time travelling?" He sounded skeptical.

I only nodded, but he probably wasn't able to see it because of the darkness.

"Finn has helped me break the seal in my head. If we can find a way to travel time, I can throw myself in front of Ramon and prevent him from being hit by the potion. It shouldn't affect me, at least that's what I hope. But since I have the powers of his Grandma, I'm positive it should work. And if it doesn't, it's a risk I'm willing to take." The words were coming out of my mouth, and I couldn't stop them.

"Okay, that's great. I'm not an expert when it comes to time travel but as far as I know, the only thing you need is in there," he carefully tapped against my forehead. "The only other thing you are missing is a watch."

I was relieved that Matt didn't declare me crazy and took my ideas seriously, in opposite to the previous séance.

"Shit," I slipped. "Does the clock on my phone count?" I asked desperately.

Who would've thought that I had now reached the point in my life where I would need an analog watch. Until now, I had always made it through life without one, simply relying on my phone.

"I don't have one either," Finn said, who had reached us in the meantime.

Damn. Damn. Damn. Why was I part of this doomed generation of smartphone users? Why did it have to be so damn easy to tell the time based on the numbers that were displayed on my phone instead of trying to understand how the hands of a clock were working?

Analog watches were simply harder to read, and if I was honest, it always took me forever to tell the time. Maybe because I had never really trained it. Maybe because humans love walking down the easy way. And using a phone was simply easier.

Ramon probably would have a watch. Although he only was a few years older than me, I had noticed in the past that he was wearing one occasionally. He simply belonged to another generation. Exactly like…

"Tim," I said out loud.

Finn and Matt looked at me confused.

"Tim has a watch. We just need to find him, and he will give it to us, and then we can get started," I cheered.

"Luna," Matt said. He sounded hollow.

Why did he always need to drag me down? Couldn't he for once leave my head in the clouds and make things sound easy? Why could he never share my euphoria?

"You don't know where he is?" I tried to find the problem he had with my plan.

"Yes, but you won't like it."

"The magicians caught him as well?" I didn't let him finish his sentence.

"No. The beast has gotten him. Tim is dead," Matt responded, and still sounded like he had no emotions even while saying this.

And although I didn't want to believe it since I was convinced Matt wasn't as cold as he pretended to be, in this moment, I realized that I might have overestimated him. He was exactly as cold as he always pretended to be.

For a moment, none of us dared to say anything. It felt as if the others were waiting for me to break the silence, though. But there was nothing I could say. There was only emptiness. The place where I had felt a spark of hope just a few minutes ago, has now turned into a hole. A hole in the shape of Tim.

My parents had divorced when I was a child, and my father only contacted me once or twice per year, but so far, I have never experienced any death in my family. This was the first time someone I knew had died, and I hated it. So, that was how it was like to lose someone. An experience that I didn't really want to make that early in my life.

My grandparents as well as my parents were so fit and healthy that it felt like there was no way they could possibly die one day. It felt as if all of them would live forever, and the thought of their possible death has never even crossed my mind. Even less would I have expected Tim to be the first person I would lose forever. He was still so young. It was even more unlikely for him to die.

On the other hand, it shouldn't be that big of a surprise. After all, we knew what we got ourselves into, but moments like this made me doubt if we actually knew for sure what we were doing.

And in that moment, I realized that I had never really thought about my own death except for that one time in the mansion. And thanks to Ramon's Grandma I would never even have to worry about it either.

Tim's death, however, was just a foretaste of what was expecting me for the rest of my immortal life, in case I would keep my powers and not give them away to another person. Whereas I needed to decide if I wanted to burden someone else with them or not? Would I have to live in torture and outlive all of my friends, my family, actually everyone that I knew? Yes, probably. I had to. Because being a grownup meant making grownup decisions and forming my own moral compass.

Ramon didn't want to kill anyone and actively tried to control or even repress his abilities. He lived with his burden, and I had my own one too. And in the way he had learned to accept his powers, maybe one day I would be able to get used to mine.

But for now, I didn't feel anything. Nothing but emptiness. Emptiness. Pure emptiness. I couldn't even cry. Nothing. I gulped. Was this normal behavior? Was something wrong with me? I somehow felt so far away from myself. And for as long as I wouldn't see his dead body in front of me – which I was trying to avoid since I was certain I wouldn't be able to bear the view – I wouldn't believe it. He wasn't dead to me; he was alive. And in my world, he would stay alive forever.

"Then let's search for the watch," I only said and started walking towards the clearing.

A cold wind was blowing into my face when I stepped out of the forest, but it didn't bother me. Nothing would stop me from trying something that could stop the magicians. In case I was doing it not only for Ramon before, now I was most certainly doing it for Tim as well.

If I was feeling anything in this moment other than the emptiness, I would be feeling anger. And this anger was like fuel to my engine. Who could know if it might even be possible to save Tim as well if I was able to save Ramon.

Since we arrived at the clearing, absolute silence had taken over. Again. Nobody said anything. Nobody did anything. It was as if the world was frozen and we could only move in slow motion.

I knew it was now that I needed to find Tim and, even more important, his watch. So far, I didn't have the time to think about how I would react if I found him. My head was too fogged by all my messy thoughts. A mess that I wouldn't be able to clean up that easily, not even with a hot bath.

And if I was honest, I had tried to repress the thought that I needed to find his body first in case I wanted to find his watch. Maybe I was hoping it was lying around somewhere far away from him, so I wouldn't even need to look at him and could keep him in my memories the way he was and not the way the magicians had left him behind.

I didn't want to say goodbye just yet, I didn't want to let go that easily. Much rather would I hold on to our memories forever, and although I didn't know Tim for as long as Ramon did, he still was one of my closest friends by now.

The whole situation sucked. Ramon was gone. Tim was gone. And I was supposed to somehow turn everything around and save the day? I felt so pathetic. But at least I didn't feel as afraid and not in control as I had felt in the mansion back then, well, even at the beginning of the afternoon.

And although I felt hilarious and I still wasn't completely convinced by my plan, I was certain, I could travel through time. Everything had its purpose. There was a reason we had moved to this town. It wasn't a coincidence we had moved just one apartment below Ramon, and it wasn't a coincidence that we met. I only needed to have faith in Ramon's Grandma and that she was absolutely sure she knew what she was doing when she transferred her powers to me. I needed to believe in her. I needed to believe in myself.

Carefully, I used the flashlight of Finn's phone to search the ground for anything that could point me towards Tim when, all of a sudden, I could feel a hand on my shoulder. I cringed.

"Luna, you don't have to do that," Matt said carefully. "Just wait here and I get the watch for you."

I turned around.

"If I save Ramon, can I save Tim as well?" I asked hoarsely.I needed to make sure that my thoughts weren't completely nonsense, and I actually had a chance to save him too.

"Sure, but there is no guarantee it will actually work," Matt admitted. "Time travels are tricky; nobody can promise you that everything will be okay. You can save Ramon, but we don't know what else will change because of that."

"Then let me say goodbye now." My voice sounded strange when I said these words.

Was I really sure I wanted to see him like that? But before I could find an answer to that question, I turned away from Matt and continued my search.

There was absolutely no reason why I wanted to find him myself, especially since Matt was the one that knew where Tim was lying. And who knew? Maybe he could even see in the dark. But I needed this moment for myself. I needed this time to rudimentary try to process the events before I could focus on saving us all. Everything was simply too much for me in this moment, but here, on the clearing in the darkness, I had the possibility of finding my peace for a few seconds. To take a break. To save my powers and clear my thoughts.

My heartbeat was way too fast, and it felt as if it was about to jump out of my chest any second. I only wanted to calm down and take deep breaths, but I couldn't. I couldn't breathe.

Luckily, this state only lasted for a brief moment, but it felt like it was so much longer. Was this a severe panic attack? Whatever it was, I needed to get a grip on myself, and suddenly, I only wanted to crawl out of my skin and leave everything behind. Suddenly, all I wanted was to go home and pretend that everything had never happened. I just wanted to run away. I didn't even know where to run to. Only far away from here. Far away from my problems and Ramon and Tim. How ironic. After all, it was them that were gone right now. They had left me, and I was still here.

"Matt," I shouted through the darkness.

I had no clue where he and Finn were.

"Get the watch. I want all of this to be over."

Within a second, Matt appeared next to me with the watch in his hand. Gratefully, I grabbed it. Suddenly, I didn't want to say goodbye anymore. I wanted this nightmare to end. And in the best case, this here wasn't a goodbye, it simply was a changing point of the whole story. It was a new beginning.

"You know what you need to do?" Matt asked carefully.

"Yes, everything is saved up here," I said, pointing at my head.

"Perfect," he said, and I could hear that he was grinning.

"Before I start, what exactly is the plan?"
I asked insecure.

"You travel back in time and throw yourself in front of Ramon so he won't be affected by the potion of the magicians, and when all of this is done, we meet here again for the final fight," he explained casually.

"Wait a second. Does this mean the magicians still won't give up on Ramon?" I asked shocked.
Why did I think it would be so easy and everything would be over after tonight? How naïve of me.

"I can't predict the future, but I doubt they will give up that easily. The magicians are way too stubborn. It's highly possible they will come back another time," he answered my question.

"So, do I understand everything correctly? I save Ramon and then the past six months will change? He will be cured, Tim will be alive, and you? You will be with the magicians?"

"Luna, I don't know. I don't know what other things the magicians have planned, and if I'm honest, I don't know how past me is going to react to these plans either. So, the odds are high that I'm still going to stay with the magicians. But I can't predict the future, especially not when everything is as uncertain as it is now," he clarified seriously but friendly.

It was one of the few moments where I didn't feel as if he was talking down on me. It felt like we were finally talking eye-to-eye.

"Wow, that's a lot of responsibility." I murmured out loud, but I wasn't sure if the others could hear it.

"I know, but if someone can do it, it's you," he tried to cheer me up.

"And you don't want to come with me?" I asked in despair.

It would definitely relieve me if Matt would travel to the past with me. Although I more or less had access to the knowledge of Ramon's Grandma, it would be helpful to have someone around me that knew more about magical creatures than me.

Additionally, he was so much stronger than me, and I was a tiny bit afraid of past-Matt. Because no matter whether Matt wanted it or not, he had changed a lot in the past months. He became a better person even though we couldn't help him in the end.

It would be tough for me to meet a person that I kind of liked, even counted to my friends by now, with the only difference that this person wouldn't be my Matt. It would be someone else. Someone that would never be my friend and even less think about helping me. I wouldn't just have a physical disadvantage; it would be tough for my mental health as well.

"No, unfortunately not. I need to stay here and try to find Ramon in case something goes wrong and our plan won't work out," he responded sternly.

"I come with you!" Finn interrupted the conversation.

With all the stuff going on, I almost forgot he was here as well.

"Are you crazy? You don't even know what you get yourself into," I blurted angrily.

I couldn't risk that he would be dragged into all of our drama more than he had already been, thanks to the magicians.

"No, I'm serious. I'll join you, and I can help you. I don't know what I'm getting myself into, but it can't be worse than all of the shit that happened today," he said calmly and held my hand.

"I won't leave you alone."

I sighed.

It wasn't as if I didn't need any help, but one additional human person would mean even more stress. I needed to not only protect Ramon but also keep an eye on Finn.

"You can do it together. Think about it, Tim was able to handle the magicians on his own. They weren't prepared for him, and they certainly won't be prepared for Finn. This is going to work out," Matt tried to remind me.

"Okay," I simply said.

Although I still wasn't fully convinced by the plan, I would let it happen. I had no other option, and deep down, I knew Matt was right. As long as the magicians wouldn't expect Finn to be there, he was safe.

"Any last questions?" Matt made sure I knew exactly what I needed to do.

"When do I need to intervene? What is Finn supposed to do? Am I allowed to meet my past self, or will space and time collapse if I do so? And will you forget us all if you stay with the magicians?" The questions burst out of me.

"I can't answer any of these questions for sure. I'm not omniscient, and although I don't know exactly what I am, I'm certain you two will find the right moment to intervene."

"But I am," I suddenly said without thinking what that was even supposed to mean.

"What?" Matt looked confused.

"I know what you are."

Apparently, Ramon's Grandma knew about Matt's existence, and she knew exactly who he was. The image of it was so clear, I could almost see it in front of my own eyes, as if it was me who had made all of these memories.

Because of her hotel for supernatural creatures, Ramon's Grandma knew everything. Everyone told her about their experiences with new or unusual magical beings, so she could write them down for documentary purposes in what we now know as the storybook. Although she had decided to keep Matt's identity a secret for some reasons, I could tell she knew about him and now I knew too. I knew everything we needed to free him.

"Don't you want to know?" I asked Matt, who had gotten surprisingly quiet.

"Tell me about it in the other timeline. It's too late for me here anyway. But if you say the words in the other future, who knows, maybe it will convince me to help you there as well."

I couldn't tell for sure because of the darkness, but I was almost sure he winked at me.

The way his voice sounded; he must've done it.

"Okay, I guess it's time to say goodbye now," I said and gulped.

Although I had never ever expected it would be that difficult to separate ways with Matt, it was damn hard. Maybe it was the fact that he was everything familiar that was left – except for Finn of course – now that Ramon and Tim were gone, or if it was because I knew that I could save those two in the past but all the moments we had with Matt would be erased forever. Who knew if we would ever meet again. Who knew when we would meet again. And who knew under which circumstances it would happen.

In fact, it was pretty impossible we would become friends. In the best case, we would not be enemies anymore. Everything was written in the stars, and I was a little bit scared of finding the answers.

"I never understood you humans, and even after countless psycho tests in teeny magazines, I'm still not much smarter. And yes, I'm confused by all of your emotions, and feelings, and relationships with each other, and especially whatever this is between you and Ramon is completely strange to me..."

"Get to the point, it's not the right time to insult me." I laughed.

Although I knew he didn't mean to sound insulting, it was still a pretty odd description of our situation. Also, it was the wrong place to talk about Ramon's and my relationship status.

"Anyways, I wanted to tell you that after all this time I have spent with you and your friends, I can maybe understand a little bit why you hang out with each other. And maybe I can understand a little bit what friendship means," he rambled.

I smiled, and there was no way I could prevent a tear running down my cheek. This was probably the best and most honest compliment one could ever receive from someone like Matt. After all, he was special.

"Thank you," I said and hugged him.

"Be careful out there," I added.

"See you on the other side." Matt waved us goodbye.

Then I concentrate and held Finn's hand so tightly, I was scared I would hurt him. He, however, didn't seem to complain.

In this moment, I didn't feel scared about what was about to expect me in the past. In this moment, I didn't even doubt myself, I simply knew I could time travel and everything would work out in the end.

Everything I thought about were my memories from that certain night in the mansion. The magicians, the basement, Matt. Tim and his baseball bat. Ramon, how he tried to get away from Matt. Ramon, how he freed me. The magicians and how they threw a potion at Ramon. All these things were running through my head while I held the watch in my hands and quietly murmured the word 'memento' with my eyes closed and without even realizing any of this was happening.

It was the memory that was the key to everything. How couldn't we notice this any sooner? Even though I didn't have an explanation for why Ramon's Grandma needed to speak to us in Latin, it would've been much easier if she had communicated in one language that we could understand, but I didn't want to complain either.

At the end of the day, it had worked and when I opened my eyes again, we were standing in front of the huge mansion and my gut feeling knew we were at the right place at the right time. It was the night that had changed everything, and it was about time we came back to change everything even more. But this time for the best.

Chapter 20

I didn't feel comfortable standing in front of the mansion for the first time after all these months, but I was glad Finn had been so stubborn; I was glad not being alone with my trauma.

"Then let's rewrite the future or erase it or whatever," Finn said and looked at me cheerfully.

I glanced at Tim's watch.

It was already early in the morning, still it was dark. Soon, we needed to make our way into the mysterious basement. We could already hear the loud squeaking noise. Everything went according to our plan; so far so good.

Carefully, I put Tim's watch around my wrist. I didn't need it anymore, but this wouldn't stop me from still carrying it close to me. A lucky charm wouldn't hurt us now either. And if we lived in a world where demons, vampires, and even ghosts were real, it couldn't harm me to believe in positive things as well.

I took a deep breath and glanced over to Finn, who was doing the same thing.

He didn't know what he had gotten himself into, we didn't have enough time to talk about everything that had changed in my life since that night in the mansion. And I obviously couldn't describe every detail about the night in the basement to him since we had been in such a rush.

Now, I needed to trust that the details I was able to tell him were enough and he wouldn't do anything stupid. Whereas I was certain the odds for me doing something stupid were much higher than for him.

The squeaking noise stopped, and I knew this was our sign to start our mission. Now we could start walking towards the basement because Ramon and past-me would already be down there.

"It's time," I said and started my way to the door of the mansion.

My heart was pounding.

Carefully, I tried to push the door, but it didn't open. Damn.

We had come this far, and not once have I thought about how we were supposed to enter the mansion. How could the magicians even enter? Was there another entrance that I didn't know about?

In the moment I realized that we couldn't enter, I wanted to scream because crying wasn't enough to express my pain. How many times have I cried in the past, and how little did it change in my life? We had come this far for Ramon. For Tim. For the future of this world. And everything that was standing between us and saving our friends was a locked door.

Hysterically, I started laughing because I had been expecting everything to go wrong but this. I didn't even think about not being able to make it to the basement in the first place. We were losers. Failures. And by that, I meant myself. I was a loser.

"Is everything alright?" Finn asked who still didn't understand how doomed we were.

"The door is locked," I said while still laughing hysterically.

I was an emotional wreck.

"Isn't there a spare key hidden somewhere? Or what about another way of opening the door?" He asked carefully.

Eventually, she was able to calm down, and despite his words still sounding strange in her ears, she tried to sort her thoughts. It wasn't easy to find a solution for this problem, but in the worst case, they needed to break the door. It wasn't about sneaking in unnoticed; it was about saving her friends at all cost.

Before she could collect all of her strength and decide to break the door – her boxing training needed to be good for something – some strange voice seemed to talk to her. Was it her inner consciousness? She didn't know. But it was obvious the voice gave her strength. And new ideas.

So far, she didn't think much about the possibility of a spare key, but if there was one, she would be the only one that could find it. She only needed to let it happen. To focus. And then the voice showed her the way.

In one of the pots with what was barely recognizable as strawberries, she could find a key. She didn't need to think twice about putting it in the lock, she knew it was the right key, and she knew they would finally be able to open the door in front of them.

The first huddle had been overcome, still I was uncertain how I should proceed next when little things like this could already make me break down that easily. I really hated losing control, and this could become my weakness.

Carefully, we entered the mansion. Actually, we didn't need to be particularly quiet or careful since Ramon and past-me should be in the basement and wouldn't even notice we were here. Only Tim was still upstairs.

Tim.

This was a great idea.

"Maybe this is stupid and will destroy everything, but what if we wake up Tim? We need every help we can get, and we also know that he can beat the magicians. We only need to be careful because of Matt," I whispered.

"I don't know what is going to happen tonight, but I trust you. And we can definitely need any help," Finn answered.

So, we made our way up the stairs and towards the guest bedroom Tim was sleeping in. We could only hope he wouldn't completely freak out when he would see Finn and me like this. We definitely owed him an explanation.

On the other hand, I was certain if someone was okay with only knowing half of the story, it would be Tim.

I chewed on my lower lip before I knocked on his door. This was my chance to do the one thing I hadn't done in that night.

I knocked on his door, and before he could say anything, I had already entered. Tim was still asleep, so I needed to wake him up. I've never felt so uncomfortable being with him. Carefully, I tried to shake him a little bit.

"Before you completely freak out, listen to me carefully. We are from the future, and we need your help to prevent something that is about to happen soon. And we don't have too much time. We need to go now. The strangers are there."

I rambled while he slowly opened his eyes.

He still looked tired and half-asleep when he looked at me, and I wasn't sure he understood what I was saying.

"Of course, and I am Batman," he murmured sleepy.

Desperate and looking for help I glanced at Finn. Maybe he could say something helpful.

"Hey, we don't know each other yet, but soon we'll meet. We can explain everything to you later, but for now we need to hurry," Finn said and held his hand in Tim's direction. "I'm Finn, by the way."

Now Tim was fully awake, at least he didn't look tired anymore and almost seemed a bit shocked.

"So, time traveling?" He summarized our situation.

Insecure, we nodded.

"Cool," he said and smiled excitedly.

Now I needed to grin too. I felt incredibly relieved. All of my doubts had been for nothing. He would help us. He would believe us, and additionally, he would find the mess that was our life fascinating. And the way Tim was now standing in front of us, alive, I couldn't stop myself from hugging him tightly.

"I'm so glad you are here," I only said.

Then I flinched.

Was I even allowed to tell him about the future or more specifically about his future, or would this destroy something?

"Are you okay?" he asked carefully.

I have never been good at hiding my emotions, so I was sure he could tell something was wrong with me. Why else did I need to travel back in time?

"Yes, it just was a long day, and it probably will become even longer," I said and gulped.

"What is the future like?" he asked while putting on a thin jacket and grabbing his baseball bat.

"Wild. You won't even believe what we have been through," I smiled.

I was full of joy that he didn't show any fear.

"And how is Ramon doing? And what about me?" he asked without thinking about it.

Finn and I glanced at each other, which Tim seemed to notice.

Carefully, he eyed me in the light of the hallway until he saw his watch on my wrist. Of course, I hadn't thought about that.

"I understand," he said a bit more quiet and less excited.

"So, the strangers are magicians that want to use Ramon's powers to control the world or something like that – pretty cliché if you ask me. Whatever. Past-me is trying to prevent Ramon from doing something stupid, and everything is going to be fine except one tiny thing. In the end, the magicians throw a potion at Ramon. And that's why we are here. So, I can throw myself in front of him and therefore protect him. All of this might sound super complicated, but I reassure you, this is our only chance. It needs to work."

I tried to explain everything to Tim while we walked towards the door that was leading to the secret basement.

I didn't need to explain to him that we weren't allowed to talk anymore as soon as we would start walking through that door and along the bizarre corridor. If he had any questions, we needed to answer them now.

"Okay, and what exactly am I supposed to do?" Tim asked curiously.

"Your task is to beat up the magicians as soon as I give you the sign," I smiled at him.

"Awesome," he said happily.

Meanwhile, Finn stayed quiet and followed us. I wasn't quite sure what his task would be, but maybe he had already fulfilled his job. He managed to convince Tim within a second to believe us, which would've been way harder without him. Of course, I had a different hair color, but he had his eyes closed and it was still mostly dark in the room, so I wasn't sure it would have been enough to wake him up in time. But because of Finn, we had saved a lot of time.

The long corridor was exactly as cold and scary as I remembered it from that night. Luckily, this time I was wearing warmer clothes. The waiting would be a little more comfortable.

Carefully, we made our way down the stairs and occasionally stopped to check if we could already hear something. It was important we wouldn't arrive too early, but exactly in that moment where Matt would kidnap past-me. I wanted to avoid that the magicians or even Ramon knew we were coming until it was time.

Unfortunately, I didn't remember how far down the stairs were leading, so we needed to be extremely careful to not accidentally walk into myself. Nobody said anything. The pressure and the tension were obvious, and I could only hope everything would work out according to the plan. We didn't need any more drama.

It became colder and colder the further down we went. Carefully, I looked around the upcoming corner and cringed. I saw myself and how I carefully observed the situation through the holes in the stone wall.

Quickly, I went back and signaled to the others that we should walk a little further up again. Although I knew we were safe from myself here, I didn't want to risk anything.

The acoustic at our new hiding spot was horrible, and we could only vaguely follow the events in the basement. Luckily, I could remember almost everything from that night. Some memories unfortunately would last a lifetime, and this was one of them.

"Are you ready to listen to our ultimatum? It's your last chance, choose wisely!" I could hear the voice from one of the magicians. From here, it was impossible to tell which one was speaking right now.

"Join us, give us the book, and in return we'll let Luna live."

It didn't matter who was talking. Everything that mattered was what was going to happen next. I knew that from now, it wouldn't take long for past-me to enter the scene. Only when we could be sure past-me was standing in front of Ramon, we could dare to get a bit further down the stairs.

Luckily, past-me was incredibly fast but not particularly quiet, so we could tell for sure when our time to get closer has come. Still, careful but relieved that we could avoid running into me, we stepped down the next stairs. Now I could observe what was going on in the room through the small hole in the wall that past-me had used just a few seconds ago.

It felt good to finally be in control of the situation again. Finally, I could see what was going on, and from now on I could make the right choices.

It wouldn't be easy, but my plan was to try to be as absent as possible. Ramon didn't need to know I was here. I would send Tim down the stairs in the right moment, and he would do exactly what he had done six months ago. And if we were lucky, Matt would still vanish like he had done in that night.

I didn't want to further think about it because I couldn't be sure we would meet again the way we did in our version of the future. It had been a chain of events that led to the point where he needed Ramon's help. It was highly unlikely the same events would happen if we changed something as relevant as Ramon's health. But in case it would happen, I was willing to welcome him back into my life with open arms. But I didn't want to be disappointed by having my hopes up too high.

Through the hole in the wall, I could see how I threw myself onto Lucius, who was squatting in front of Ramon and therefore fell to the ground.

"Don't worry about me. Worry about yourself because if you accept their offer, you just wish I would be dead." I could hear past-me say.

I needed to smirk.

Although this was absolutely spontaneous, I was highly satisfied with what I had said. Unfortunately, I couldn't be happy for too long because I had to watch how Matt threw Ramon against the wall of the basement room. And while he was lying there without moving, Matt was already on the way to grab past-me, and pushed her into the direction of the dark corridor where he would later chain her to the wall, like a dog.

Immediately I had goosebumps all over my body. But I couldn't change anything about where past-me would be. I wanted to change as little as possible to not ruin the future.

"Where did they go?" I could hear Ramon ask.

From now on, everything that was going on in the basement was unfamiliar to me. Since I wasn't in the room while this conversation happened, it was the first time I would see it. Now I would know for sure what had happened while I was gone, but did I really want to know?

I already knew that at some point, Matt and Ramon would fight against each other. A fight that would be exhausting for Ramon and even leave a little scar behind as a memory.

Although Matt wasn't back in the room yet, I knew I wouldn't be able to watch their fight. And there was no way I could stop it or prevent it. It would be too dangerous to send Tim into the basement room just now. So, I followed the completely irrelevant conversation between Ramon and the magicians.

It was easy to see that both parties were running in circles. Ramon wouldn't join them, especially not now after past-me had basically threatened him to not do it. The magicians, on the other hand, wouldn't give up that easy either. It was only a matter of time until they would call for Matt so he could further pressure Ramon. They knew they couldn't kill me, but they could let Ramon believe they would do so. And to prove their position, Matt only needed to demonstrate his powers.

While past-me was sitting in the little room far away from everything, I had lost every track of time or something like that. I didn't know for how long I was chained to the wall or even how long Matt had stayed with me. But the conversation in the basement room felt longer than expected. It definitely explained how we were able to spend a whole day down here without any of us noticing.

"We didn't put so much effort into finding you just to get back home empty handed," Antonius yelled and jumped towards Ramon.

My heart pounded faster. I didn't know the magicians tried to fight him.

"Antonius!" Titus called him back. "You know exactly that we're out of that age where we can fight."

And like on command, Matt was rushing out of the darkness.

Reflexive, I took a step back. If there was one thing I hadn't thought about, it was Matt's supernatural abilities. If we would make one wrong movement, he would be able to hear us. Now we needed to be even quieter than before.

Carefully, I tried to signalize Tim and Finn that we shouldn't move anymore until I would give Tim the sign to intervene. However, this would also mean that I needed to forbid myself to watch through the hole in the stone wall. And if I was honest, I didn't want to see it anyway.

The noises I could hear were enough to assume what was going on. I even knew a few things that would be happening while I was gone. He had told me enough about their fight. I really didn't need to witness how he was beaten up by Matt.

And although we were officially broken up, my feelings for him were still there. And nobody wanted to see the person that they loved in a situation like that. Additionally, the idea of past Matt broke my heart a tiny bit. If those two would know that in one specific version of the future they would call each other friends... It was crazy.

"Don't get any closer!" I heard Ramon shout.

He already sounded out of breath even though Matt and him weren't fighting for that long. Or has more time passed than I thought? I didn't dare to glance at the time. I was almost afraid of breathing. Matt could probably sense us already. He was just too busy with fighting Ramon.

I heard that the situation in the basement room was getting more and more tense. The magicians were screaming and complaining about Matt. Ramon had told me that he was sure Matt was about to kill him during their fight. It was the only time he was going against the order of the magicians, or has this already been a desperate attempt at fighting for his freedom?

He probably knew by then the magicians wouldn't let him go as easily as they had promised. Maybe this was the changing point of everything. The point we needed to reach to guarantee Matt would run away as soon as he would get the chance.

Suddenly, I could feel hopeful. We could do this. We just needed a little bit of luck, and then everything would be alright.

"Do you have enough, or do I need to punch you again?" I could hear Matt ask.

He could be so incredibly cold; it hurt seeing him – or rather listening to him like that. This wasn't Matt. Well, somehow, he was, but somehow, he wasn't.

"I still won't tell you anything," I heard Ramon pant.

Whatever it was that was happening in that room, it was exhausting him, and I was afraid he wouldn't be able to hold on much longer.

"You are tougher than I thought," Matt complimented him.

"Maybe, but I still won't help you," Ramon answered, and one could hear he was about to break down.

It was now or never.

I tried to find Tim's glance.

He was already in position.

He too looked at me.

I only needed to give him the sign, and he would start running. No matter what would happen, I would never forget him.

With a heavy heart, I nodded at him.

This was his signal.

He stormed down the stairs and into the unknown.

So far, we were actually doing fine. Our plan seemed to work, but who knew what would happen next? These were the things I couldn't plan. And these were the things that scared me the most.

"Am I interrupting this party?" Tim asked when he arrived at the end of the stairs.

I was so damn proud of him and his confidence. He would manage this. I was sure of that.

"There is another one?" Lucius asked confused.

Matt had been right. The magicians didn't expect him to be here, which was quite stupid of them.

I always thought Matt had spied on us. Was it possible that he purposely kept this information from the magicians? Or did he simply assume Tim wouldn't be a threat to them because he was only human?

Now the magicians were distracted, and I took my chance to step closer to the wall so I could observe what was going on inside of the basement room again.

I could see Ramon, who was talking to Tim. I saw Ramon stumbling in the direction of the dark corridor. Watching him like this, it was a miracle he was able to save me.

Tim ran without hesitating towards the magicians. Those weren't prepared for the attack. They were still too deep into their discussion. What had started as a discussion about their plan turned into a discussion about Matt and his inability to follow simple orders.

Everything happened so quickly, it was hard for me to grasp that he had already beaten up the magicians. They must have been pretty bad at multitasking if they didn't notice Tim was ready to fight them.

Relieved, I could breathe again. I didn't even realize that I had held my breath in the first place.

The only problem we had left was Matt. I had no idea what he would do next. And even though I was expecting every possible thing to happen, and tried to prepare myself for the worst, there was no way I would have been prepared for what would happen next.

Slowly, Matt walked a bit closer to Tim.

"Thanks," he said appreciating.

Then he looked in the direction of the spiral staircase where we were hiding.

"I don't know where you are coming from or why you are here, but for today, I'll leave you alone. Today, I only want to be free," Matt said with small eyes.

My heart was in my mouth.

And before I could respond, he had already vanished.

All of my attempts at being quiet were for nothing; of course he was able to hear us.

Was it already too late for me to tell him who he was? I didn't know for sure, but my gut feeling told me it was more like the opposite; it would have been too early to tell him.

Exhausted, Tim sat down in the other corner of the room, and we all waited for Ramon and past-me to come back. Because as soon as the three of us – them, whatever – were back in the basement, my mission would start. My mission of jumping between the magicians and Ramon.

My pulse was racing, now everything needed to work. So far, the night was a huge success, everything worked out, maybe even too well. The pressure was on me; I wasn't allowed to ruin it.

All of a sudden, I had one thought crossing my mind. Something I hadn't thought about before, and now that I did, I hated it.

I wouldn't be able to prevent Ramon from seeing me. For a brief moment, we all would be standing in the same room, and I could only hope he wouldn't recognize me. After all, I had a new hair color, and therefore wouldn't immediately be identifiable as Luna.

I had an unwell feeling in my stomach. I was afraid. What if they were able to stop me? What if I wouldn't be able to travel back to the future because the future where I came from didn't exist anymore? So many questions.

Where was the Matt from my future when I needed him, and why hadn't I asked all of these questions before the time travel?

Now I was on my own, which meant I needed to find the answers to my questions myself. I could already hear voices. Soon Ramon and past Luna would be back. Shortly after hearing the voices, I could already see them.

"Where is Matt?" Ramon immediately asked when he entered the room and saw the magicians.

"You mean the tall, scary guy?" Tim askes. "I made him run away," he bragged.

What a weird Deja-vu. All of this, I had experienced before, like I had literally been in that exact same situation, and now I was living through it once more but from a different perspective.

"Okay, maybe I didn't have to do anything. He just vanished because he was tired of obeying these three guys. Kind of shitty of him, but better for us," Tim added.

Now I needed to get ready. It could happen any second.

"Where is this good-for-nothing fool?" I could hear Antonius ask.

Meanwhile, I had left my spot from where I could observe everything, I was already at the bottom of the staircase, ready for the most important sprint of my life.

"Gone," I heard Tim answer.

"Did he…?" Titus asked panicky.

I knew he was looking for the missing pages from the storybook in his pockets.

"No, fortunately, he didn't." I could hear Lucius say in relief.

The three magicians sighted.

My heart was skipping a beat all of a sudden.

He didn't take the pages with him. Did this mean he was sure he wouldn't need our help? Why else would he ignore these pages?

Although this wasn't a huge change, it made me realize that things were already alternated, and this was frightening. It scared me so much, I almost forgot to focus on the conversation.

"Change of plans," Titus yelled.

Soon, it would happen.

"You might think you defeated us, but we'll be back," Antonius threatened.

Oh well, they would definitely come back.

"It's not over, and remember, the next time we'll see each other, you'll be begging us to let you join us and then we'll get what we asked you for," Lucius said calmly.

Everything happened in slow motion. I jumped out of my hiding spot. For a second, nobody even noticed me because all eyes were still resting on Antonius. But things were about to change quickly.

"Never," I shouted while I threw myself between Ramon and Antonius.

At the same time, I tried to push the magician as far away as possible. All of this before he could even throw his potion at Ramon. The potion fell on the floor, and the flask broke. Ramon wasn't even touched by it.

"What the…" I could hear Ramon murmur from behind.

Before anyone could figure out who I was, I ran back to the staircase where I had come from. I could only hear how the magicians became even more uneasy.

"Until we meet again," they said and didn't sound anywhere near as confident as they had done in my memories.

It seemed as if I had done it. Their plan didn't work out, for now. And the only thing left for me to do was to run away with Finn and hopefully make it back to the time we came from.

Together we sprinted upstairs until we both couldn't breathe anymore. Although I had told Tim beforehand to distract the others for a short moment so we had enough time to leave, I wasn't completely confident in my powers. The more distance I brought between me and the basement, the more comfortable I felt. Now I could try to bring us back to our time without any pressure.

Afraid, I looked at Finn, who still seemed to be surprisingly calm.

"Are you ready?" I asked him.

"Of course. No matter what will change in the future, one thing will always be the same: our friendship," he answered and gave me a cheerful smile.

That was exactly what I needed to hear.

"Then let's travel back to the future." I smiled as well and took his hand.

It was time to go back home.

And when I thought back then that the road trip to the mansion was an *incredibly tremendous journey*, I would've never expected the tremendous journey that was in front of us now.

Back then, when we drove to the mansion, we knew that afterwards a lot of things would be different, however, we didn't know exactly what would change, in opposite to now.

Now, we knew that things would change as well. We didn't know what would change either, however, we knew how things could've been instead, which was the hardest part of all of it.

I only hoped our trip to the past was worth it and I had changed the right things. And if I hadn't, then I was at least happy I could talk to Tim one last time...

Chapter 21

When I opened my eyes again, it was dark outside. But what did I expect, after all, we had traveled into the past while it was already dark? It only made sense we popped up exactly where we left – or when we left?

Now, we were standing in the forest close to the clearing where we had said our goodbye to Matt with a heavy heart because it most likely was a goodbye forever.

But in contrast to before our time travel, Matt wasn't here with us. It didn't need to mean anything since he wanted to go and look for Ramon, but any kind of change calmed me down a bit. It was a sign that our plan had worked, at least that was what I told myself.

I took a deep breath of the fresh winter air. We had been through too many season changes within one night, while in our timeline, not even a whole night had passed – which I didn't know for sure. I didn't have any feeling of time anymore, nor did I have any idea of what would expect us when we would leave the top of the mountain.

"We made it," I said flabbergasted.

"No, you made it," Finn said and wrapped his arms around me.

We were standing like this in the dark forest for some time in silence because nobody knew what else to say. We probably were both afraid of leaving the forest because, as soon as we would, reality would await us. Then we would know if everything had worked out for sure.

"Shall we?" Finn asked, and carefully let go of me.

I nodded, even though I knew he couldn't see it because of the darkness, but I had a lump in my throat; I couldn't say a word.

I noticed the first change when I felt my cellphone in the pocket of my jeans. In the other future, I didn't have time to take it with me when we left Matt's cabin. Something must have changed.

Armored with now two flashlights, we walked across the clearing. The full moon was clearly visible, and despite the darkness, it was surprisingly bright outside. We probably wouldn't even need our flashlights, but we used them anyway.

In the other future, it had been so cloudy that it was impossible to tell what moon phase we had. Was it possible that we could have even changed the weather?

The way across the clearing felt long because we only walked slowly and carefully since we didn't know if anything or anyone would expect us here. Against all odds, we didn't find neither Ramon nor the magicians, and there was no sign of Tim as well. It felt like we were the only ones up here, and, in some way, it even felt a bit peaceful. It was as if I was at peace with myself.

The moonlight was shining particularly brightly on one spot on the clearing, and it wasn't until we almost reached it – we walked towards it like we'd been hypnotized – that we realized the moon was leading us nowhere. The spot where the light was meeting the grass of the clearing was absolutely empty. Something was missing. It was as if the moon wanted to prepare us for what had now become our reality. Or for who was missing; Matt.

His cabin was nowhere to be found. Not even the remains of it. It was as if it had never existed. As if Matt had never moved to our town.

"Do you think we've lost the Matt we know forever?" I asked Finn and broke the silence.

"I don't think so. If he really was the person, we thought we knew, he can't simply vanish. Maybe this Matt is hidden pretty well on the inside, but he will never be gone completely. We just need more time to find him," he said and tried to cheer me up.

I smiled.

I liked the idea that our Matt was still somewhere in this big world. I preferred this idea over the truth: our Matt was in another timeline, he was nowhere to be found in our world, and the Matt we had in our new time, would never let us get close enough to him, so we would never be able to trigger his good sides.

If he wasn't here, where else could he be? Did this mean he didn't need our help? Was he reunited with the magicians? Or was he still on the run?

All of these things would take some time to figure out. But they could wait. Now, we needed to climb down the mountain without hurting ourselves. Could I even fracture my bones? Anyway, I didn't want to find that out.

"Then let's go home," Finn said as if he could read my thoughts.

"Into the unknown," I said, and honestly, my fear had disappeared. I was way too curious.

Finn dropped me off at the beginning of my street, then we separated ways since none of us had any clue what we had told our parents to justify our late-night adventure.

Relieved that we managed to hike down that hill in no time and fortunately, found Finn's car at the bottom of the mountain – in this time he wasn't kidnapped by the magicians since they weren't here either – which made the way home easier than with public transportation. Especially at this time, we would've needed to wait forever for the bus since it would only drive once per hour and then later not at all.

Carefully, I turned my key around in the lock of the front door, then I opened.

Immediately, my mom entered the hallway, and I could see the worry in her eyes.

"I thought you wanted to sleep at Ramon's place tonight?" She said confused.

Oh. This was unexpected. I had used the same excuse in this timeline as I had in the other one. Now it was too late to change something anyway.

And before I could answer, she added: "Did you fight? Are you okay? I knew he wasn't the right guy for you. You'll find someone better. What about Finn? He is such a great guy."

I only looked at her in confusion.

Then I hugged her happily.

Even though we had changed the past, she had stayed the same. Of course, I wasn't particularly happy about her negative opinion of Ramon, but at the same time I was incredibly glad she hadn't changed. It was the little things in life that counted, and right now, in this moment, where it was impossible to even imagine all of the changes, I was glad about everything that stayed the same.

"I'm glad to have you," I murmured.

Then I got rid of my shoes and walked upstairs into my room.

I could hear my mom say something that sounded like: "Why do you even look like that?"

But luckily, she didn't follow me, so I could pretend that I hadn't heard her question.

And she was damn right. I must've looked horribly. I was sweaty from all the changes in season and from walking down the mountain. I had cried a lot because of all the things I had been through in the past night. And it wouldn't have surprised me if I had a lot of little branches in my hair because I got stuck in a few bushes on our way down the mountain. I didn't even want to think about all the insects that might be crawling around somewhere on my clothes.

When I arrived in my room, I took a deep breath. I had done it. I was back home. And although I didn't know what had happened in the past six months, I knew, no, I felt, that the magicians hadn't arrived yet.

I looked at my phone.

Ramon had tried to call me, but I missed it since I had only used my phone in plane mode to save battery. I would call him back as soon as possible, but first I needed a shower to feel a little bit more human again.

Tired, I grabbed fresh clothes from my wardrobe and walked to the bathroom.

The bright light was blinding me a little bit – my eyes were still too used to the darkness after spending so much time on the clearing and in the not-so-well-lit basement of the mansion – but this was okay.

Sleepy, I looked into the mirror to figure out how bad I actually looked.

Suddenly, I was wide awake again.

The person that was looking at me from the mirror didn't look like me. It was me, but somehow it wasn't. And actually, not much was different from how I looked except for my hair color.

I had gotten so used to my colorful hair that it became part of my identity. The person in the mirror, however, had brown hair. As if I had never existed.

Chapter 22

What had just happened? In one moment, I saw one of the magicians come closer while fumbling in his pocket, and in the next moment, some blue-haired creature was throwing themselves between us and pushed the magician away.

A weird liquid was spilt on the ground. And before I could say anything, or even show my gratitude, the person vanished as quickly as they had appeared. As if they never really existed. I didn't even see their face.

"Did you see that as well?" I asked after the magicians had disappeared to make sure I wasn't crazy.

I was pretty exhausted and hurt, the wound on my head was still bleeding a bit, it wasn't completely unlikely that I was simply hallucinating.

"What exactly do you mean? I have seen a lot of things tonight," Tim said and laughed.

"I mean the thing that threw themselves between the magicians and me," I explained more clearly.

"I have no clue what you're talking about," Luna said and gave Tim a conspiratorial wink.

Did I miss something?

No matter what these two were trying to hide from me, it didn't matter anyway. Everything that mattered was that we were still alive. We now knew who the strangers were, which made them appear less scary, since we weren't fighting against some unknown power anymore; we knew our opponents.

Although it was likely, we had to meet them again in the future – something told me they wouldn't give up that quickly – but until then we would have time to figure things out.

"Let's walk back up," I said and together we started the exhausting way upstairs.

Luna and Tim needed to help me walk through the staircase since I was still weakened. It was still too exhausting for me to actively use my powers, but I would continue working on that. So, in the future, it hopefully won't bother me anymore. And maybe, one day, I wouldn't have any issues with feeling weak or exhausted after using them. The thought of that made me happy even though I knew the road to get there would be long and hard.

When we arrived in the living room of the mansion, I broke down on the couch. I felt some sort of fatigue that I had never felt before. However, I had never used my powers as much as I had done it last night. And never have I been more in control than last night either. I was damn proud.

Although, physically, I had no chance against someone like Matt, I was able to control my abilities despite being stressed and emotional. I was able to fight him without any vision. Without murdering anyone. Maybe it wasn't that wrong to have feelings. Maybe it was okay to not always be in charge of my emotions as long as I could control my abilities, everything was fine.

Tim and Luna looked worried at me and desperately tried to find something to clean my wounds, but I was too dazed to properly answer their questions. I only wanted to go home, far away from the mansion.

"Please, just drive me home," I beseeched them.

It didn't take them long until they had packed and stored everything in the car, but it felt like eternity to me.

I was fighting hard against myself to stay awake; I didn't want to fall asleep for now. Not yet at least. But if one was tired and exhausted, it became even harder fighting the urge to fall asleep.

Not for nothing, there were too many accidents on highways that were caused by people dozing off for only a second behind the steering wheel. And even I wasn't completely guilt free if it came to not driving the car while being tired. Fatigue was something one should never underestimate. And because of that, I didn't even need to say anything else, Tim overtook the driver's position without hesitating.

It wasn't like we had another choice anyway. I was absolutely not able to drive, and Luna didn't have a driver's license.

Absolutely done, I lied down in the back of the car. I only noticed that Tim started the engine, then I fell asleep and only woke up after we had arrived at home.

Tim and Luna carefully woke me up and helped me climb up the stairs to my apartment. My wound wasn't bleeding anymore – I had stopped the blood with one of my T-shirts before we had started to drive back – still, it didn't change anything about my terrible headache.

Matt didn't hold back his powers, and I wondered if I had some more powers than I might've thought since I had been hurt pretty badly during our fight, but in comparison to the pain I was feeling, I was doing surprisingly alright. Despite all of the punches and hits in my face, I had neither a broken nose nor lost a tooth – something that could even happen during a fight among humans.

Matt, however, wasn't human, which led me to the conclusion that I was probably resisting violence better than normal people. This wouldn't help me to win over him in the future, but it would help distract or even provoke him – after all, I was tougher than he had thought. He wouldn't be able to break me that easily.

Luna quickly disappeared while looking for a dressing to keep the wound sanitary after cleaning it. The last thing I needed was a nasty infection. Unfortunately, I was still too dazed to tell her we had a med kit in the trunk of the car since it was mandatory for all cars to have one. But there was no way she could know that; she didn't have a driver's license. Tim, however, should've known this, but maybe he was simply too stressed out.

"What a wild night," Tim murmured while he cleaned my wound with water.

I could only agree, but I was too weak to respond. But no matter how exhausted and powerless I felt in this situation, I could also tell that it would pass. Soon, I would feel better, and then I would only become stronger.

At some point, Luna returned with a first-aid kit. Tim helped her wrap my head with the dressing, and after a long discussion, he was able to convince her he would take good care of me.

Still, she only vanished after Tim had promised multiple times to sleep over at my place and keep an eye on me in case my condition would get worse. Although it felt unnecessary to me – after all, I could feel how my strength was slowly coming back – still, I was too weak to properly communicate that.

"Could it be possible that this is the first sleepover we have since our childhood?" he asked motivated after Luna had walked away and he had grabbed one of my spare toothbrushes from the bathroom.

"Probably," I said and smiled.

It already felt as if normality had returned into my life. Now I could finally make all these experiences I couldn't do in the past years. But before we could've done anything special, I fell asleep again.

✻✻✻

As expected, my weakness didn't last forever. My exhaustion had only been caused by the frequent use of my abilities, and within a week after we had left the mansion, I was feeling great again. My wounds were healing without any issues, and against all odds, the wound on my forehead didn't even leave a scar behind that would forever remind us of our adventure in the mansion. I was feeling good. No. Even better. I was feeling great. Because now I knew my abilities were working and I was pretty close to living a normal life.

On a closer look, my life was already normal. When Luna invited Tim and me to her birthday party, I didn't hesitate for long; I agreed. Nothing – especially not my visions – would stop me from having a normal life with normal activities.

Finally, I could properly get to know Luna's friends, the last time I had seen them at that party, we could barely talk with each other. And even Tim got along well with her friends, which didn't come surprising to me. After all, he was Tim. He would get along with everybody, and everyone simply had to like him.

Shortly after the birthday party, Luna and I had planned how I could coincidentally bump into her mother on the staircase so she would finally meet me. Up until that point in time, she had lots of prejudices. Beyond everything, it was me who had run away with my best friend, and her daughter to an unknown place for an unknown timespan. Who could blame her for feeling that way towards me?

It must've been strange to have a neighbor that nobody except for Luna had ever seen. And because I wanted to change that negative view Luna's mother had of me, I agreed to meet her.

I had no reason to avoid people anymore. Now, I could control my visions, and I started wondering how much of my isolated life was really caused by my fear of having a vision and how much was simply just an excuse to shut everyone out and live alone in my own misery?

Although I had hoped my encounter with Luna's mother would change her view of me, I had to come to the conclusion that I was wrong. In the moment she saw me, her face changed, and it almost seemed as if she was feeling uncomfortable in my presence, even though I hadn't done anything special. I had only introduced myself to her.

But I guess I had to learn to live with that. Not every person in life would like one from the beginning, and maybe I had reached a point where I had to learn this lesson. After all, I had spent most of my life without meeting new people. Nobody could've disliked me in the past because nobody knew me.

Luckily, the fact that Luna's mother disliked me didn't have any impact on Luna. She still enjoyed spending time with me, and we texted almost daily. Even after she had moved away, she tried to visit me as often as possible. Everything was normal. So human. So new.

It was like a first relationship should be. And if Luna's mother would like me a little bit more, everything would be perfect. Maybe things would be even more perfect if Luna hadn't moved to the other side of town, because if she was still living one apartment below, we might be able to see each other more often.

If Luna wasn't coming over, Tim was by my side. Together we tried to figure out more about my abilities, and we learned how I would be able to control them even better. It was scary how easy it had become to push glasses down from the table after some time. It was as easy as recovering from using my powers.

In the mansion, I had reached my lowest point, but from there, things only moved uphill. I didn't feel exhausted or tired after using my abilities; I had learned how it felt to live a normal life.

Luna and I were able to go on dates without me being afraid of murdering someone. I had the possibility to do all of these things I had never expected I would be doing. Like ever. I even went to the cinema alone, and although I felt a tiny bit stressed while doing that – I might or might not have developed some social anxieties during my time of isolation – I didn't have a vision. I was finally alive. I was finally free.

Time passed, and summer turned into autumn, and suddenly it was almost winter. The temperatures were sinking with every day, and I felt this odd feeling of being satisfied with the way my life had unfolded.

This Christmas was the first Christmas I would be celebrating with my family again. After all this time. It was the first time the thought about Christmas movies and music didn't horrify me. It was the first time I would feel like a part of my family again, and I deserved it.

I was sitting at my kitchen table waiting for Luna. She wanted to sleep over at my place tonight, but so far, she hadn't arrived yet. Worried, I called her, but she didn't pick up. I didn't know what I should do, so I decided to distract myself and watch a TV show. While doing that, I must've fallen asleep because I couldn't remember anything that had happened in the show. But I wasn't surprised; I had a tough day at work.

Although I was self-employed, it was the first time since I had moved out of my dad's place that work was really popping off in the best way possible. I finally, enjoyed what I was doing again, and it seemed to attract even more positive things.

In general, everything in my life seemed to be working out great. There were almost no things that I would consider bad. And what should I say? Maybe I had deserved more in life than being sad and alone all of the time. Maybe even I deserved to be happy.

I twitched when the loud ringing of my doorbell woke me up from my involuntarily nap. I stretched and, still sleepy, made my way to the intercom.

"Hello?" I asked carefully.

After all, I didn't know who would stand in front of the door.

Chapter 23

R amon?" I asked confused.

Since when did he talk while using the intercom?

On the inside, I was overjoyed. It must've meant that he was feeling better, and our little trip into the past was a success. He wasn't affected by the potion anymore. How could he? It had never touched him in this time line.

And because I was too impatient to see all of these changes with my own eyes, and apparently, I wanted to sleep at his place anyway, I immediately took the next bus to Ramon's apartment after I was done with my shower. My mom was more than just confused about my behavior that evening, but she would get over it. I would tell her I went on a spontaneous hiking trip with Finn, which wasn't even a lie. She would believe me and continue disliking Ramon.

"Oh, it's you," he said through the intercom.

With a buzzing noise, the door opened, and I entered the staircase. The familiar smell of this apartment complex filled my nose. It was nice that this hadn't changed.

My heart pounded when I walked up the stairs to the fifth floor. Although I knew I was supposed to meet up with Ramon today, I didn't know if we were still in a relationship, broken up, or if all of this had never happened. I gulped and hoped it wouldn't be all too awkward.

"I thought you had ditched me." He greeted me with joy and kissed me.

This should answer all of my questions.

Hesitantly, I kissed him back.

I wasn't prepared to find all of my answers about our relationship status that quickly. In the other future, things were so much more complicated between us.

"Are you okay?" Ramon asked after I had followed him into the apartment.

"Yes," I stuttered, and desperately tried to figure out what to say next.

Of course, he had realized something was wrong with me, but in case he didn't know anything about time traveling so far, I didn't want to confront him with that topic tonight. Tonight, I only wanted to be normal for once and discreetly observe how Ramon was actually doing since that night in the mansion.

"I think about dyeing my hair blue," I answered slowly and looked at him with my eyes wide open.

"Then go for it," he said and shrugged, then he helped me get out of my jacket since I was still a little bit too disturbed by everything to move.

"What kind of blue?" he wanted to know.

"Midnight blue," I said and smiled.

It was amazing, he simply accepted my choice and didn't even second guess why I wanted to change my hair color that badly.

"I think it would suit your eye colo…" he said.

But I didn't even let him finish his sentence.

I simply kissed him.

Here, in the light of his lamp – we had made it to the living room by now – I could clearly see that he didn't look weak anymore. And something about the way he hugged me and slowly pulled me closer to him was different than in the other future. He was different. He was healthy. And all of our efforts had been so worth it.

Although it was already pretty late when I had arrived in front of his door and although I would have school the next day, we still had a good time together. It was the first time it felt like actually being in a relationship with him because it was the first time my head was clear and I didn't need to be worried about him anymore. He finally didn't seem to be fragile, and I didn't need to be afraid of accidentally hurting him while touching him. It felt like we could finally be honest with each other. Well, almost. The only thing I hadn't been able to talk to him about was my time travel. But I definitely planned on telling him everything, just not tonight.

Finn and I pretended our time travel never happened when we met again at school the next day. He didn't seem too shocked or dragged down by the events from the past night. Actually, he seemed surprisingly okay with everything. He behaved like he always did.

315

The only extraordinary thing he did was to ask me if everything had worked out while greeting me. I had nodded and therefore signaled him that everything worked out the way we wanted it to. Ramon was healed, stronger than ever, and it hadn't been too hard for me to figure out that Tim was still alive.

I had hidden Tim's watch that was still in my possession in my room before I had made my way to Ramon. Maybe I would need it again one day to prove to Ramon that my time travel was real, in case Tim hadn't told him about it so far. But I would only find these things out on the weekend, since Tim, Ramon, and I wanted to meet up, and if necessary, I would tell him everything he needed to know.

After all, we weren't allowed to feel too safe. Even though Matt wasn't here and therefore couldn't attract the magicians, we had no idea whether they were following us or doing other things right now. And especially because we didn't have Matt anymore who could've told us when the magicians would come closer, we needed to be prepared. All the time. I wanted to share these worries of mine with Tim and Ramon so they could start getting ready for the fight, like I was.

"Are you free today?" I asked Finn during lunch break after I had made sure all of our other friends were busy right now.

"Sure, what for?" he asked excitedly.

I grinned at him and said: "I think I need someone that can bleach my hair."

"Not again," he moaned playfully annoyed. "It feels like I've done it not so long ago," he added and laughed.

Finn and I met in the entrance hall of our school after class to walk to the city center together. This time, I knew exactly where to go to find the right bleach and toner for my hair. Additionally, I trusted Finn a tiny bit more with my hair, since I already knew he would have a bright future ahead as a hairdresser if he wanted to. At least, last time everything worked out fine.

"Why do you think your hair color has changed back?" Finn asked, after we had arrived at my place and locked ourselves into the bathroom.

"I don't know. I think I dyed my hair during my identical crisis to change something. Like, if I can't be in control of my life at least I can control the way I look or something like that," I tried to find a plausible explanation.

"But why does the Luna from this future not have this problem?" He asked further.

I thought about it.

He was right, something must've changed within me so that I had never thought about dyeing my hair. Until now, obviously.

"Maybe Sina didn't come back to meet up," I considered.

"There is only one way to find out," Finn said and looked at me expectantly while mixing the bleach.

"What exactly do you mean?" I wanted to know.
Somehow, it wasn't as obvious for me what to do next as it was for him.

"Well, don't you think you can see it on your phone? You probably texted with each other, and if you actually met up in this future, you can find the chats on your phone," he proposed.
What a great idea.
Immediately, I grabbed my phone and looked through my contact list to see if I could find her number. From the corner of my eyes, I noticed that I also still had the number of someone saved that shouldn't be in my life anymore: Matt.

For some reasons, his number hadn't been deleted from my phone despite our time travel, even though it was mostly impossible, I could've gotten his number in this version of the future. Unfortunately, this would also mean that the chat with Sina would exist anyway, even if we hadn't met up during vacations. Still, I clicked on the chat, which was full of messages where we talked about spending the vacations together, just as expected.

"It's not helping me. I even have Matt's number," I pouted disappointed.

"Have you checked the text messages with Matt? Maybe there is some kind of sign that he isn't in our lives anymore." Finn tried to find another approach and started massaging the bleach onto my head.

"You're right!" I screamed excitedly and moved so quickly that I almost knocked the brush out of Finn's hand.

"The chat with Matt is empty. As if it never existed."

It was strange that everything pointed towards the fact that Matt and I didn't know each other in this future, still I had his number saved as a contact. But on the other hand, who knew if it was actually his number? Maybe he even had another phone number in this future.

"Although nothing makes sense right now. It's time traveling, nothing needs to make sense to us. But if the chat with Matt is empty, the one with Sina, however, isn't, it could be a sign that she actually visited you," Finn tried to conclude.

"But what other thing didn't happen that led to me dyeing my hair?" I asked desperately.

Why should Finn know that? He knew even less than me.

"Well, you have enough time to think about it," he laughed while still bleaching my hair.

And he was damn right. I had all the time in the world to think about it while he was focused on my hair. What other thing than Sina and her bleach blonde hair triggered me so hard it made me change my hair color?

What if it really was a way to feel like I was more in control of my life after it had felt like I completely lost it?

And then I remembered.

Luana.

The connection to Ramon and his Grandma, and the fact that I actually didn't know who I was anymore. This must've been the real reason for my blue hair.

"I got it," I said.

Finn was finished with my hair.

By now we were only waiting until we could finally wash the itchy bleach off my scalp again.

Immediately he looked up from his phone.

"Matt didn't take the missing pages of the storybook with him. That's why he isn't here. He doesn't need our help, or for some reason, he simply doesn't want to cooperate with us. In conclusion, this means we don't know more about these missing pages. In this version of the future, Ramon, Tim, and, somehow, I as well, don't have any idea about the connection between Luana and me until now," I blurted out.

In this moment, I didn't know if Finn could follow my thoughts, after all, he hadn't been with us at that time. And when I finally told him about everything, it was a lot of information at once, there was no way he could have remembered everything.

"Despite your names sounding so similar. Shocking." He joked.

And I needed to laugh too.

He was right. Sometimes the truth was so obvious, the only thing stopping me from believing it was myself.

We spent the rest of the time making bad jokes and simply talking in a way we had always done it before last night. He still had a lot of questions, which I didn't hesitate to answer, but all in all, he did a great job at coping with everything. Way better than I had back then.

And after we had washed out the bleach, he helped me, like he had done in the other future as well, to dye my hair *midnight blue*. It was as if I had found myself a little bit despite still having an identical crisis.

"I think I have a Deja-vu." Tim greeted me after I had entered Ramon's apartment.

A wide grin hushed across my face.

Although it wouldn't have surprised me if he had even forgotten about our encounter in the mansion, it was nice to know he still believed me that I had traveled through time.

Ramon only looked at us confused but didn't say anything.

"Looks good," he complimented my – for him – new hair color.

I thanked him and sat down on the couch next to Tim.

"Great to see you're back again," I said as if we hadn't seen each other for a long time. Which somehow was true for him.

After all, in his time, almost six months have passed since we met for the last time, while for me, it was only a little bit more than a week.

In the meantime, he had seen Luna, who, in theory, should have been me but practically wasn't at the same time. And now, after I had dyed my hair blue, he knew for sure that I had arrived in his future. God, this was so complicated.

"You only met like a week ago or something." Ramon figured out.

Of course, I couldn't know about that. At this time, I had been in a different future. In my future.

"True." I laughed and tried to overplay my insecurity.

I had no clue what I was talking about.

"So, what do you want to talk about?" Ramon asked and looked worried.

Before we had arranged our meeting, I had let him know there was something important that we needed to talk about together.

"I was thinking about the magicians and came to the conclusion that we can't avoid them forever. It's time that we prepare for another attack from them," I said.

"I'm better prepared than ever. They can come, I'm not afraid anymore," Ramon immediately answered.

"And I have my baseball bat," Tim intervened.

I shot him a warning glance.

He knew, as well as I, that he was pretty easy to harm. Also, there was no guarantee that Matt would leave Tim alone again. There was no guarantee for anything.

"I want you to take me seriously. Who knows what the magicians are planning for when they come back? Who knows who is fighting on their side? I thought maybe we can ask Finn for additional help. We can be glad about everyone that wants to help," I proposed.

"I thought you wanted to keep him out of this?" Ramon questioned my words.

Damn. I hadn't thought about that.

Of course, I wanted to protect him, but now he was already in too deep anyway. He could be pretty useful for us.

"Did you tell him about me?" Ramon sounded angry.

I didn't answer but looked at the ground.

Only the truth could help me to get out of this situation.

"Luna?" he asked again and this time he sounded even more serious than before.

"I promise, I can explain everything." I tried to calm him down.

"You don't need to," he said and stood up to lock himself into the bathroom.

"You haven't told him, I guess?" I asked Tim.

"No, I thought you would like to do it for whenever you would come back," he admitted.

It was pretty kind and thoughtful of him, after all, I knew more details and therefore could explain everything better. Tim didn't know much about the future other than me having blue hair and him being dead.

"Do you think he is very mad?" I carefully asked.

After all this time, Tim knew Ramon best. He could tell if it was worth to explain myself now or if it was better to let him calm down first.

"If you tell him everything, he will understand," Tim said.

So, I stood up and carefully knocked against the bathroom door.

"Ramon? Can we talk? I promise, everything makes sense. You only need to listen to me." My voice was shaking a bit.

I have never seen him that angry. At least he has never been that angry at me. What if he would have another vision?

I could hear a sigh from the other side of the door, then it slowly opened.

"Your explanation better be good," he grumbled and together we walked back to Tim.

"There are two rules. Rule number one is that you don't think I'm insane, and rule number two is that you won't leave before I'm done talking." I quoted him from that evening when he had told me the truth about himself.

I didn't know if he would understand this homage or if, in this timeline, he had even said it – he should've said it because it should have happened before our time travel, but to be honest, I couldn't be certain about anything anymore. Still, I knew one thing. Today, our roles were reversed. Today it was me who needed to tell him everything.

In case he didn't understand my joke, he was good at hiding it.

He only nodded.

"So, where do I start?" I murmured and sighed.

I had so much to tell him, and still I hadn't said anything useful at all. How would I explain to a person that I would trust with my life that, in another future, he almost killed me?

"You were right from the start. There is a connection between Luana and me," I started.

This information should be the least shocking for him.

"I knew it," I heard him say. "But how do you know?" he added confused.

"This will sound completely batshit crazy, but please, you need to believe me. I traveled through time, and in the other future, we found out about this connection," I tried to explain myself.

"So, time travel," he murmured.

I had no clue if he believed me or not. On the one hand, there was no reason why he shouldn't believe me after everything he had seen so far. On the other hand, however, my story sounded so much more unrealistic than the other things we have been through. I desperately glanced over to Tim.

"Maybe I haven't been honest with you either," Tim said and looked at the ground.

"I met Luna from the future during that night in the mansion. It was her, who woke me up and led me into the basement. Even back then she has talked about time travelling." Tim took my side and told his version of the truth.

"How could you believe her so quickly?" Ramon wanted to know.

"Well, she wasn't alone. Finn was with her. And she was wearing my watch, I simply had to believe her."

"Finn was there too?" Ramon asked further.

He still looked skeptical.

"Yes, Finn was there too. And believe me, in the other future, he didn't know about the magicians, or your powers, or anything else that would be somehow supernatural. Until the day we met the magicians again. They used him to pressure me, and I had no other choice than to tell him the truth," I justified myself.

"Why did you bring him with you when you time traveled? Why was he so important? Why couldn't you take one of us?"

"Why can't you just trust me that I had my reasons? What's going on with you? I don't know you like this." I was furious.

Why was it so hard to convince him that everything I had done in the past, I did it for him?

"But in case you really want to know... In the mansion, the magicians wanted to put a spell on you. It has worked in the other future but not in this one, thanks to Tim, and Finn, and me because now I was prepared to step in and be actually helpful. In the other future, the magicians eventually came back, and how do I phrase it nicely... You were abducted and Tim was dead."

Ramon looked at me with his eyes wide open.

"That night, in the mansion, that was you?" He slowly seemed to realize what I had done.

I only nodded.

"Thanks," he said and smiled.

It seemed as if he could finally believe me.

"Are there any other differences between our time and the alternate future? Except for the ending and the fact that we figured out you and Luana have a connection?" He wanted to know.

Now he was curious.

I quickly thought about it.

"So far, I don't know. I'm not here for super long yet, and if I'm honest, I have no clue what has changed," I admitted.

Still, I started telling them about my version of the future. I told them about the consequences the potion had on Ramon. That he became weaker and weaker and therefore wasn't able to control his visions anymore. When Ramon heard that, he seemed visibly shocked. In the new future, he was doing so great. It had definitely been worth it to protect and save him.

I told him about his visions that almost killed Tim and me. I told him about the mysterious savior, but I left out the fact that it had been Matt. I firstly, had to process the fact that it was certain he had never moved to this town and everything we had been through never happened for him.

Although I knew that eventually I would need to tell the others about it, after all, it were important information that we could hopefully use for our final fight with the magicians. But for now, a brief summary of the alternate future was enough. And for that, Matt wasn't important either.

I told them about the missing pages of the book and further explained the connection with Luana. I didn't even spare out the details about my following identical crisis to loosen up the mood a bit. And even though it didn't feel quite normal, I had come to peace with the fact that I had gotten a second chance in life.

Additionally, I let them know more about our second encounter with the magicians and how Finn and I managed to travel back in time. It was weird to have all of this knowledge when, in this future, we weren't supposed to have it.

We shouldn't know the spell book of Ramon's Grandma was actually in my head. And we weren't allowed to know anything about Luana and me. Also, we weren't supposed to know that the book wasn't a physical book because, as far as I knew now, in this timeline, Ramon had never driven back to the mansion after we had left it that night; he hadn't searched for the book.

After all, he didn't need it. He was healthy and better prepared than ever. He never left, and I never left him. Even though only little things had changed, it was a lot of little things that had changed.

Ramon and Tim curiously listened to me until I was done.

"And that's why I think it's important to lure the magicians to us somehow. Any more questions?" I ended my explanation.

First, everyone stayed silent.

"How did we get the missing pages of the storybook?" Tim wanted to know.

Of course, he picked up on this tiny detail.

"From a friend," I said and noticed how tears were filling my eyes.

Carefully, Ramon hugged me.

"It's okay. You don't need to talk about it if you don't want to," he calmed me down.

I sighed.

It was time to fill them in.

"Do you remember Matt? Tall, dark haired…" I started, but Tim didn't let me finish.

"Scary," he added.

"In my future, he joined our side after he left the magicians. Back in that night we first met him, he stole the pages from the magicians to give them to us as a trade. We received the pages, and he received our help," I explained.

"So, we only need to wait a bit, and suddenly he will pop up in front of our door and hand us the pages?" Ramon wanted to know.

"No, he won't show up at all. While you were saving past-me in the basement and Tim was beating up the magicians, Matt left, but for some reason, he didn't take the missing pages with him. As if he has never planned to ask us for our help. Everything that we had been through has never happened and will never happen."

"Will he be back with the magicians then?" Ramon asked further.

"I don't know. Everything I know is that he has never come to this town. His home isn't where it's supposed to be, as if it has never existed. And all the other traces he has left in my future have been erased. It's very likely he went back to the magicians, after all, in my future, he was still bound to them," I explained.

"What if he isn't here because he doesn't need to save anyone?" Tim thought out loud.

I looked at him astonished.

Everything he said sounded surprisingly plausible. Of course, it didn't explain why he hadn't taken the missing pages from the magicians, but it explained why he had never come here.

Ramon was fine. He had never put anyone in danger. And Matt, who needed to save us in the other future, never had the weird urge to save us or anyone else; it wasn't necessary after all.

"This is brilliant," I exclaimed.

Tim always continued to surprise me with his understanding of supernatural things. Sometimes, I wondered, if it wasn't him who actually inherited the knowledge of Ramon's Grandma.

Ramon, however, didn't seem fully convinced yet. But after we explained everything in more detail and clarity, he started to believe in Tim's theory as well. In the end, it didn't even matter why Matt wasn't here. It was a fact that he wasn't, and we needed to expect to meet him at our next encounter with the magicians.

"Although I always knew that we would have to face the magicians again, I never knew how important it really is," Ramon admitted.

"So, what's the plan? How do we lure the magicians to us? And where do we lure them to?"

"I don't know the how and the when, but I know where," I said and grinned.

"That's already a good start."

Ramon smiled.

I told them about the clearing in the forest, where we fought against the magicians in the other future as well. After all, this was the only place that was far away enough from town while at the same time easy to reach.

Additionally, my gut feeling told me this was the right decision. Some things simply felt right, and this was one of these things. And maybe I had hopes that up there, where Matt used to be at home, it would be easier to convince him to fight with us and not against us.

Chapter 24

Luna had a lot of news for us. Nothing I could've done would've prepared me for what she had to say, and still there were no doubts about her telling the truth. She was right. I believed her. And even if I wouldn't, there was still Tim who had witnessed what had happened in the mansion back then. He was there when Luna traveled through time; he only kept it a secret for now. Maybe it was for the best. Who could know if I would've believed him without any evidence?

The whole topic was pretty complex, and I still couldn't understand everything that had happened in the other future and what hadn't. But actually, it didn't really matter, it was more than enough if Luna understood these things.

After all, she was the one with my Grandma's knowledge which, by the way, was another thing I couldn't really grasp. All the time, she wanted me to believe she didn't feel a connection to Luana, and now, all of a sudden, she told me they were the same person. It was crazy, but it only confirmed my theory. And maybe I was a little bit relieved about it because now she noticed it herself, and I wasn't insane for seeing a connection that didn't make any sense.

Tim seemed to be able to follow the conversation better than I was, but, to my defense, he was a little bit more prepared for this conversation. For me, everything was new.

At least I now had an explanation for the strange creature that threw themself between me and the magicians. Never in my life would I have thought of this creature as Luna, and even less would I have expected her to be from the future. Now that I saw her with blue hair, it seemed astonishingly logical that it had been her who we saw that night.

"Great idea!" I heard Tim say.

It interrupted my thoughts.

Confused, I stared at the others and tried to follow the conversation without anyone noticing I hadn't been paying attention previously.

"Wow, I had never thought it would be so easy to convince you to lure the magicians here," Luna said enthusiastically.

I had never thought it would be here, where we would meet them again. Actually, I had hoped we would never have to see them again. Maybe they had forgotten about me by now and were looking for something else. Someone else.

Although they hadn't kept it a secret at the end of our last meeting, that they planned on meeting me again, after all this time, I hadn't really thought much about them actually still caring about me. Even though it didn't make any sense, I felt in safety.

On the other hand, I was surprisingly unafraid of them. They could come if they wanted to. I was prepared, and especially if we would lure them to us, we could use this as an advantage. It could only be good for us if they would underestimate us.

"But how exactly do we lure them here?" I asked.

I had no clue how they were supposed to find us. Did they know we were here? And if they knew, why haven't they come to this town already? And if not, how could we signal to them that we were here without giving away we were expecting them? Would they even come?

"That's a great question, and if I'm honest, I hoped one of you guys has any idea. We can't just simply write a text message to Matt and tell him where we are going to be at which time." In the end, Luna's voice became quieter.

It was obvious that whatever had happened in the other future was still messing with her head. Time simply can't heal every wound, especially not the ones that weren't supposed to be there in the first place.

And even though I couldn't imagine that in the other future we were in some way friends with Matt, after everything he had done to us in the mansion, I believed Luna when she said that it had happened. And it would even be helpful since it was hard for me to judge Matt, but maybe she was able to help us out because of their shared past – or future? What am I supposed to call it? – which would be another advantage for us.

"Why not?" Tim asked confused.

Luna and I eyed him critically.

Did he actually just propose we should write Matt a WhatsApp message?

"Well, just because I have his phone number doesn't automatically mean it still belongs to him. What if he doesn't have a phone in this future?" Luna stuttered.

"Also, even if he would receive my messages, why should they go to a place of our choice? They would expect this to be a trap," I said and sighed.

No matter how long we would sit here, we wouldn't find a solution for this problem.

"There is only one way to find out. Of course, it won't work if the phone number doesn't belong to Matt anymore. And the odds of the magicians actually coming to a place we choose are probably low, but do you know what will work even less? To not try it. Because then nobody goes anywhere. If we try it, we at least have a small chance that it could work. And what are the other options? To use a spell to lure them to town? Let's first start with the most obvious thing, and then we can still make things unnecessary complicated," Tim explained his train of thought, and when he said it like this, he was right.

Of course. Like always.

"Okay," Luna said quietly. "What should I write him?"

If one was listening closely, the shaking in her voice was hard to ignore. And even I felt a bit nervous. At least I could stay quiet and observe the others while trying to spell out the perfect message to Matt or someone else since we didn't even know whose number it was.

"Yo Mattiboy, long time not seen. What about you and your weird friends coming over for a fresh visit? Somewhere behind the mountains but not with the seven dwarves. Maybe we even have a nice spell book for you. YOLO," Tim dictated to her without laughing.

Luna only looked at him deeply disturbed until we all started laughing.

"What?" I asked confused.

"I thought this is how young people talk," Tim said shily.

"Tim, you are 21 and not 80. You ARE young." I tried to explain.

"Pfff," he only said. "If you have better ideas what to write to Matt, you can also use them," he said playfully mad.

"But you should definitely talk about the book. It would be too unrealistic that Ramon would want to join them all of a sudden," he added.

"Oh, brilliant. Idea. What if we would actually hand them a book? They don't need to know that the book isn't a real book." Luna shared another idea with us.

"But who would get the fake book?" I wanted to know.

"I'll take care of it," Luna said and smiled as if she knew exactly what she wanted to do.

That was great. One problem solved.

"Hey Matt, in case this is your actual number, I just want to let you know that Ramon decided to give you the book if you still need it. But in return, you leave him alone. If you are still interested in the book, come to the following place next Saturday at 4 p.m." Luna read the message out loud before she sent it.

"That sounds good," I said.

"Hm," Tim took some extra time to think about it. "I couldn't have phrased it any better," he finally admitted.

Luna hit the send button and added another message with the location that she had chosen.

And even if I had no idea what would expect me on top of the mountain, I liked the idea that we wouldn't put anyone in danger. We wouldn't lure the magicians in town, we would only lure them close enough to hurt only us, but they wouldn't know.

"Now we can only wait and hope it works out," Tim said and clapped his hands.

The rest of the meeting, we spent planning the possible encounter with the magicians. In case they would actually come, we needed to be prepared as well as possible. Luna would take care of the false spell book, and I would have to train my powers every day. In case I needed to fight Matt again, because this time, I wouldn't lose. That was for sure.

Finn would be part of our team as well; he was already in too deep. And even though I still needed to get used to the thought he knew about everything, I wasn't angry at Luna anymore. After all, it wasn't her fault. The magicians just were horribly good at finding our weak spots.

Luna was immortal, they couldn't do anything to harm her, and I should by now be able to protect Tim with my powers.

In the last six months, we all had become stronger than ever. We weren't the same old group of confused teenagers that had no clue who or what would expect them.

We knew what we were fighting for, and we were prepared. And I found the idea of the fake spell book a bit too brilliant. If we were lucky, we could maybe avoid a fight. But then again, this wasn't an option either. If they would run off with the false book, they would return another time. We needed to fight them for good if we wanted this to have an ending.

And this was the only thing none of us had any answer to. Nobody knew how we should end it and nobody dared to say it out loud.

Chapter 25

I n case our plan would work out, we had exactly one week to prepare ourselves, and even though Tim, Ramon, and I have planned everything, I still felt insecure about it.

Of course, our chances to fight them were way better than in the other future, still, I wasn't as optimistic as Ramon and Tim. After all, I had seen things they hadn't. And even though the magicians weren't able to harm me, I was still scared of them. They could hurt Tim or Finn, if not worse...

All of these things were in my head when snowflakes were landing on my hair and my hands while I waited for the bus that would bring me home. Like always, the bus was late. As soon as there was a little bit of snow, the infrastructure in this town would completely fall apart. At least it felt like that. Maybe that was a problem in all of Germany and not only here.

Although Ramon had offered, I could sleep at his place, I didn't want to. I wanted to go home and clear my head a bit. Also, I needed to take care of the fake spell book. And even though I already had an idea where I could find it, I was still depending on Finn. He was part of my plan.

With a squeaking noise, the tires of the bus stopped. I entered and looked outside of the window. The further away we drove from the city center, the fewer lights I could see through the glass pane until they fully vanished when we hit the country road that would lead towards my new home.

"I should do what?" Finn asked confused.
I had already asked him the day before if he would be free today, and, fortunately for me, he was.

"You should write some Latin or Greek words in this old notebook," I repeated his task.

"Why don't you do it yourself? You know how uncreative I am." He sighed desperately.

"Because I'm scared, I'll actually write down real spells or something like that," I tried to explain.

But before I could continue saying that I wasn't sure how to separate my thoughts from my hidden knowledge, Finn responded: "I understand."
I was surprised how easily he could understand my fears, but I didn't second guess if he actually could comprehend why I didn't want to do it myself or if he was just being Finn. Because Finn was uncomplicated.

Then I handed him an old note book, which I had bought at a flea market in the past because I liked the vintage style of it. However, I had never been a fan of writing down notes, so I didn't actually use it until today. It was fitting perfectly to our plan.

Carefully, I observed Finn, who had opened a Latin dictionary on his phone and eagerly wrote down words with a pen. The book needed to be a good fake.

It was important that it would distract the magicians for long enough. Because even though I didn't know how we should win for good, I could at least do everything that was in my power so they would lose their best fighter: Matt.

We only needed to unobtrusively tell him that we knew who or what he was, so he would switch to our side. How exactly we were supposed to do that, I didn't know, though. So, I planned to write a message on one of the last pages that was dedicated to Matt.

In case the magicians would figure out the book was a fake, maybe they would hand it to Matt and he could read my message, and then... What then? Maybe I had watched too much *Harry Potter* in the past if I was actually convinced, I could liberate him like this, but I was desperate, and any plan – no matter how unrealistic it was – would be better than doing nothing.

In an emergency, I could yell at him what kind of mythical creature he was, but that was by far my worst idea.

"Done," Finn said, and triumphantly closed the notebook.

"Superb, thank you so much," I said with a wide smile.

I didn't deserve a best friend like him.

"Do you think Matt will remember us?" Finn asked out of nowhere.

Until now, I hadn't even thought about the fact that he was also affected by losing Matt as a friend. After all, the two of them had been friends as well, and especially at Finn's birthday party, where Matt didn't appear, Finn was sad about his absence. Knowing that absolutely everything about this friendship had never happened hurt him as much as it hurt me.

"I don't think so, but I hope he will," I admitted.

"I don't know if I can get over it. That he's simply not there anymore. It is so weird to hang out with everyone at school and nobody notices that something is different." Finn explained his feelings.

"I feel the same. I'm not even afraid of the magicians anymore. I'm scared of what they could've possibly made out of Matt. And I'm even more scared they won't come at all." I opened up as well.

If someone would be able to understand my feelings, it would be Finn. After all, he had seen everything I had seen as well. How ironic that I had tried to keep him out of this mess, and now he was the only one that could actually relate to me. The only one that remembered Matt the way I did.

Finn only nodded.

"I don't even know what I should be afraid of anymore. We have seen pretty much everything by now," he murmured.

"Then don't be afraid." I tried to cheer him up and smiled.

He didn't say anything.

"Thank you," I said after some time.

"What for?" he wanted to know.

"That you didn't let me go alone. Without you, I would go insane here."

"No big deal. That's what friends are for." He smiled.

Unfortunately, it was time for Finn to go back home. Writing the fake spells into the notebook had been more time-consuming than I had expected. But at least my part of the preparations for the weekend was done. The next day, Finn and I would have to go back to school. And again, we would need to pretend everything was normal. As if we weren't trying to save the world next weekend or something like that. But now, we could only wait and hope the magicians would actually show up.

The week passed by incredibly slowly, or maybe it just felt this way to me because I was super impatient. Tim and Ramon updated me every day on how Ramon's training boot camp was going and apparently controlling his abilities worked out pretty well. Ramon was now able to lift Tim up only with the power of his mind. I could understand well why Ramon wasn't even worried at all. He had no reason to. He had become everything his Grandma had predicted: strong and in absolute control.

"Are you ready for the most important hike of our lives?" Tim asked motivated after Finn and I had joined them.

We had met in front of Ramon's apartment complex to drive to the mountains together.

"I've never been more ready," I said despite my doubts and fears.

But it wasn't even a lie. I was ready to get these turds out of our lives once and for all.

"Let them arrive and calm down before you bomb them with questions." Ramon laughed and kissed me as a greeting.

I smiled, and looked into my backpack for the note book.

After Finn had left, I wrote a small text on the last page of the book for Matt to find, which I was pretty satisfied with.

"That looks great." Ramon whistled through his teeth, appreciating what we had done after I had handed the book over to him.

"It was a lot of work. My wrist is still hurting because of that." Finn complained laughing.

"That was worth it. There is no pleasure without pain," I said while thinking about one of my favorite characters from Yu-Gi-Oh! GX and most certainly not about Christian Grey. Despite it sounding like something the latter would have said as well.

"Are you ready?" Ramon asked us after a brief moment of silence.

I nodded, Finn nodded, Tim nodded.

Nobody said anything.

Then we entered the car and drove towards the mountains. We wanted to be there earlier than the time we had told Matt. In case they would show up – which still was a huge question mark since Matt hadn't read the message – we didn't want to be late, and we couldn't estimate how long we would need for the hike up the mountain.

Ramon turned the radio on, and I heard Tim sing along, but I didn't really listen. Lost in thoughts, I looked out of the window and observed how we drove further and further away from town until we were only surrounded by forest. It was fascinating how small this world felt and how even smaller this town was. And although I had never really thought about what I would do after graduating, I was sure, I wanted to move away from here. This city restricted me. The memories that I had made in that little time would haunt me forever. In case we would be done with the magicians, I wanted to start over somewhere new, maybe even with Ramon, in case he still wanted to get away from here.

The drive didn't feel long at all. I just had to blink, and suddenly, we had arrived at the parking space where Finn and I had entered his car and driven back home almost two weeks ago. It was almost scary to know there wasn't much time between our last encounter with the magicians and today.

Hiking up the mountain was surprisingly easy for me, and with the help of Finn, we could even find the correct way first try. Still, there was an unwell feeling in my chest. We were so well prepared, why was I so stressed out?

Maybe it was the fact that I didn't know if the magicians would show up or the fear of the unknown? Even though the magicians weren't strangers to us anymore, who could know which new plans they have made to try to convince Ramon to join them?

"It's nice here," Tim said when we arrived on the clearing that used to be the home of Matt less than two weeks ago.

"This really is the perfect place to wait for the magicians." Ramon figured.

And that was what we did. We waited.

In case the magicians wouldn't show up, Ramon and I had thought of a plan B. Neither he nor I liked it, though.

In an emergency situation, we would try to lure only Matt to us. Ramon would try to trigger a vision in which he would see me die. If there was one thing Matt from my future had taught me, it was that Ramon's visions couldn't harm me, and we would take advantage of that. We had nothing to lose anyway. And in the best case, this vision would lure not just Matt to us; maybe the magicians would follow him.

Of course, we could only speculate about it, and there was no guarantee that our plan B would work out. That was why it was only our emergency plan. Ideally, we wouldn't even need it, and the magicians would come because of our message. Ideally, they believed us and were on the way to us, and all we had to do was wait.

"Nervous?" Ramon asked and carefully held my hand.

"A little bit, but thanks for asking," Tim answered, grinning.

Ramon smirked.

Of course, he meant to ask me and not Tim, but I was glad he had answered because I wasn't exactly sure how I should respond to that question. I didn't know what I should think or expect anymore.

Even though it was only 4 p.m., and therefore still the afternoon, the sky was grey and cloudy. It started to get dark. Stupid December. And why did we always choose such bizarre times to meet up with the magicians? Couldn't we meet them outside in summer and in the middle of the day? Why did it have to be odd, dark basements, or now, the clearing? The darkness added more tension to the atmosphere, as if it wasn't already tense enough.

4 p.m. passed and nobody came. We completely forgot to plan how long we would wait for them. How long we should wait to trigger Ramon's vision. The more time passed, the more tense the situation became. Even Tim seemed more restless than usual. He didn't joke anymore to loosen up the mood and only starred at the horizon.

But not even 10 minutes later, we saw a group of torches slowly heading towards us.

"They are here," I whispered quietly.

"As punctual as the Deutsche Bahn." I heard Tim murmur.

It seemed as if he was relaxing a bit more.

Faster than I would've preferred, the magicians and Matt were standing in front of me. My heart was in my mouth. In case I had any completely unfounded hopes that he wouldn't be fighting on their side but live a nice life on some Caribbean island far away from all of this, I needed to realize that it wasn't true. He was here, next to the magicians, exactly as I had feared.

"Hi there," Tim chirped and smiled politely at everyone.

The three magicians were standing way closer to us than in the other future, and to my relief, they didn't have Brutus with them. A spark of hope formed in my chest. If Matt was supposed to be their most dangerous fighter, we would be able to make him switch sides. We could actually defeat the magicians, and Ramon would finally be left alone.

"I would say it's nice to see you, but that would be a lie," Ramon said while looking at the magicians with small eyes.

"It's nice to see you as well," Titus responded untouched by what Ramon had previously said.

"Our offer is that we give you the book and you leave me and especially my friends alone forever."
Ramon got straight to the point.
We had no time or motivation to debate with the magicians much.

"Just a quick moment. I see, you have another friend in your gang."
Lucius eyed Finn as if he was trying to figure out how he could use him to his advantage. But this wouldn't work. Finn was part of our plan. They couldn't turn him against us. They couldn't use him as a distraction. He was safe here, as bizarre as it might've sounded.

"I don't know why you should care about it," I hissed and stepped protectively in front of Finn.

"What a great friend he must be if he even accompanied you into the past and all of that only to protect him," Lucius glance shifted towards Ramon. "How noble of him."

I looked at him in confusion.

"No matter what he says, don't listen to him," I whispered to Finn.

"Isn't it amazing that he endangered himself and his life to save Ramon so your little summer romance can go on? How friendly of him." Lucius emphasized especially the last part of his sentence.

I had no clue what he was hinting at, but I was certain he was trying to manipulate Finn. But why?

"What do you want from him?" I asked.

"We don't want anything from him. It's just extremely honorable of him to give up on his feelings for you, so you and Ramon can live happily ever after in this future." Lucius grinned mischievously. "Or do you actually think a friendship between a man and a woman is possible?"

I looked at Finn, who seemed exactly as confused as me.

I stepped closer to Lucius and looked him deep into the eyes.

"I don't know which century you are coming from, and I highly doubt you have any friends, and especially not friends from the other gender. But well, to answer your question, yes, I believe it is possible. We're in the 21st century, of course, it's possible."

I searched for Finn's glance, and when our eyes met, he nodded and smiled.

"And since you find it so great that I have traveled time with Luna, I want to add that this is a thing people do for their friends without even thinking about it. But what do you know about that? You probably don't know shit because you wouldn't even do it for each other," Finn said unbothered and shrugged.

I couldn't have phrased it better. I was so proud of Finn and a little bit of myself because I was able to verbally fight against the magicians. Not like in that night back then when I was helpless and emotional. I wasn't the person from back then anymore, this person was exactly as deeply buried within me as the memories of Luana.

"Are you done playing games?" Ramon asked bored.

The three magicians didn't respond.

From the corners of my eyes, I could see how Matt was staring at Finn and me. My glance wandered in his direction so that I was looking at him as well, but before I could do anything, he had already looked away again. Maybe it was just a coincidence or a product of my imagination.

"The book?" Antonius asked and stepped closer towards Ramon.

Requesting, he held his arm in Ramon's direction.

"Only if you leave us all alone. Forever." Ramon sounded serious.

"Okay, I promise," the magicians responded in unison.

In this moment, we couldn't care less if they were honest about it or not. It was more important that they would be distracted so we could… Yeah, what exactly could we do? We needed to free Matt. That would be our only chance to defeat the magicians for good.

Carefully, Ramon handed the faked spell book to Antonius. He immediately gave it to Lucius, who started flipping through the pages.

My heart pounded.

Would they notice our lie?

"Interesting," he murmured.

This could mean everything.

"Memento," he read out loud and looked at us.

While he was saying the word, something in Matt's face changed for a millisecond, as if he had actually remembered something. As if he knew that it was him who helped us to travel through time. As if there was a connection between him in this future and him from the other future.

"Do you really think we are that dumb?" Lucius let the book fall to the ground and looked at us.

"Yeah, somehow we did," Tim responded and shrugged.

Antonius looked at him angrily.

Why did he had to let the book fall to the ground? Why didn't he throw it away in anger so Matt could find it and read the page that was specially prepared for him to read? Why couldn't this be a movie? And why did plans like this only work in movies or books? Why couldn't anything in this world work out to our advantage?

"Of course, we were prepared that you wouldn't bring us the real book. Or maybe you have done exactly that without knowing about it," Titus said calmly, and his glance wandered from Tim to Ramon and from Ramon to me.

I knew what he was hinting at. So, he knew that I knew more than the others. Damn. Again, we had made the mistake of underestimating the magicians.

"Matt, don't you want to have some fun as well?" Titus asked directed towards Matt.

When Titus said these words, an evil smile, hushed across Matt's face.

It was so evil that it scared me. All the hopes that he could still remember some things about us were gone. This wasn't the Matt I knew. This was a monster.

Chapter 26

Within a second, Matt was about to lunge at Tim. He was already well prepared for the attack and held his baseball bat in a position from where he could hit Matt with as much force as possible.

A loud cracking noise could be heard when the bat was hitting Matt at the height of his belly button; the bat was broken.

"Nice try!" Matt said, laughing.

Although it didn't seem to bother him much that he had been hit by a baseball bat, it seemed to slow him down and throw him off track a little bit. That was great. We could use this to our advantage.

Quickly, I focused Matt with my glance and immediately felt the familiar tingle everywhere in my body. I wasn't the Ramon from six months ago. Using my powers had become ridiculously easy for me. Controlled, I pushed Matt away from Tim, so he fell to the ground.

From the corner of my eyes, I could see how Luna and Finn looked at me amazed. It must've been the first time she could see the progress I had made during that time where she technically wasn't in my time with her own eyes.

"Not bad." I heard Matt say as he slowly got up again.

Immediately, I stepped in front of Tim and said: "Don't you want to fight someone that can actually defend himself?"

An evil smirk formed on his face.

"Whatever you prefer." Matt shrugged.

Even faster than before, he leaped forward, and I could only ditch his punch by a few millimeters.

Although I had no idea what to do from now on – I had hoped Tim would have a plan – I realized that I didn't need to be stronger than Matt to stand a chance; I only needed to be faster.

And this was one of the things Tim and I had practiced for the past few months, and without bragging, I had become incredibly good at being fast. Of course, during our training we had no comparison to other supernatural creatures, but we were confident that I could beat them.

Now, it was time to prove this theory right or wrong. It was time to figure out if my powers were enough to distract Matt while someone else would come up with a plan.

Matt tried to come closer for a second time, but this time I was better prepared. Quickly, I focused my glance at one spot on the ground. Until here, I would let him pass, but not further. It was almost as if I had built an invisible wall around all of us because every time Matt tried to throw himself at Tim or someone else, as soon as he stepped further than my spot on the ground, he was dramatically pushed back.

"Wow, I didn't even know you could do such things." I could hear Tim say in the distance.

He probably laughed while saying that or showed his enthusiasm in another way, but I had no time to look at him. I still needed to concentrate.

Matt's efforts to try to hurt us almost reached a comedic effect after some time because he didn't show any learning progress. Every time, he fell, he stood up just to throw himself back at us a second later to again get pushed back by the invisible wall. If this wasn't the real life but a movie, I would have probably started laughing. But this wasn't a movie.

Unfortunately, we have reached a point where no one really knew what we should do from now on, even though we had prepared ourselves so well for the meeting with the magicians.

"Matt. You moron! You won't get through that." I could hear Antonius yell.

The magicians seemed to show a bigger learning progress than Matt. But he ignored them. What was his mission?

Why did he continue doing this even though it wasn't making any sense?

Why was he fighting a battle he couldn't win? At least not like this.

And then I realized it. He wasn't fighting to win. He wasn't fighting for the magicians or himself either. He wasn't fighting. He only tried to distract the magicians from something that he hoped would happen.

He was like me.

He was exactly like me in that night back in the mansion. I didn't stand a chance against him, and still, I never gave up, even though he hurt me. Matt, however, didn't get hurt, still, his behavior was pointless.

Maybe we were more alike than I had thought all along. This thought was sending a shiver down my spine. Usually, Matt wasn't a human or a supernatural creature that I wanted to identify myself with. Especially not, because after all, he was the murderer of my Grandma. Still, in this moment, I couldn't deny the similarity between us.

Back during that night in the mansion, I would've given everything so my friends could be in safety, and in the end, we got lucky that Matt had run away when he had the chance to do so. Without his help, I wouldn't have gotten through that night as well as I did. Who even knew if I would've survived that night at all?

And even if Matt wasn't fighting to protect his friends, his behavior was coming from somewhere. He was Matt, did he even have friends? Somehow it was pretty hard for me to imagine him with friends, and it was even harder to imagine a future where he had befriended Luna and me.

That was it. That was the solution. Matt wasn't playing on the side of the magicians or on our side. He was playing on his own side and right now it meant he was trying to reach something by acting like a bird that was flying against a window. Over and over again.

But before I could figure out what exactly it was, I could see from the corners of my eyes that Luna was carefully coming closer.

"Guardian angel paired with demon," she said with a shaking in her voice.

Matt, who just got up from the ground again, looked at her and automatically stopped everything.

"What?" he asked perplexed.

"Your mother was a guardian angel, and your father a demon. There is no page in the storybook about you because you're one of a kind." Luna repeated her words and sounded very vulnerable.

I couldn't say what Matt was thinking right now, but he seemed to be remembering something. As if he was able to understand what she was saying, even though not even I had any idea what her words were supposed to mean.

"You think you are one of the bad guys, but still, you have this unexplainable feeling that drags you to different places where you suddenly save people." Luna continued talking and looked him deep into the eyes.

"You know it for quite some time, don't you?" Matt asked and tried to grin; however, he still seemed a little bit too shocked to fully be himself again.

Luna nodded.

"Thanks," he said almost whispering.

"Matt, do something," Antonius screamed at him.

But he was just shaking his head.

"I'm not your slave anymore. I'm free."

The three magicians looked at us in shock.

"How did you do that? Impossible." We could hear them murmur.

"Don't take my friendliness personally. I really don't care about you guys, but I would love to get some revenge against these three," Matt said towards us.

"It depends on what you want to do," I answered pretty chill.

As long as he wouldn't kill or even torture them, I was fine with everything that would make me never see them again.

"You seem to have a pretty false idea of me. It's too crazy that she remembers." His glance shifted towards Luna. "And he." Now he looked at Finn.

"And even I do. Only you don't," he ended his sentence incredibly untouched by everything that had just happened.

"You remember?" I heard Luna say astonished.

"A little bit. But we can talk about this later. Now, we need to get rid of the magicians. Forever. And I have the perfect plan for that."

Quickly, Matt shared his plan with us.

As always, it was shocking to see how different our abilities were. In general, he seemed so much more confident and stronger in comparison to when we had met before. As if he hadn't been unjustly fast and strong in the past.

"Maybe you remember my little experiment." In the end, he got quieter.

Luna's face darkened, and I could only guess he was hinting at the party where he had played with Finn and almost got him killed.

"I'm particularly good at playing with people, and I think now that I have unlocked my full powers, since I'm not bound to the magicians anymore, I could try to manipulate their memories in a way that they don't remember anything. Neither you, Ramon, nor your Grandma, nor the fact that they even are wizards," Matt explained.

"This is genius," Tim shouted.

"Nobody needs to die, and we don't have to worry about them anymore," he added and playfully boxed me against the arm.

"It sounds good," I responded.

I couldn't grasp his plan at the moment. Especially because I didn't know if he would actually be able to change their memories in a way that it would work out for sure. But then again, it was our only chance to get rid of the magicians in the most pacifist way possible. Enough blood and tears were spilled because of the magicians. It had to come to an end. Ideally, forever.

So, we put our fate in the hands of Matt, someone who wanted to fight us just a few minutes ago. And I had to admit, if Luna hadn't trusted him based on their history, I wouldn't be able to trust him that quickly. But I had no other choice.

Matt walked towards the magicians and looked them deep into the eyes one by one. It all happened so casually, we couldn't even tell that something was changing or if something was even happening to them. When he was done, he returned to us and gave us the signal that everything had worked out.

"What a beautiful clearing!" It was Titus who broke the silence that had taken over.

"I'm cold. Why did we decide to go moon watching today? There are too many clouds, we can't even see anything," Antonius complained.

"I've told you before, we aren't the youngest anymore. Going for a hike at this time was a horrible idea. What if we won't find our way back anymore?" Now Lucius was talking as well.

While the magicians continued discussing, I looked at my friends. They seemed to be as relieved as me. We made it.

The magicians didn't know anymore why they were up here. They had become human. We couldn't take away their powers, but we could take something even more powerful than that from them: their memories of what they used to be.

"I think it worked," Tim said and held his hand in front of Matt so he could give him a high-five. Matt, however, ignored him.

The magicians now seemed to notice us. Their glances wandered to us as if they hadn't seen us before. For a second, my heart was in my mouth when I realized our views were crossing.

"Oh, look at that. There are other humans up here too. Hello!" Titus said overly excited and waved at us.

Confused, I waved back.

"Are you here to watch the moon as well?" He asked and sounded a bit stupid.

Shouldn't he be afraid, seeing a group of strangers at this time on a desolate mountain? I, at least, would have a certain amount of respect if I had met strangers here and if I wouldn't have my abilities to protect me.

"Yes, but unfortunately, we can't see much today. That's why we will leave again," Luna answered and turned around.

"It was nice meeting other moon lovers," Lucius said friendly and waved us goodbye.

Chapter 27

Although Matt had clarified that he didn't care much about us or our well-being – yes, it did hurt to hear it coming from him – he brought each of us back to the parking spot where Ramon had left his car.

We did it.

The magicians weren't a hazard anymore and Matt was finally free.

"Oh wow, can we go again?" Tim said excited when Matt dropped him off close to Ramon's car.

"Thank you for everything," Ramon sounded honest when he talked to Matt.

"I think it's time to drive back home," Ramon said to Tim and smiled at him.

"You're right, but this was insanely cool. We need to work on your powers so you can let me fly or something like that." Tim was already coming up with new plans for the future when he entered the car and climbed on the passenger seat.

Finn looked at Matt for one last time.

"Farewell. And thank you for everything," he said and hugged him.

Matt seemed a bit overwhelmed with that situation but he didn't push Finn away, he let it happen. After that, he looked confused at him while Finn was vanishing in the car.

"Are you coming as well, Luna?" Ramon, who was still waiting for me at the opened door of the car, wanted to know.

"Give me one moment," I shouted back at him and observed him sitting down in the car now as well. I heard the door close. Now, Matt and I were the only ones left.

Silence.

I didn't know what to say.

I had so many things that I wanted to say to him.

"Okay, listen, I don't know why everyone is so emotional here, and I don't know what I have to do with all of this, but I'm honestly very grateful that you freed me." Matt started talking.

I gulped.

Again, he was so incredibly Matt.

"No big deal. I owed you big times after everything you have done for me, or not at all. I mean, it never happened, but I remember it, so somehow it is still real." I couldn't stop myself from rambling.

"Yes," he smirked. "Although I haven't lived through it, I have some memories of the other future. Don't ask me why, I don't have an explanation for it either."

I felt hopes inside of me. Maybe the Matt from the other future was still somewhere hidden deep inside of him.

"But unfortunately, I have to tell you that these memories don't feel as real to me as they do for you," he added and looked at the ground.

That hurt. But if I was honest with myself, I had already expected that. It wasn't a surprise anymore. I just had no clue how I should respond to that.

"What I remember is that you always wanted to protect your friends and keep them away from all of this mess. This didn't work out well, did it?" He laughed.

"That's why I offer you my help, only this time – disgusting I know. But it feels like I owe you something. So, if you want to, I can delete Finn's memories, so he won't remember me or the fight with the magicians or even Ramon's powers," he offered.

If he would erase Finn's memories, he would at least save him from the pain that Matt's absence would leave behind.

I couldn't imagine that Matt would stay here and pretend we were all friends and happy. No matter how much I wanted him to stay, I needed to be realistic. There was nothing that would make him stay in this town. Neither the humans nor the memories.

"No, it's okay. I think we have played enough with time and humans. It's time for normality." I made my decision.

"I almost expected you to decline my offer."

"Well, maybe you do know me better than you refuse to believe." I teased him.

"I don't want to destroy your hopes, but before we met in the mansion, it was my task to observe Ramon and you," he said.

Playfully insulted by that, I boxed against his arm only to figure out that, again, this was more painful for me than it was for him.

He laughed.

"And there is no chance that you will stay here? We could help you build your little cabin on the clearing, and if you want to, I could even buy you the latest Bravo." Nevertheless, I tried to convince him to stay.

"Unfortunately, not. It's the first time I'm actually free. This was everything I ever wanted. I always was, and still am, a loner, and now I can finally live my life the way I want to," he explained patiently.

"Also, I don't need a Bravo, I already know I'm team Jacob," he added while laughing.

Apparently, he could remember more than I had expected. Whereas this was a super important and character-building information which would always help him out in life.

"Not even team Edward? I'm shocked." Now I was laughing as well.

"I'm sorry that I'm not the person you think I am. But this doesn't mean that it will never happen. Maybe we will meet again. I've heard you have a whole eternity ahead of you." He winked at me while saying that and brought me back to reality.

"It's okay. I was already prepared for this," I admitted.

"Even you seem to know me better than I have expected. At least, thank you for everything." While he said this, he awkwardly put his hand on my shoulder as if he didn't know exactly what to do. It seemed as if he tried to show me that even if we weren't friends in this version of the future, he still worshiped the memory of what used to be, in his own rather peculiar way.

I threw myself into his arms.
I didn't care if he would think this was weird. It was the last time we would see each other and I wanted to properly say goodbye to him.
Slowly, a tear was running down my cheek.

"It was nice to get to know you, and I'm glad we met," I said quietly.

"I never thought I would say that, but so am I," he answered even quieter, so that I couldn't be sure if he had actually said it.

"Enjoy your freedom and until someday," I said and smiled.

"Thank you, enjoy your normal life. Until someday."

I went back to the car and squeezed myself on the backseat next to Finn since Tim had already occupied the passenger seat.

"Wow, that was emotional," I said when I sat down.

"Understandable. I only wonder why almost everyone can remember the other future except for me." Ramon speculated while he started the car.

None of us had any answer to that and even Tim couldn't come up with a fitting theory.

It probably was the same reason why Matt's phone number had still been saved in my phone; there must've been some kind of connection between us. Maybe because I was the only one that knew who Matt really was. However, I didn't have a real explanation either.

I only realized that everything was over when we arrived in front of Ramon's place. It wasn't until then that I could feel the endorphins fill my body. We had actually made it and even though we went into the battle without a real plan on how to defeat the magicians, we had done it.

We had survived.

Tim was doing better than ever. Matt was liberated. And Ramon was cured. We had accomplished everything we wanted to do.

Fortunately, Tim agreed to drive Finn back home. I, on the other side, stayed at Ramon's place.

"I didn't expect this to be so easy. And your abilities are absolutely amazing. I didn't know you could do such things," I rambled after we had closed the door that led to Ramon's apartment.

"And all of this only thanks to you," he said and shrugged.

Although I would never claim that everything only went that smoothly because of me, I had to admit I wasn't as weak and helpless as I had felt at the mansion. And even thought my boxing lessons didn't turn me into a tough fighter, I had become more and more confident within myself. I would never feel weak or small again.

If it wasn't for my friends, I would've never realized what was hidden inside of me. And if it wasn't for Finn, I would've time travelled all alone. But that was what friends were for, wasn't it?

To give each other so much more than just friendship. We gave each other hopes. We gave each other a normal life back.

"And what do you want to do now that the magicians aren't a threat anymore?" I asked Ramon.

"First, I want to sleep," he answered and yawned.

"And tomorrow I just want to be with you."

I smiled. I liked that plan.

Epilogue

D o you really want to do this?" Ramon asked another time. He looked nervous.

"Yes," I answered exactly like I had done the previous times.

"Then I won't be standing in your way." He smiled, sat down next to me, and finally closed the door behind him.

"I've got my driver's license for two weeks now, I can do that. How difficult could this possibly be?" I shook my head.

"You're the boss; I'm only the passenger," he agreed and observed me amused.

I turned the key around and let the clutch rise but before it had completely risen, the engine had stopped already. But this wouldn't stop me. Motivated, I tried again, however with the same result.

"You need to hit the gas pedal while you let go of the clutch. This is a car that runs on petrol and not on diesel," Ramon explained patiently.

Although the teacher at my driving school had taught me to fully let the clutch rise before I was allowed to touch the gas pedal, I listened to Ramon. After all, he knew his car better than I did.

When I tried to follow his instructions, it worked and we finally started rolling.

"I made it. We're driving," I yelled excitedly.

More than six months have passed and winter was over. It was the first time since I had moved to this town that nothing extraordinary had happened. Everything was normal.

Ramon was living a normal life like he did before our encounter with the magicians but now he didn't need to worry about meeting them again. Tim finally had a normal life as well, since Ramon wasn't depending on his help anymore. And even though Tim hadn't met his soul mate so far, he used his new found free time to have an active dating life. According to him, it was unfair that it was so easy for Ramon to find someone to be in a relationship with despite never searching for a partner.

And me? Well, I had spent the free time between final exams and prom with getting my driver's license, and now that I had finally turned 18, I wanted to make the most of the time I had between graduating and the start of university. This summer would belong to me. I was free.

At the beginning of the summer, my school friends and I had gone to a festival for the first time in my life. But my main goal this summer was to return to the mansion, with Ramon, of course.

Although we didn't have any questions left unanswered, I still had a very important and personal mission that I could only fulfill in the area around the mansion; I wanted to find closure.

I wanted to make my peace with Luana and finally stop wondering if she would be the way I was now or if I was only a restless soul inhabiting the body of a stranger.

And that was what we were about to do. However, it wouldn't be an adventure if I would've let Ramon drive his car. That's why I wanted to be the one to drive. Because one thing I had learned through earning my license was that nobody was able to drive a car after receiving their license. I would learn how to drive by collecting experiences, and that was what I wanted to do now.

After this summer, I could become more reasonable and make grown-up decisions. I would start to study and maybe even move to another city depending on which university would accept me. Finn and I already made plans to become roommates as far as it would be possible. After all, we couldn't know to which city we would have to move, but one thing was certain: we would study at the same university.

But now I didn't need to worry about these things. This was for later. Now, I was still young. I had nothing to lose. I could make dumb decisions and mistakes.

I still had my whole life ahead of me. And if I was honest, growing up scared me more than the magicians ever could.

Despite a few problems with shifting gears, the drive to the mansion went surprisingly smoothly. Ramon looked only a few times as if he was afraid to die, but I swear, I had everything under control.

The whole drive, I was following the speed limit, which Ramon seemed to dislike as soon as we drove on the lonely and curvy country roads – after all, it was way harder than it sounded to drive around the corners at 70 km/h.

So, understandably, Ramon was glad when we arrived at the mansion. And even I needed to figure out that this time it seemed so much more welcoming to me than it had been the last time we drove here.

Even though it was already dark, we decided to take some time to calm down before we would start with following my plan. It was completely insane that Ramon was supporting my idea, but maybe this was the good thing about our relationship. We were able to communicate openly and honestly with each other without being afraid the other one would judge you.

We let some hours pass until we decided that it was time to go. Completely dressed in black and armored with a shovel, we made our way to the graveyard that wasn't too far away from the mansion. Although it had surprised me that Luana's grave could still be found at the same graveyard where she had been buried a long time ago – after everything I had been through, it shouldn't have surprised me anymore.

Actually, I was even glad it was still there because, as long as there would be a tombstone, she couldn't be forgotten even if Ramon was the only person that could remember her.

The saddest thing in life was being forgotten, and the second saddest thing was burying an empty coffin. Although, Luana's coffin wasn't empty during her funeral since Ramon's Grandma took her time to revive me, I still felt uneasy by the thought of the empty coffin that was left at the graveyard. That was why I had come up with a plan to change that.

Ramon had immediately agreed to help me without even knowing the full plan, and I wondered if he already regretted it or if he was still cool with the fact that we were about to desecrate a grave.

But then again, it wasn't harmful because it was my grave, wasn't it? I preferred to leave this question unanswered, and even if it wasn't desecrating for myself, it was basically impossible to explain this to someone that didn't know me. So, I choose to rather not think about the possibility of someone else catching us in the act.

Carefully, we climbed over the fence of the graveyard. Somehow, I had never found the idea of walking around at a graveyard at night particularly attractive, and especially now, where I could be sure that ghosts and everything else were real, I was even more worried.

These doubts and worries vanished immediately after I put my feet back on the ground on the other side of the fence. This graveyard wasn't a place where ghosts were wildly running around and attacking everything that was in their way, no, more like the opposite, it was a place of silence. And I could feel some sort of calmness inside of me.

Being here, felt peaceful. The only noise we could hear was the sound of our shoes on the gravel. In the light of my phone flashlight, insects were flying around. And the wind was peacefully shaking the trees around us. I had never felt as much at peace with myself as I did now. And even Ramon seemed to feel similar.

Maybe that was why he had never questioned my plan or told me how dumb the idea actually was. Maybe he needed this too. He was never able to say goodbye to her. He had never been to her grave until today. Everything had started with her, everything needed to end with her. He needed to let go of his past life as well, and there was no better way of doing it than at her grave.

Luckily, he had informed himself before we had started our trip, where exactly we could find her grave, so we didn't waste much time looking for it. Below a small tree at the edge of the lonely graveyard, we could find the tombstone of Luana.

"It feels odd to finally be here," Ramon murmured quietly.

"Definitely," I agreed.

Then Ramon handed me the shovel.

"Do you want to start?" he asked.

Uncertain, I took the shovel in my hand.

"Do you think we need to dig deep?"

"Probably, we can be glad if we'll find some leftovers of the coffin. After some time, it decomposes." Ramon answered my question honestly.

"Hm... then let's get started. Maybe your Grandma has casted a spell so it wouldn't decompose." I laughed and started digging.

It was a warm night in the middle of the summer, and I was starting to sweat almost immediately.

I actually had hoped I would have more stamina, but Ramon offered to take over for some time until I could breathe again. I handed him the shovel and regretted that we didn't bring anything to drink with us.

"What are we doing if somebody sees us?" Ramon wanted to know.

"I don't know. You'll run away, and I'll see what I'm doing."

"Do you want to go to jail that desperately?" He teased me.

"No, but I have all the time in the world." I grinned.

I had accepted my immortality by now. The thought of seeing my friends die one day was scaring me, but if I was able to prepare for it, maybe it would get easier one day. And who would know what the future would bring. Maybe I wasn't even as immortal as we all thought. Only time could tell.

When Ramon needed a break, I jumped in and took over again. In the meantime, we had already dug quite a hole in the ground. Sometimes, we felt like someone was observing us, but not in a bad way, as if someone was staring at us, more in a good way. It felt like the ghosts of the graveyard knew that I had come home. They were curiously observing what we were doing.

The shovel made a loud noise when it hit the coffin, which was surprisingly well identifiable as a coffin. Quickly and with newfound motivation, we got rid of the last bits of dirt, so we would be able to open it soon.

"Should we really do this?" I asked hesitantly.

Even though we knew Luana wasn't lying in the coffin, it still felt weird to open an already buried coffin. What if it wasn't empty after all?

"We came that far, we'll have to do it," Ramon tried to cheer me on.

He was right.

We didn't just spend the last hour digging out a grave to now stop and go back home.

My hands were shaking while I was opening the lid. As expected, the coffin was empty.

I gulped.

Even though it was everything I had hoped for – I didn't want to imagine what would've happened if we had found a body on the inside – it was still hard for me to look at this empty coffin. It was impossible to imagine that I used to lie in there. While at the same time I had never been in the coffin. Why was everything so complicated?

I grabbed a folded piece of paper from the pocket of my jeans and threw it inside the coffin. Then I closed the lid. That was my plan all along. That was the reason we went through all of this. Now the coffin wasn't empty anymore.

Ramon helped me climb out of the hole we just dug. Before I wanted to reach for the shovel to start getting the dirt back into the hole, he stopped me.

"There is an easier way for this," he said, and within a second, I could see the pile of dirt that was next to the grave fly towards the hole on its own. All of our work we had spent an hour on was buried, as if we had never touched anything.

"You're such an idiot." I laughed.

Ramon looked at me confused.

"You could've told me that you can use your powers for that. Everything would've been so much faster."

"I could've, but I thought you wanted the full experience." He laughed.

I could only shake my head in disbelief.

Together, we made our way back to the mansion.

"What did you even put in the coffin?" He asked me after we had climbed over the fence again. Now we weren't on the graveyard anymore.

What a great question. Actually, I had never told him what I wanted to put in the coffin. I had only vaguely told him about my plan to lay something down in the coffin so it wouldn't be empty anymore. And since I was certain words were more powerful than anything else in this world, I had decided to share my favorite poem with her.

Since the day we had read Shakespeare's 18th sonnet in school, it had left a special impact on me. And even though it was a love poem, I still found it fitting to put a handwritten version of this poem down in the coffin. As a sign of loving myself again. But what I liked the most were the last verses of the sonnet, and I wanted Luana to know how I felt about her:

So long as men can breathe or eyes can see,
So long lives this, and this gives life to thee.

Acknowledgements

It took me longer than I would have liked but now the translation of the second part of my *Midnight Blue* saga is finally done.

A special thanks to Beni who proof read and corrected the German version of this book. Without his feedback I probably would've never felt confident enough to publish this novel.

Another thanks to my Mama who always enjoys to hear me rambling about my book without being annoyed by it.

And another huge thanks to everyone that bought this book. I hope you were not disappointed with how the story of Luna and Ramon continued. I put a lot of pressure on myself to make the book as good as the first part but in the end, it will be on you to decide if I have fulfilled my job. I personally am more than happy with how things went and who knows, maybe there will be a third part in the far future because I simply can't let go of all the characters I have created.

Consider following me on social media to be updated about other book projects in the future. Because there surely will be more ☺

Instagram: likemidnightblue
Tiktok: likemidnightblue

Also, I would always appreciate positive reviews. It's harder to do the marketing for a book without reviews (especially when you are a self-publishing author).